Buckeye Legends

Buckeye Legends

Folktales and Lore from Ohio

Michael Jay Katz

Ann Arbor

THE UNIVERSITY OF MICHIGAN PRESS

1997 1996 1995 1994   4 3 2 1

A CIP catalogue record for this book is available from the British Library.

Library of Congress Cataloging-in-Publication Data

Katz, Michael Jay, 1950–
    Buckeye legends : folktales and lore from Ohio / Michael Jay Katz.
       p.   cm.
    ISBN 0-472-09558-7 (alk. paper). — ISBN 0-472-06558-0
(pbk. : alk. paper)
    1. Tales—Ohio. 2. Legends—Ohio. 3. Ohio—History. 4. Ohio—
Social life and customs.   I. Title.
GR110.O48K37   1994
398.2'09771—dc20   94-2379
                                                            CIP

Map and illustrations by Nancy A. Burgard

Contents

Ohio

These Ohio stories were created from bits and pieces scattered through a variety of written narratives; specifically, the kernels were found in:

Bareis, G. F. *History of Madison Township, including Groveport and Canal Winchester, Franklin County, Ohio.* Canal Winchester, OH: Geo. F. Bareis Publisher, 1902.

Bond, B. W., Jr. *The Foundations of Ohio.* Vol. 1 of *The History of the State of Ohio,* ed. C. Wittke. Columbus, OH: Ohio State Archaeological and Historical Society, 1941.

Botkin, B. A., ed. *A Treasury of American Folklore: Stories, Ballads, and Traditions of the People.* New York, NY: Crown Publishers, 1944.

Corrigan, M. J. *Life and Reminiscences of Hon. James Emmitt,* revised by J. Emmitt. Chillicothe, OH: Peerless Printing and Mfg. Co., 1988.

Darby, E. F. [Webb, D. K.] *Idy, the Fox-chasing Cow.* Chillicothe, OH: Ohio Valley Folktale Project, Ross County Historical Society, 1953.

Darby, E. F. [Webb, D. K.] *Three Chips on a Mulberry Tree.* Chillicothe, OH: Ohio Valley Folktale Project, Ross County Historical Society, 1953.

Dolan, J. *Adam Puckett: A Few Adam Puckett Stories from Lawrence County Ohio.* Chillicothe, OH: Ohio Valley Folktale Project, Ross County Historical Society, 1956.

Dorson, R. M., ed. *Buying the Wind: Regional Folklore in the United States.* Chicago, IL: University of Chicago Press, 1964.

Edwards, S. E. *The Ohio Hunter, Or a Brief Sketch of the Frontier Life of Samuel E. Edwards, the Great Bear and Deer Hunter of the State of Ohio.* Battle Creek, MI: Review and Herald Steam Press Print, 1866.

Frary, I. T. *Ohio in Homespun and Calico.* Richmond, VA: Garrett and Massie, 1942.

Federal Writer's Project. *The Ohio Guide.* New York, NY: Oxford University Press, 1940.

Federal Writer's Project of Ohio. *Chillicothe and Ross County.* Chillicothe, OH: Ross County Northwest Territory Committee, 1938.

Galloway, W. A. *Old Chillicothe, Shawnee and Pioneer History: Conflicts and Romances in the Northwest Territory.* Xenia, OH: Buckeye Press, 1934.

Galbreath, C. B. *History of Ohio.* Vol. 1. Chicago, IL: American Historical Society, 1925.

Gill, W. W. *Myths and Songs from the South Pacific.* London: Henry S. King and Co., 1876.

Glines, W. M. *Johnny Appleseed by One Who Knew Him.* Columbus, OH: F. J. Heer Printing Co., 1922.

Hildreth, S. P. *Genealogical and Biographical Sketches of the Hildreth Family: From the Year 1652 Down to the Year 1840.* Marietta, OH: privately published, 1840.

Historical Society of Geauga County. *Pioneer and General History of Geauga County, with Sketches of Some of the Pioneers and Prominent Men.* Burton, OH: Historical Society of Geauga County, 1880.

Howells, W. C. *Recollections of Life in Ohio, from 1813 to 1840 (1895).* Gainesville, FL: Scholars' Facsimiles and Reprints, 1963.

Hulbert, A. C. *Red-Men's Roads: The Indian Thoroughfares of the Central West.* Columbus, OH: Fred J. Heer and Co., 1900.

Izant, G. G. *This is Ohio: Ohio's 88 Counties in Words and Pictures.* Cleveland, OH: World Publishing, 1953.

Leasure, J. E., Jr. *The Ghost of Lindy Sue: A Folklore Tale of Ross County, Ohio.* Chillicothe, OH: Ohio Valley Folktale Project, Ross County Historical Society, 1953.

Leasure, J. E., Jr. *The Headless Horseman of Cherry Hill.* Chillicothe, OH: Ohio Valley Folktale Project, Ross County Historical Society, 1953.

Miller, A. B. *Shaker Herbs: A History and a Compendium.* New York, NY: Clarkson N. Potter, 1976.

Millspaugh, C. F. *American Medicinal Plants.* New York, NY: Dover Publications, 1974.

Morgan, V. *Folklore of Highland County.* Greenfield, OH: Greenfield Printing and Publishing Co., 1946.

Owen, E. T. *Johnny-Cake, etc. in the Ohio Country at the Muskingum.* Beverly, OH: Elizabeth Thorniley Owen, 1932.

Roebuck, M. E. *Genealogy of the Chapman Family: Relatives of John Chapman (Johnny Appleseed)*. Fort Wayne, IN: Mary Elizabeth Roebuck, 1947.

Ruggles, A. M. *The Story of the McGuffeys*. New York, NY: American Book Co., 1950.

Schneider, N. F. *Blennerhassett Island and the Burr Conspiracy*. Columbus, OH: Ohio State Archaeological and Historical Society, 1950.

Schoolcraft, H. "The Celestial Sisters" In *Indian Legends*, edited by M. C. Williams. East Lansing, MI: Michigan State University Press, 1978.

Scully, V. *A Treasury of American Indian Herbs: Their Lore and Their Use for Food, Drugs, and Medicine*. New York, NY: Crown Publishers, 1970.

Shoemaker, H. W. *Duyvelscar (Devilscar) or The Ways and Wonders of Wolves*. Chillicothe, OH: Ohio Valley Folktale Project, Ross County Historical Society, 1957.

Shoemaker, N. *Two Iron Kettles: An Ohio Folk Tale About Buried Treasure*. Chillicothe, OH: Ohio Valley Folktale Project, Ross County Historical Society, 1956.

Thwaites, R. G. *Afloat On The Ohio: An Historical Pilgrimage of a Thousand Miles in a Skiff, from Redstone to Cairo*. Chicago, IL: Way and Williams, 1897.

Volz, J. A. *Rambles in Ohio*. Carthagena, OH: Messenger Press, 1935.

Weiner, M. A. *Earth Medicine—Earth Foods: Plant Remedies, Drugs, and Natural Foods of the North American Indians*. New York, NY: Macmillan, 1972.

Wilson, S. A. *Ohio*. Supplementary volume to Tarr and McMurry Geographies. New York, NY: Macmillan, 1902.

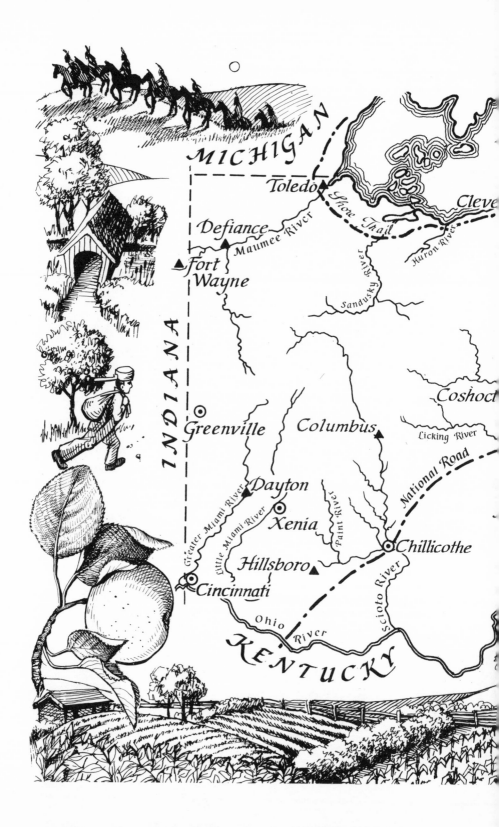

MICHIGAN

Toledo

Shore Trail

Cleve

Defiance

Maumee River

Huron River

Fort
Wayne

Sandusky River

Sandusky

INDIANA

Coshoct

Greenville

Columbus

Licking River

National Road

Dayton

Greater Miami River

Little Miami River

Xenia

Paint River

Hillsboro

Chillicothe

Cincinnati

Scioto River

Ohio River

KENTUCKY

Erie

Grand River

Chagrin River

uyahoga River

Youngstown

Pittsburgh

Steubenville

Wheeling

nesville

gam River

etta

VIRGINIA

PENNSYLVANIA

Ohio

·1·

The Ill-Fated Blennerhassetts of Blennerhassett Island

ALL RIGHT I'LL tell you one of those stories; you know what I mean, a story where somebody laughs and somebody cries, where somebody knows and somebody cares. In my day, the young folk used to get together on long evenings in the winter and tell stories; there was Sadie McIntosh, Major Clark, Joelle Regnerson, and Enoch Shepard. Who else? Well I shouldn't leave out Calvin Shard, Luther Stringfellow, Ethrezial Zephyr, and Clem McGaughlin. Everyone had to sing a song, tell a story, or dance a jig; otherwise he'd have his nose smudged with the burnt candle wick.

There were good stories then. I don't much like today's stories, the ones you read in a book or a magazine; they don't begin any place and they don't end any place and they wander round and round in the middle. Ah well . . . anyways just sit down and listen and I'll tell all I know about folks hereabouts, and then I'll tell some more too.

Well here we are in Ohio. It's a good old place. The French were the first Europeans to come here—that was at the end of the sixteen hundreds—and they claimed the area and put military posts on the Ohio River. American Indians lived here before the French. And who came before the Indians? No one knows—but someone was here, there's no doubt about it. Someone built the mounds, the big earthy hills, the mysterious tumuli. Were these Mound Builders the lost tribes of Israel? Were they wandering Aztecs? Maybe they came from the North—who knows.

Since the Mound Builders, many other people have lived in Ohio, but it could hold them all. Ohio's a big state: it's a hill state and a tree state, and it's an old oak of a state. Once there were dense forests with butternut, cherry, elm, maple, oak, sycamore, and walnut, with ash, beech, buckeye, chestnut, and hickory. To-day the lowlands have been cleared, but there's still a patch of woods on every farm. The old trees were cut on most of the hillsides too, but the hills are getting covered again by thick young timbers.

Ohio has its blackberries, cherries, cranberries, elderberries, pawpaws, raspberries, and wild plums. There are anemones, butter-cups, Indian turnip, spring beauties, trilliums, and violets. The hills have got columbine, laurel, orchids, and wild honeysuckle—and in autumn you find asters and goldenrod.

At one time bears were common; European settlers ate bear meat and they ate buffalo and deer too. There were so many wolves that the government paid a fee for every scalp turned in to the local Land Office. There were American elk (that's the large wapiti elk). There were wild turkeys and wild pigeons, now long gone. I'm sorry to say that no large wild animals are left in the state. Oh, you see a deer every once in a while, but bear are nearly extinct. Wapiti are gone. The gray wolf and the coyote—well they're both gone too. Of course, you can still find foxes, opossums, raccoons, and skunks, and chipmunks, mice, rabbits, and squirrels. In the pioneer days there were Namaycush trout. Eagles still live on the edge of Lake Erie; they have six-foot-wide nests in the tops of the tallest trees, a hundred feet above the ground.

Ohio's got no mountains. There's a divide, a watershed, that runs across the state; it separates the waters that go up into Lake Erie from the streams that go down into the Ohio River. In the east there are rolling hills. In the west there are the beginnings of the prairie plains. Some of the hills in the southwest, between the Scioto and the Miami rivers, are pretty tall, as much as thirteen hundred feet high. The Ohio River's on the south. Lake Erie is on the north. And that's the whole state. . . . Now let's see—I'd best start my stories at the bottom, by the Ohio River; we can go north later.

The Ohio River is four hundred and forty-six miles long. It's the bottom of the state, where there's a narrow valley. The river turns and it winds. Sometimes its low bank—its flood plain—is on one side, sometimes it's on the other. The lowlands and most of the islands are good for farms even though they're flooded in the spring and fall. On either side of the valley there are tall banks that are steep and covered with forests. Here and there are a few big clay banks, and nowadays you can also see some quarries and coal mines along the edge of the river.

The river runs along a whole pile of Ohio counties—Columbiana, Jefferson, Belmont, Monroe, Washington, Meigs, Gallia, Lawrence, Scioto, Adams, Brown, Clermont, and Hamilton. Adventurers floating down the Ohio River would stop off in these places and sometimes they decided to stay. Marietta, one of Ohio's oldest cities, was settled by these floating New Englanders coming from Massachusetts and Connecticut. Marietta's in Washington

County on the north side of the Ohio River; it's where General Rufus Putnam first set up a town, on Monday, April 7 of 1788. . . .

What? Well I mention Marietta because of another place, an island nearby. I'm talking about Blennerhassett Island; it's in the Ohio River just below Marietta. Once upon a time, Harmann Blennerhassett built a mighty ornate mansion there. He had a Garden of Eden—until Aaron Burr arrived. That was in the year 1805, after Burr's fatal duel with Alexander Hamilton. Burr enticed the Blennerhassetts into a secret scheme to invade Mexico, but the plan was discovered, Burr and Blennerhassett were arrested, and the Ohio militia wrecked the mansion; the Blennerhassetts led a miserable existence ever after.

Blennerhassett's Island is two miles below Parkersburg. It's broad and dark and now it's pretty much forest. There's a dam joining it to the West Virginia shore—but that's a new addition. How big is the Island? Oh perhaps three or three-and-a-half miles long. Once the whole island was a single estate, but fire and looting and the wear and tear of time left only a bit of the mansion's foundations and one water well to show for all its former glory. A few farmers live there in the summer because the fields are such fine planting grounds, but in the winter they move back to Ohio or to West Virginia.

Blennerhassett's wharf was at the upper end of the island. There's a small farmhouse near the original site of Blennerhassett's mansion. Now they call that area "The Blennerhassett Pleasure Grounds." A seedy-looking man is the proprietor. His name is Otis Elderby, and he accosts all and sundry, levying a landing fee, which, he'll tell you, includes the right to remain overnight. There's thirty acres at the head of the island that actually belong to Otis and he rents the farmable parts to a local gardener. Otis Elderby is a grizzled old coot. He told me that fifteen thousand people come to the island each summer at the end of railway and steamboat excursions, and this provides his main income—but I'd say it's a pity that so famous a place isn't free to the public.

Here's Blennerhassett's story: Harmann Blennerhassett was

very rich but he was completely impractical. He and his wife came to America from England in 1798 after he'd sold his family estate for a hundred and sixty thousand dollars. Blennerhassett was tall and stooped. He had eyes so weak that he had to hold books touching his nose in order to read. When he hunted quail, a servant pointed his gun and told him when to pull the trigger. Blennerhassett was awkward, but he was six feet two inches tall and he looked impressive, especially in his old English dress—a coat of blue broadcloth, red knee breeches, silk socks, and black shoes with silver buckles.

In America, Harmann bought an entire island in the Ohio River on impulse. Before this, the island had been called Backus Island, Long Island, and Belpre Island; Blennerhassett renamed it Isle de Beau Pre. After purchasing the island, the Blennerhassetts had plenty of money left. They built a huge white mansion. They imported fancy French furniture, pictures, and statuary. They had local workmen make graveled walks and plant hawthorn hedges and erect arbors and grottoes covered with white and yellow honeysuckle and pink eglantine. There were orchards, a stable, ponds, and a dairy.

Harmann lived the life of the English aristocracy. He ordered books on every subject. He taught himself astronomy, chemistry, galvanism, and music. His wife, Bessie, organized a fancy old-world kitchen. Visitors slept under silk coverlets in flower-filled rooms. There were parties weekly—and there was no lack of eastern visitors because in those days every wealthy young man was expected to take a journey down the Ohio River into the "western parts" and then to write a book about his adventures.

This went on for a few years. Then a snake, an evil serpent, came into this Eden. Every famous person traveling down the Ohio River stopped at Blennerhassett Island. On a Monday in March of 1805, Aaron Burr arrived on his way to New Orleans. At the moment he had no formal job—but he had a plan. Burr had been one of the most powerful men in the United States. He was young and he was smart and now it was time to advance still farther. With his skill and knowledge he felt he should head a country, so he planned to set up his own republic on land that he would capture in Texas and Mexico.

As they did for many of their guests, the Blennerhassetts gave a ball in honor of Burr. Burr charmed the ladies, Marigold Borden, Emma Cowper, and Faith Danielle McCoy. He bowed, he spoke lightly and gallantly, he admired their clothes, his speech was poetic. Cladis Comfort, Lewis Alden, and Top MacIntosh shook their heads in envy. Burr spoke smoothly. He was like a dream; he was polished, light, quick, and slick; he knew politics and famous people. Burr talked easily of the president and the senators and of famous lawyers and writers. He described how he would soon organize a strong southern government in Mexico funded by native gold and silver.

Aaron Burr had been the vice president of the United States but he wasn't well liked in the government. He'd managed to make most politicians, even the president (that was, Jefferson), angry. Nonetheless he was brilliant—there was no doubt about it. He knew how to maneuver, and he was a skilled president of the Senate. But Burr was also selfish and he was extreme. He acted swiftly and boldly, and he had killed Alexander Hamilton in a duel on the eleventh of July 1804 at Weehawken, New Jersey.

Burr was filled with lightning: he was irresistible, charming, articulate, witty, and wild. He won over the Blennerhassetts. Harmann had already used up a considerable amount of his inherited money, spending wildly, and he was in a hurry to rebuild his supply. Burr told stories aglow with vast rewards from the golden southwest, where the Spanish had found such riches. But, to carry out his plans, Burr needed start-up money for men and supplies. He'd already recruited soldiers at Chillicothe, at Cincinnati, and at Lexington. Also, he purchased from Colonel Charles Lynch four hundred thousand acres of land on the Washita River in Louisiana— this was called the Bastrop Grant because the former owner was Baron Bastrop. Burr was using the Bastrop farm as a staging grounds and a cover for his military expedition.

The plan was supposed to be a secret, but Burr talked grandly about the empire he intended to establish in Mexico. He would have money, he would have power, and jealous American statesmen would tremble at his decrees. He would be Emperor Aaron I. Blennerhassett listened wide eyed. He himself had never been fully appreciated. Now he could triumph over the people who looked down on him. Burr assured Blennerhassett that he would be their first ambassador to England.

Blennerhassett signed on. He was the son of an aristocratic Englishman. He knew how to behave with royalty and he would be proud to serve in Burr's new government. Blennerhassett shook hands with Burr and pledged money. He wrote letters of credit and letters of support. Burr clapped him on the back. We will do great things together, he promised.

Burr left Blennerhassett's Island and went to Cincinnati and then on to Lexington. Two weeks later Blennerhassett joined Burr in Lexington. He came with thousands of dollars in gold coins. He also brought servants and a boatload of dried grains—wheat, oats, and barley. He had ordered wagons and guns and flatboats. Burr welcomed Blennerhassett warmly. One of Burr's men took the gold and bought dried meat and corn meal and grain, rum, and ammunition—much of this was shipped back up the Ohio River to be stored on Blennerhassett's Island. Money was also sent to pay debts in Louisiana.

Harmann Blennerhassett returned home. He felt strong and invigorated; he was important. He hired some men from West Virginia to build two wooden cabins where the accumulating supplies were stored. The cabins were in the bayou that runs near today's dock site. You can still see the foundations of one of those cabins. The shore there is lined with old sycamores and the banks of the river are mossy; everything has the feel of a different time— an old-fashioned time of plotting and mystery and adventure.

Now you may ask, exactly what was going on? What was this expedition really all about? It's simple—Burr wanted to go onward and upward; he wanted influence, he wanted power, he wanted money. Burr walked in our world but he dreamed in his own. He didn't see things through others' eyes—the world had Aaron Burr's colors and it was filled with Aaron Burr's motivations. His scheme was big, it was grandiose, it was golden, and it was secret and selfish—just like Aaron Burr.

Aaron Burr shook his head. This was a monumental venture. It was of global importance—it would change the world. He talked freely to everyone he met, and people spread the word. Soon President Jefferson learned of the plot. Nothing like this can be allowed to take place in the United States of America, he said. On November 27th of 1806, the President signed a proclamation: the government of the United States of America dissociated itself from any plans to conquer Mexico and no American citizen would be allowed to overrun another land.

Burr heard of the proclamation. He paced. He waved his arms. He swore. The president officially broke all connections with Burr and his men and declared the whole enterprise unlawful. It was against the principles of the American constitution, said Jefferson: It was treason. The federal military was ordered to arrest the participants, and Blennerhassett's estate was invaded by a boatload of soldiers. Some of Burr's men, such as the young army lieutenant James Canter, escaped. Blennerhassett himself slipped away on a boat, and he joined Burr in a small camp at the mouth of the Cumberland River. The weather was cold and sad, damp and grim—it was foggy, the tall grasses were bent low, the jipajapa plants were wet, gray, thin, and forlorn.

After months of hiding, Burr and Blennerhassett were finally arrested. This was in the winter of 1807. The two men were brought up before a federal judge on charges of treason, but they were acquitted on technical grounds. At the conclusion of the trial, Burr and Blennerhassett parted company. Burr was distant and cold. He owed Blennerhassett somewhere between twenty and fifty thousand dollars but he was now poor—he could hardly support himself, much less repay Blennerhassett

In the meantime, Bessie Blennerhassett and her two small

sons left Ohio country and moved to New York. The Blennerhassett servants had long gone, and people from West Virginia and Ohio had stolen things from the Blennerhassett estate. In the spring, Zebulon Raleigh came down from Marietta. He was a major creditor and he and his men seized Blennerhassett's property, carrying off everything they could fit in their wagons. Dishes, linens, statues, and pictures went on the first trip; furniture, saddles, tools, and carpets were taken on the next trip. Folks from Ohio dug up plants and took fancy cut stone. A group of young men from West Virginia took pieces of carved woodwork from the dining room. Then one day the mansion was burned. If you go there now, all that the proprietor can show are the well, the outlines of the mansion's foundations, and a few ancient trees that once graced the side lawn.

Aaron Burr was free—he had been acquitted. He left America and traveled to England, Scotland, Denmark, Sweden, and France. He used his best charm, trying to become an advisor or an ambassador for royal families in Europe. He was greeted respectfully but distantly, and no one would give him a formal position. In 1812 he returned to New York, where he became a lawyer for wealthy friends. Burr remained a braggart—unscrupulous, insincere, and immoral—at the same time he surprised people by being kind and generous with his own little family. Aaron Burr died at Port Richmond on Staten Island in New York, on Wednesday, the fourteenth of September 1836.

And what about the Blennerhassetts? They were ruined. The family wandered about and everywhere they went they had problems. They had little money and they lived with relatives. People thought that they were foolish. Harmann became bitter and Bessie became quiet. Like Burr, Harmann repeatedly asked government officials to appoint him as an ambassador and repeatedly he was turned down. Finally Harmann died from a stroke—his third—this was on the Island of Guernsey, where his sister Avis owned a farm; it was Wednesday, February second in the year 1831.

Bessie returned to America. What was left for her? Would

Congress repay her for the ruin of her estate? She went to Washington, she petitioned, and she waited. Nothing happened. Back in New York, Bessie sat silent day after day, looking out of sad black eyes that were like two burnt holes in a blanket. The government did nothing and finally Bessie passed away; she died at 75 Greenwich Street in New York City on Thursday, June sixteenth 1842 in the presence of her two sons, Harmann Blennerhassett, Jr., and Joseph Lewis Blennerhassett. Bessie Blennerhassett was buried by the Sisters of Charity—but it isn't known where her grave is.

One son, Harmann, was an artist; he never married and he died of cholera on Thursday, August tenth, 1854 in the almshouse on Blackwell's Island in New York City, where he had been under the care of the ladies of the Old Bowery Mission. Joseph, the other son, died at Troy New York in 1863. At his request, his tombstone reads:

> Joseph Lewis Blennerhassett
> Died: Monday, March 23 in 1863.
> Beneath this stone poor Joseph lies;
> Nobody laughs and nobody cries.
> Where he's gone and how he fares,
> Nobody knows, and nobody cares.

·2·

The Formidable Abigail Mink

WHEN YOU THINK of Ohio, you probably think of raccoons. Raccoons were here before the white man and even before the Indians. We got our word *raccoon* from the Algonquin Indians of Virginia—the Powhatan tribe—who called them *arrathkune*. However, in Ohio, Indians called these animals *geauga*. Today, Ohio has a Geauga County, a rural and raccoon-filled place with no big cities, unless maybe you count Chardon or Burton.

Geauga County's got woods with spectacular red, orange, and brown fall colors. This region of the state—way up east—has forests of old sugar maples. Ohio is one of the top three maple syrup-producing states, and Geauga County is Ohio's maple sugar capital. Like much of Ohio country, Geauga is farmland. Geauga County rolls up and down, with wonderful pastures for grazing cattle. Grain was the main export, but cheese was never far behind. You see, milk spoils easily unless you keep it in a springhouse or an underground cellar with heavy oaken doors, but cheese—well, there's something that keeps for a long time and can be shipped to distant places.

Ohio cheeses were well known a hundred years ago, and northeastern Ohio (Connecticut's Western Reserve) was called "Cheesedom." Every Ohio township had a cheese-making creamery—in Geauga County alone there were more than sixty. Cheese was shipped from the cities of Aurora, Hudson, Solon, and Windham, hauled in wagons to the Ohio River where it was loaded on boats for the long journey to all manner of river ports.

In the beginning, only the wife was the cheese-maker. Soon, cheese became extremely profitable, children were enlisted to help, and it turned into an industry. Cheese factories sprang up. In the

mornings, farmers emptied the milking buckets into large cans and hauled the cans to the factories. Now, to many people, the cheese factory workers were alchemists—they knew some mysterious magic—but it was just a homey craft like any other. I knew one of Geauga's most famous cheese men, Skreete Staner, and after all these years I guess I can tell you his secrets, so listen carefully.

Skreete Staner was a patient man. First he'd set aside the day's milk. The next morning he skimmed off the cream and he warmed it gently and stirred it. And then what did he do? Why, he added the warm cream back to the rest of the old milk of course.

Next, Skreete put in new milk; that's when he added his special ingredient, a bit of the crumblings from his best earlier cheeses. Skreete heated this whole mixture and added carrots (which he'd already softened by boiling them in milk). . . . What's that? . . . Yes, I said carrots—just listen a moment. Skreete stirred all morning. Stirring, stirring, stirring, he mixed and he heated and soon the vat got thick and curdled. The mix stood, the cheese curds sank, and old Skreete Staner sat whittling until he could pour off the liquid—he called this liquid whey the mother.

Now it was time for squeezing the cheese bits. Skreete pressed and kneaded them into a solid loaf. He set the cheese loaves in a salt bath and he let the water dry away into the air. That might take days or weeks—I forget which. Anyways, the last step was washing: after everything was dried out, he washed the cheese and he put it into wooden boxes to age and to flavor. Skreete was in no hurry, and his orange-colored cheeses—three, six, and even nine months old—were prized throughout the Grand River valley.

That was how Skreete Staner treated the milk brought in by neighboring dairy farmers. Skreete paid the farmers in money and also in pig food—on his return trip from the factory each farmer had his milk cans filled with leftover mother, and back home the farmer fed the mother to his hogs.

Geauga County is cheese country—that's its true rock-bottom self. But maple syrup's pretty important there too. The city of Burton is the maple syrup center of Geauga County. Today, maple syrup is a treat, even a luxury, but once upon a time it was the main sweetener in Ohio households. Cane sugar was rare and expensive, so maple sugar and maple syrup sweetened puddings, cakes, and pies. Maple topped the pancakes and the muffins and the cookies. And Christmas candies were all *maple* candies—sugary, sticky, crunchy, and crumbly.

Maple syruping's an uncertain business. Everything depends on the atmospherics, and of course "weather is as weather does." The way it works is this. The maple farmer bores holes through the sugar maple bark at the end of the winter. Into these holes he pounds spiles—short wooden pipes where the sap leaks out of the tree and into buckets. Warmth and sunshine start the sap climbing from the roots to the branches, and as the sap passes the spiles it drips out into the buckets.

To the maple syruper, bouncing cold spells are heaven sent. If the temperature drops below freezing, then the sap slips back down to the roots. Next morning, the day warms up and the sap starts to rise again. Each time it flows past the buckets, it drips in, and if the temperatures go up and down then so does the sap. A plain old steady warm spell is great for the city man, but the sap in the maple trees passes the buckets only once and goes right into the buds: the sap never falls back, and the poor maple sugarer gets a mighty thin haul.

In any case, the next step in maple sugaring's a hard job. In pioneer days they boiled the sap in iron kettles over a wood fire. Geauga woods are slippery and soggy in the maple-sugaring spring-time. The snow is melting, there's mud everywhere, and the streams are rushing. It's no child's play to collect sap. You have to trudge through thick, wet leaves with the buckets, two at a time, down to the sugaring house. You pour the sap—which tastes almost like water—into the steaming kettle. Then you go back out again. Meanwhile your partner keeps the fire going with thick chunks of wood hauled into the sugar house. If the fire gets too low, the sap doesn't evaporate, but if the fire gets too hot, the syrup boils over.

If you're a sugarer then you're carrying and dragging something all the time. A work day wears on mighty slowly. If you sit a moment, you get hynoptized by the fire. Suddenly the syrup boils up wild and angry and you have to grab a piece of salt pork and stir it into the hot volcano, hoping to calm the savage maple waves and not to lose anything flowing over the edges and hissing into the fire.

At the end of a sweaty day of syruping, you get a few different things. Of course there's syrup. But some of the syrup's boiled further until it's very thick; this is "sugaring off." The thick syrup is poured into little forms to cool. My grandmother—Grammy Win—used to make her maple cakes in fancy shapes with scalloped edges. These were the joy of our little hearts, and they tasted much better than the chunks broken off corners of the big cakes from exactly the same run of sugar.

Another good thing is to take a dipperful of boiling syrup and drop it on clean snow. You get a dark brown treat that's the ally of all poverty-stricken dentists because of the great ease with which it separates loose fillings from teeth. This wonderful candy has a flavor that I can't describe. But there's something still better, which we called "white gold." At a certain magic stage, you pour the hot maple syrup into an iron pot and stir it and stir it and stir it. Then a miracle happens. Somehow the mix turns lighter and lighter and whiter and cream colored. You have to keep stirring until it's cool—but if you don't stop, you'll have the greatest creamy stuff every discovered, a candy that makes the nectar of the gods seem commonplace in comparison.

As you might imagine, our native Indians knew all about maple sap and the wonderful foods that it can make. We white men learned from the Indians, and it didn't take long for settlers to turn maple syrup into a cash crop, so the Sugar Bush areas got a good regular income from their maple farms. In fact, for a time Geauga County made more maple syrup than any other place in the country. Geaugans say that they make the best maple syrup in the world—though people in Vermont don't agree.

For a few years Archibald Mink tried his hand at maple syruping. This was too much work for him, especially in the spring, so he took up school teaching in Burton at the Academy; this was in the year 1804 . . . . Archibald Mink? I thought I'd already mentioned him. Archibald was a graduate of some eastern college, and he came west with his wife to set up a new life. Formally he claimed to be a lawyer. He wore vests. He smoked a pipe. He spoke like a scholar, and he wrote with a fancy quill. Soon after his arrival, he was chosen to be deacon of the Geauga Congregational Church at its organizational meeting on Monday, August twenty-second 1808.

However, if the truth be known, Archibald was not much of a worker—mainly he sat around and smoked and whittled and talked. He was sloppy, and when you looked at him close up you thought that he dressed like a scarecrow. No one wanted to hire him, so Archibald was poor. But words are cheap and Archibald Mink was an expert talker.

Archibald would stop nearby to men who were working out-of-doors, on fences, outside cabins, and in the fields. He smoked his lazy pipe. He whittled his sugar pine stubs. He sat on a log. He talked and talked until the men had worked their way some distance off. Then he would get slowly to his feet and move closer, sitting on a new stump or log or rock. In this way he followed you around all day.

Geauga County's Edwin Ferris was an archivist. He kept a diary and his grandchildren's grandchildren still have it today. Ferris wrote that he and his father were working in their tree nursery one day. The rotund Mr. Mink sat on a nearby fence, talking, talking, talking. Edwin and his father shook their heads. Archibald Mink began to yawn, and soon he fell asleep. The skies turned dark; the air got heavy. Thunder rumbled afar. Edwin and his father ran to the house, but Archibald slept on. The rains came and Archibald got soaked. He woke up and shook himself. He wiped his face with his hand. Then he slogged and sloshed back in the wet and the mud. He passed the Ferris house, where the men were sitting on the porch. Archibald called out to them: "You could've woken me before the rain, you know!" Edwin's father yelled back: "I know."

Archibald was married. His wife's name was Abigail. Abigail said that Archibald read extensively. Often he read himself to sleep, dozing off over some weighty tome. Archibald must have been quite a reader because you could always find him asleep. Archibald snored loudly and he dreamed deep dreams. In the morning (or in the evening following an afternoon nap), he recited his dreams and he thought about writing them down in a book. Abigail said that Archibald could've filled piles and piles of manuscript paper.

Somehow Archibald managed to get hold of a farm lot in Burton—I think it was with the dowry money from Abigail's father. Archibald always owed people money, and under financial pressure Archibald eventually moved from Burton to Parkman and then to Pittsburgh, where he died from too much wife. . . .

What's that? Well just be patient and I'll explain. Let me see, how can I put this mildly? Mrs. Abigail Mink was a person who disregarded the rules. She did whatever she wanted, and she did it her way. She had a violent temper and she was built like a stove; and this combination made her a woman of influence, a force of nature to be reckoned with—as the poet said:

Her dove-like eyes turned to coals of fire,
Her noble nose to a terrible snout,
Her hands to paws, with fierce sharp claws,
And her bosom went in and her tail came out.

Abigail Mink didn't know any way to talk but just to yell and to scream. The world would not defeat her—no siree. She fought with everyone, even officers of the law, just like she would fight with a wild beast. In the Mink household things were always tense because Mr. Mink had the habit of contracting debts without making provision for their payment: he bought on credit and he forgot to pay. One time the deputy sheriff, Uri Hickox, came to take back a sack of beans, some coffee, and some salt. Mrs. Mink seized the deputy by the back. She twisted a bed curtain around his neck. She choked him until he was purple in the face. At that moment Archibald stepped into the room. He raised his eyebrows, he cleared his throat, and then he went over and tried to free the deputy. Abigail took a tailor's goose and hurled it at her husband, smashing his foot. Archibald winced. "My dear," he cried, "you've hurt my toes exceedingly." "Good," answered Abigail, as she pushed poor Uri out the door.

Then there was the time when Archibald Mink neglected to pay Ladd Herriot for three bear skins. The sheriff himself, big Joe Paine, tried to get Ladd Heriot's bear skins back. Joe had shoulders as wide as a yoke. His arms were like tree trunks. Joe opened the Mink's cabin door without knocking. Abigail screamed. She jumped up and grabbed a wooden, square-bottomed candlestick and hit Joe on the forehead, cutting a hole in his scalp. Blood oozed and ran down his face and he was temporarily blinded. He staggered back out the door. He pressed his bandanna against his forehead, he sat down a moment, and then he walked home weak and dizzy.

Once Yonnie Ford, another powerful man, was sent to retrieve a bed that was never paid for. He got in the kitchen door. Abigail jumped at him. She grasped him by the neck like a wildcat. In the scuffle she shut her teeth on his finger (accidentally, she claimed) nearly taking it off. Yonnie abandoned the bed, running wounded from the field of battle. Ah well:

When the Himalayan peasant meets the he-bear in his pride,
He shouts to scare the monster, who will often turn aside;
But the she-bear thus accosted rends the peasant tooth and nail—
For the female of the species is more deadly than the male.

Eventually the troublesome Minks left Burton for Parkman. Everyone breathed a sigh of relief. The air seemed fresher. The sun shined more often. Cellar doors were left unlocked again. After they'd moved to Parkman, the never-resting Abigail, angry at the world and at all the bones and stones and animals in it, became furious at Fred Kirtland, who owned the Parkman general store. In stormed Abigail one day. Fred was charging too much for sugar and flour, she shouted. He'd sold her a tin of coffee that had damp beans in it, she yelled. She wanted her money back.

Abigail's tongue flamed. She spit words like lightning. She roared in a voice like thunder. Fred stood back. He held up his hands. Slowly he followed her around as she ranted about his high prices and poor quality. Another lady hurried out the door. Eventually, Abigail passed the front door herself. Fred jumped and gave Abigail a push, but as she tripped out the door she caught him by the shirt. Out they went together. He fell on top of her and she screamed. "Murder," she shouted. "Killer, rape!" She held tightly to his shirt. Esquire Parkman came running. "Why don't you let the poor woman up?" he called. "Ah, man," Kirtland groaned, "I would if only I could."

Life with Abigail was too wearing. In a weakened state, Archibald succumbed to some disease or another in the city of Pittsburgh. After her husband died, Abigail made her way back to Burton. She came into town and word spread instantly. Abigail stomped into stores. She clomped and clattered into the City Hall. She shouted at the city agent. Her husband, she declared, had owed her money. Now he was dead. When he had forced her to leave Burton and move to Parkman, she still rightfully owned property. There was her dowry in land. There were possessions left behind. Townsfolk in the office shook their heads and stopped up their ears.

For years afterward, Geaugans remembered that day well—it was a Tuesday in April when Abigail Mink returned. Before she made her way into town like a vasty thunderstorm, Abigail showed up at the household of an old acquaintance, Asabel Barnes, a mile southwest of the village of Burton. The terror of the Mink name had preceded her, especially for the children—you see, mothers sometimes threatened that Abigail Mink would return at night and steal misbehaving children.

As I've said, Abigail was a loud and fierce traveler and rumors of her return had preceded her. The children kept their eyes peeled. In fact, two little girls living near Asabel Barnes had been having bad dreams for a week. As they came home from school on that Tuesday, the girls saw a horse and a wagon tied at the horsebars outside the Barnes's farm. The girls and all their friends crowded around. They were scared and shy and some of them shivered. They didn't dare to come too close. Little Julianna Barnes (afterwards Mrs. Mensah Chase) remembered that a woman built like a keg with legs like fence posts was standing at the door. She asked little Julianna for a dipperful of water. Julianna ran and brought it, and, to Julianna's utter astonishment, she was thanked politely.

Then Abigail stormed into town and stirred up everything, and it was Yonnie Ford (now Yonnie Ford, Esquire), the same powerful Yonnie Ford with whom the Minks had already had dealings, who made out the papers for her to sign that night. Abigail received one hundred dollars for her dower interest in lands, possessions, and "accidental matters." Surprisingly, Abigail smiled and seemed satisfied. Of course during that evening, when the townsmen were there witnessing this transaction, she called Ferris a catamount, Mr. Umberfield an owl, and Mrs. Umberfield a goose. She had strong names for Hitchcock, Punderson, Clearmont, and Hickox, too, but these I can't mention without embarrassment.

Later, Abigail Mink was charged with burning the Burton

School—the Academy it was called. Some men claimed to have heard her singing the old schoolboys' song:

> Now we're met like jovial fellows,
> Let's all do as the wise men tell us—
> Sing "Old Rose" and burn the bellows.

But Edwin Ferris saw the fire and he wrote in his diary that Abigail Mink didn't do it—he knew for a fact that she was in the house of Lyman Durand at the time.

Abigail said: "Well, lah-dee-dah to you!" and she ignored the accusations. She frowned at everyone she saw. She walked fast. She clomped loudly on wooden floors. She called people "skinny thieving raccoons," and she continued in her unrepentant ways. Amazingly she managed to marry again—I suppose that's like the saying: "It's better to marry a shrew than a sheep." Nonetheless, when Abigail died, her new husband, Heywood Lentil, had inscribed on her tombstone:

> Here lies my wife
> Here let her lie;
> Now she's at rest—
> And so am I.

And if you don't believe me, then just go to the pioneer cemetery in Burton and you can see for yourself.

·3·

The Child from Nowhere

YOU'D THINK YOU'D know who you were if you lived in the middle of Ohio. Ohio is solid homey territory—it's a place full of folks who know their great-grandparents. They certainly know their family histories in Highland County. Highland County's in the southwest of the state. It's where the Mound Builders left their great and mysterious hills. But the Mound Builders aren't the ancestors of today's Highlanders. Mound Builders are lost in prehistory; they left Ohio even before the Indians.

Europeans first came to Highland County in 1801. Many of these pioneers came from Virginia and from North Carolina. In the mid 1800s Eliza Jane Trimble Thompson of Hillsboro in Highland County, the daughter of Ohio governor Allen Trimble, launched the Women's Temperance Crusade; that was in 1873 and the whole country heard about it. Eliza Thompson closed all Hillsboro's bars—everyone called her "Mother Thompson." In Highland County there have been big events like this and then there have been small events, there have been large mysteries and tiny ones. One small story that I've heard is about an unknown woman.

The unknown woman was Sarah Dorney Stroup. Sarah was a familiar town figure and she died in a familiar place on Wednesday, January twenty-first 1942—it was at the home of her daughter, Mrs. Lewis Cecil Vance, on West South Street. Still, Sarah Stroup died with a mystery unsolved.

Sarah never knew her true identity because she had been abandoned as a child in Hillsboro. Even in her last years, Sarah hoped for a miracle. She hoped that something magic would happen, clouds would part, the sun would shine, an unknown person would knock on her door, and he would reveal who her true parents

·21·

were, where they had lived, and how she came to be deserted by a woman believed to have been her nurse. All her life Sarah had searched for some clue to her history. At one point a local professor took an interest in her case and spent his own time and money trying to locate her parents. But today the mystery remains as deep as ever.

Exactly what *is* known? Well, Mrs. Stroup knew that she was brought across the ocean from England. The courier was Ellen Dorney. Ellen said that she was Sarah's mother but there is no doubt that this woman was really Sarah's nurse. Ellen was tall and dark with brown hair and with a fiery temper. Ellen also had another child with her, a little boy named Wystan. Wystan resembled Ellen and she claimed that he was her son, Sarah's brother. It was known that Ellen had come to America following her husband's death in order to live with her sisters, Mary and Margaret, and that an American brother-in-law, William Park Dorney, had sent her the money for the ocean voyage.

At one time, Margaret had lived in Hillsboro. When Ellen Dorney reached Hillsboro she found that Margaret had been widowed and had taken her three children to Indiana in order to join Mary. Ellen was tired and upset and angry. She returned to the depot to take a train to Mary's house. It was a Wednesday and it was raining—it was a wet midweek day in an April of long ago.

Why did it happen? Was it the weather, cloudy, gray, wet, and miserable? For some unknown reason little Sarah stopped and pulled back at the station. She cried. She shouted. She would not move. Ellen Dorney was furious. According to the conductor, a

Mr. Grant Wood Clark, Ellen turned and said angrily: "Whoever wants this child can have her! I don't want to be bothered any more."

Ellen pushed the child away. She jumped onto the train with her son. The steam shot out of the wheel pistons. The train started up, and suddenly it vanished. Ellen and her son were gone completely and dramatically from the little girl's life. People stood dumbfounded. Had this really happened?

Sarah was blue eyed. She was sandy haired. She had dimples and delicate features. Little Sarah was dressed in expensive, hand-tailored clothes, quite different from the plain clothes worn by Ellen and Wystan. The old ladies of Hillsboro sighed and shook their heads. A child could not be left alone. Four prominent women of St. Mary's Episcopal Church took Sarah under their wing; these ladies were Mrs. William A. Scott, Mrs. Roger Smith, Mother Thompson, and Alice Postelthwait, who was the minister's wife. The women contributed a monthly stipend and they paid a widow, Bessie Jones Harper, to care for Sarah. The four women also took turns making clothes for Sarah.

The life of an orphan was the life of a serving woman. When she was seven years old Sarah was bound out, as was the custom for poor children in those days. Sarah was taken to the dark, ancient mansion of General Charles Sheif and his mother, Clarrisa, to work for her board.

Poor Sarah was upset by these old and formal adults. She missed Mrs. Harper and she cried and cried, so she was taken back to Bessie's house where she continued to work for her keep. Not long after, Bessie Harper moved to Indianapolis and she took Sarah with her.

Sarah grew into a fine girl. She kept at her education. After the age of nine when she left school she still practiced her reading and her writing. She was serious and she was modest. In her later years she looked back proudly on all her hard work. She had had a good life, she reported. Why, she had shaken hands with nine governors and four presidents. As the oldest woman bearing the name of Stroup at the annual Stroup family reunion at Dodsonville, Sarah was presented with an inscribed Shaker chair. And she recalled, as though it were yesterday, her amazing adventure when still living with Mrs. Harper in Indiana. There, she had seen Abraham Lincoln's body lying in state at the State House in Indianapolis. Two years later Mrs. Harper and Sarah moved to Cincinnati, and soon thereafter Mrs. Harper was killed by a train.

Sarah was ten years old. She was sent sent back to Hillsboro. Sarah was mature and neat and well thought of, and the four townswomen who were acting as her godmothers arranged for Sarah to work at the James Stroup farm west of Dodsonville. This was a large estate and a quiet place. Sarah cooked and washed and cleaned the house. She grew up. One day her employer's son, John W. Stroup, proposed to her.

John was a widower. He lived in his parents' home with his child, Eldora. John Stroup was tall and thin. He was an outdoorsman and he was intrigued by natural herbs and spices and medicines. John had many friends in the Shaker communities, especially Union Village to the west of Hillsboro. The Shakers knew the healing powers of plants and they raised and sold medicinal herbs, including aconite, angelica, bittersweet, black elder, borage, and lady's slipper. John was always trying this herb or that and he kept a stock of all manner of healthful dried plants.

In any case, John married Sarah and he bought a farm near Danville. John and Sarah lived there for, said Sarah later, the thirty-seven happiest years of her life. And what was Sarah's life like? The Stroup farm was one hundred acres. They grew wheat and corn and they had some apple trees; there were ten cows, twenty or more sheep, and a great many chickens. In the spring and summer there was planting and cultivating. After the harvest in the autumn and the winter they cared for the stock, cut the year's supply of fuel, and split the rails for the fences. In the fall they cured their meat and they stored the potatoes and the apples in the cellar along with beets, cabbage, celery, and turnips. There was always enough flour and meal made from their own wheat and corn and there was plenty of milk, butter, and eggs.

Sarah lived happily on the farm. Generally she was content. The seasons were regular, the summers were hot and the winters were cold. Her mornings were bright. The clouds were white and spadgers sang in the trees. Sarah got along well with Eldora and Sarah also had her own daughter, Harriett. Around the turn of the century, Sarah took in an orphaned boy and she raised him like a son. Still there was a nagging problem, a hole in her past; there was an empty space somewhere inside of her and she felt it in the deep dark hours of the night.

"All through the years," Mrs. Stroup said, "I prayed to find my real parents. One time I went to Indiana and found Ellen Dorney's sisters, Mary and Margaret. They were quite old and somewhat confused. They wouldn't tell me anything. I cried and they said that Ellen had remarried and moved to some place in Missouri. Finally I left. I was sad and disappointed. I guess the sisters died soon afterwards."

In a little town everyone knows everything. People shook their heads when Sarah walked by. They pointed her out when they were entertaining visitors and there was always a wind of whispers around her. One day a retired professor, Isaac Ishmael Sams, moved to Hillsboro. Originally he came from Bath in England. Professor Sams heard the stories about Sarah Dorney Stroup. He raised his eyebrows. Perhaps I can help, he thought. He looked closely at Sarah when she passed him by. He studied her face; it seemed familiar. Professor Sams was certain that Mrs. Stroup had English and Scotch-Irish parents. I wouldn't be surprised, he thought, if Sarah descended from some sort of nobility.

Professor Sams had a theory. The landowners in England kept close hold on their wealth; it was a closed society and it was a men's society. When an English girl was first in line for an inheritance she was pushed aside. She was sent to a far-off school where they wore prim starched blouses and long, modest leggings. She was encouraged to stay away from home. As she got older she would travel abroad and be hurriedly married to a foreigner. Sarah must have had some scheming male relative who wanted to inherit and who had arranged for her to be brought to America and hidden. Undoubtedly she was lost on purpose.

But there was no hard evidence—there were really no clues. Mrs. Stroup had only two relics of her childhood. She had a child's cup of the finest china, which she had brought with her across the sea. Also she had a picture taken of her in a dress from England and standing in a summer Hillsboro garden when she was five years old. Sarah often looked at that little five-year-old girl. Was that really her? The photograph was weightless in her old and wrinkled hands; it felt like a piece of cotton paper, like a cloud. The child in it, the tiny serious girl of long ago, was a child of air. Sarah held the picture out at arm's length. Had she really been that little girl?

Sarah remembered the old nursery rhyme

> Monday's child is fair of face
> Tuesday's child is full of grace
> Wednesday's child is full of woe
> Thursday's child has far to go
> Friday's child is loving and giving
> Saturday's child works hard for a living
> And during the whole of her Sabbath bright
> Sunday's child is good, wise, and right.

Had she been born on a Tuesday—somehow she thought so. What was the full Tuesday verse?

> On Tuesday morn when I awake
> My bedspread's like a strawberry cake,
> The pillows are biscuits that I bake,
> The sheets are a white and fluffy lake.

All that day I'm full of grace,
Quiet at meals with a fresh-scrubbed face,
I clean my plate—I don't leave a trace—
Then put my dolls in their hiding place.

And Tuesday night from my fortress bed
I fight great battles inside my head;
Wolves and bears wait to be fed,
They want to eat me—but get pillows instead.

Ah, but Sarah was a child of woe; undoubtedly she had been born on a Wednesday, the same day of the week that she had been abandoned in the Hillsboro train station.

On Wednesday morn I'm out of my room
As sunshine lightens the nighttime gloom
I creep downstairs to the kitchen-room
To stare outside at a morning moon.

But during the day I'm full of woe
My buttons have bunched in a crooked row
And after breakfast I stubbed my toe,
Pricking it where the rassle-berries grow.

Late that night through the rains I ride
Flying on the clouds I slip and slide
Through misty-wisty stars in the cosmic tide
With trusty Teddy at my side.

Had it actually been a Wednesday? Would she ever know her true birthday?

Mrs. Stroup took a deep breath. She looked out the window. Here she was in the fine town of Hillsboro, sixty miles east of Cincinnati. Hillsboro had four banks; it had two newspapers and two hotels. There were mills for grain and there were storage sheds and railroad loading docks. Mrs. Stroup tried to feel a part of Hillsboro life. Everyone was related to one another in Hillsboro, but she was not. She sighed again. Maybe it was just her old-lady ailments—nowadays she was always feeling only fair to middlin', and at night she had heavy leg pains and she drank Monkshood tea that she bought from an herb farmer in Union Village.

Sarah Stroup leaned back in her chair. She knew Hillsboro well. She could close her eyes and picture its old stone buildings. She could feel its warm worn park benches. In the summertime everyone sat on his porch or walked in the town square. Hillsboro's a family town, but Sarah Dorney Stroup was an incomplete person with no family. Had she come from a mist? It seemed as if she had—and it seemed as if into a mist she would go. In fact, it was a misty day in the year 1942 when Sarah Stroup finally died in Hillsboro at the age of eighty-nine.

When Sarah Stroup died she left only one known living descendant; this was her daughter Harriett with whom Sarah had lived in her last, elder years. Sarah's husband John had died in 1906. Sarah's step-daughter Eldora Stroup Jonte was also gone. The boy Sarah had taken to rear when he was deserted at the age of seventeen months, she had named Charles; Charles was lost in Europe during World War I. And as to brothers and sisters, parents, cousins, aunts, and uncles? Well, once upon a time and long long ago Sarah had been captured. She had been kidnapped. She had disappeared from her home, and her relatives had disappeared from her life.

Sarah died without roots and almost without family: at age eighty-nine she was still an orphan. "Where is my history? Where is my family?" asked Sarah Dorney Stroup. "I've lived in Highland County for a very long time. I've married and raised a family and I have many friends. But as long as I live I'll never stop wanting to know who I really am and where I really came from."

That's the end of the story; I know no more than this—but perhaps Sarah does now.

· 4 ·

The Zanesville Earthquakes

OHIO IS SOLID COUNTRY: it's built on limestone, shale, and sandstone. Of course there's a bit of crumbly scattering scree here and there but there are few actual slips or slides or earthquakes. Basically the place is firm, solid, and homey—it's good settling territory, and its also good substantial travel-through country. Ohio was always a passage land. There are waterways and long Indian trails. The Indian trails are as old as humankind, crossing those areas that have no waterways and leading to the headwaters of the navigable streams. Sometimes the trails followed alongside the water routes. And why would you have a land route when you had a river right next to it? Well, in dry seasons the water was too shallow for boats and in the winter the streams froze up—besides, some Indians preferred land travel rather than having to carry canoes with them everywhere.

Most Indian trails followed the high ground, so the Eastern settlers called them ridge roads. The patterns of cities on the maps of Ohio follow the Indian ridge roads, along which white men set up their first towns and forts. In fact, the old Indian trails became the white men's military routes and later the public roadways. The most important of these highways was the Great Trail. It was the major Indian road westward from the Chesapeake Bay. Beyond Pittsburgh, the Great Trail crossed northeastern Ohio to Sandusky Bay and then it went around the west end of Lake Erie, turning north to Detroit; later this was used as a white man's military highway, connecting Fort Pitt, Fort Laurens, Fort Sandusky, and Fort Detroit.

There was also the Scioto Trail which ran north and south between Sandusky Bay (at Lake Erie) and the Ohio River at the mouth of the Scioto River. At the top it followed the Sandusky River; then it crossed overland and descended through the state along the Scioto River. After crossing the Ohio River, the Scioto Trail became the Warriors' Trail, which wound far and away, disappearing deep into the southern United States.

The Easterners followed these preexisting trails but they weren't satisfied. They wanted real roads because they coped with plenty of other hardships. The settlers had few supplies, they had to carry everything themselves, and they were darned if they were going to suffer just getting from one place to another. The feet of man and beast were the only powers available inland and they plodded tiredly over roads that didn't deserve the name, along trails marked by gashes chopped on the tree trunks deep within the forests, wading or swimming through streams. Although they had horses and oxen, people walked most of the time, mothers carrying their babies, children dragging and lagging behind. The paths wound up and down and around, along, and beside. The mountain crossings were especially painful—the slopes were so steep that settlers used ropes and chains to haul their wagons up or to ease them down.

Ohio country was more travelable than many other areas. It had no mountains and it had boatable rivers. People coming from the East could ease into Ohio country through the flat areas of New York or they could come by river and lake to Niagara Falls and then float down Lake Erie or follow the northern trail along the shore. Settlers coming from the South faced endless ups and downs through the mountains in Pennsylvania and northern Maryland.

Eventually, there was the National Road. The National Road was built along the route used by George Washington when he took his surveying trips into the Western Territory and later for his ill-fated campaign with General Braddock against Fort Duquesne. During the administration of President Jefferson, the government decided to improve the Washington-Braddock route. Congress authorized the building of a great highway called the National Road. The road began in Cumberland, Maryland, it went to

Wheeling, West Virginia, it extended across Ohio through Zanesville, Columbus, and Springfield, and it ended in Indianapolis, Indiana.

In the great annals of the National Road, Ohio has a special city: it's Zanesville in Muskingum County. In 1796, Congress designated Ebenezer Zane to carve out the Ohio portion of the National Road, from Wheeling, West Virginia, to Limestone (now called Maysville), Kentucky, on the Ohio River. Zane took his brother Jonathan, his son-in-law John McIntyre, and two other strong young men. They surveyed and they marked, and they cut a highway wide enough for two horses to walk comfortably through Ohio country. This section of the National Road is known as Zane's Trace.

In the middle of Zane's Trace is Muskingum County, hilly and rolling and green. Before the white men moved in, Delawares, Wyandots, Shawnees, and Senecas all lived there at one time or another. The most famous Indian town in the region was near Duncan Falls and was called Oldtown by the early white settlers. While he cut his road, Ebenezer Zane stopped to set up his own little city in Muskingum County where Ohio's Licking River empties into the Muskingum River. Ebenezer staked out a mile-square tract of land, which he was allowed to claim in accord with the terms of his contract with Congress. It was here that Zane's Trace crossed the Muskingum by ferry and the town began as the homestead of the ferry keeper. Soon the town attracted other settlers, men who were carpenters, potters, shoemakers, stonemasons, and weavers.

Ebenezer sold the site of the town for one hundred dollars to Jonathan Zane and John McIntyre. At first the place was called Westbourne. Westbourne was a fine area for homesteading; there's black soil and plenty of water power. John McIntyre and a partner, Increase Emeree Mathews, opened the first Westbourne store in about 1800. Do you want to know how much things cost then? Well, I'll tell you. MacIntyre and Mathews sold green tea at $1.21 a pound, stockings at $1.66 a pair, muslin at $1.93 a yard, and gingham at $1.58 a yard.

Pottery-making clay was discovered nearby. By 1808 the town had been renamed and all manner of dishes, stoneware, and bricks were stamped with the Zanesville imprint. Zanesville became the center of Ohio's glass industry—it turned out window glass, glass dishes, glass bottles, and glass flasks. Today, Zanesville is the county seat, and from 1810 to 1812 it was even the capital of Ohio.

Life was simpler in those early Zanesville days. The children got together every afternoon and every evening in the town square. They played ball and any number of forgotten games, some with names like The Farmer Sows His Seed, Marching to Quebec, Sister Pheba, Oats, Peas, Beans, and Barley, and Pass the Button. They played with dolls and tops; they played bull-pen, town ball, and sockey-up, and most especially they played baste. Baste is Prisoner's Base. It's a game you can play with lots of boys or girls—the more the merrier.

You've never played baste? How could you have missed out on it? . . . Oh? In that case I'll tell you a little about the game. You begin with a playing field, any big open area. You pick two bases; these can be stumps or trees or stakes or rocks that are maybe fifty feet apart. Two captains choose teams. (In Zanesville they decided who could pick the first player by spitting on one side of a wood chip and giving it a toss in the air and then calling out either wet or dry.) Each team stands near its base. They begin with a chant like: "Red clover, red clover—let the prisoners come over!" Then all the players run toward each other, trying to reach the other base without being tagged. If you're tagged then you have to stand as a prisoner near the base. On the other hand if you touch the other side's base without being tagged, you free all the prisoners. The game is over when one side takes all the other team as prisoners. We played baste many, many a time, with the game never fully ending because it got too dark and our parents called us in for the night.

Baste was the most popular game in Zanesville. But today's old men, even those who grew up playing baste every single summer night, won't tell you about it, at least not first thing. Instead they'll always talk about earthquakes. Earthquakes came with childhood for these men. Tremors are the crystal clear and dramatic scenes remembered even by old men with the weakest memories, and you still hear endless earthquake stories on the porches and in the stores and along the park benches during Zanesville summer evenings, although it's decades and decades later.

Nature's rumblings, grumblings, and crumblings were on everyone's tongue in those days. Back in their grandparents' homeland—in old and settled Europe—there had been violent earthquakes in 1755 in Lisbon and in 1783 in Calabria. News came across the sea as word of the troubles spread worldwide. Was it Divine retribution? Was it the foreshadowing of still worse disasters? In 1757 Halley's Comet appeared. People shook their heads. Some felt chills in their back. Wonders of the heavens followed mysteries of the earth: northern lights were seen in southern Europe. Will-o'-the-wisps were everywhere, even in the daytime. Biela's Comet came in 1758. Enchke's Comet came in 1783. In 1784 hail the size of melons fell in France's wine fields.

People in Connecticut's Western Reserve talked endlessly of these cosmic events and natural disasters. Mother Nature was angry; she was shaking herself like a wet dog. In the fall of 1811 a huge comet visited the night skies over Ohio. The next winter the whole western valley of Ohio was rocked by earthquakes. Of course everyone expected this—hadn't Noah Webster deduced that comets and earthquakes are boon companions and always accompany each other?

In December and again in January, earth shivers and shocks were happening all the time and the tremors continued on and off into the late spring. Some quakes were light—little bitty jiggles. Others were so strong that they shook bricks from the tops of chimneys and cracked the walls of houses. After a major shake there was silence and then small tremors; these small shakes were the earthquake echoes, and they could go on for hours. One day in Zanesville, dishes, books, and guns were knocked off shelves. The potmen and glassmakers moaned at the damage. That evening there was just one real bad shaking but there were little knocks and shocks on and off for the rest of the night.

Around about that time, a great many Indians of the Shawnee and the Delaware tribes had come into Ohio for their winter hunt. These Indians were a little irritable at the moment; they'd been on the move, continually bothered by raids from other tribes. What's more, these particular Indians were friendly with the English who encouraged them to fight against the settlers. This made the settlers in Ohio country very nervous. A band of forty or fifty Indians had set down near Zanesville that winter and they often appeared in town with meat and skins for sale and in order to exchange their goods for meal, salt, gun powder, and so on.

You know how we make up our whole worlds: the feel and appearance of where we live is pretty much something that we dream. Are the skies sunny and bright or are they glaring white and garish? Are the winds gentle and warm like clouds or are they hot and dry and irritating? It's all in our heads—it's made up. . . . What's that? Yes, yes, I'll get to earthquakes in a moment. You see, in Zanesville, Micah James, a friend and neighbor of my great-grandfather, was awakened one night. It was in May, late in the week—I think it was a Thursday. Suddenly there was a terrible rattling. His whole house shook. His doors and windows and pots and pans jiggled. It must be the Indians trying to break into his house, thought poor Micah. He sprang from his bed. He seized two axes and he stood by the door, shaking and ready to cut down the first Indian who stepped in.

For May it was cold, a startlingly cold night; it was cold enough to freeze the hairs in your snout. The doors shook every quarter hour. The dishes rattled. The chairs shivered. Micah stood next to the door. His hair was damp and stringy and it stood out in all directions. He was frozen because he'd been in such a hurry that he hadn't put on any clothes. He stood wide eyed and (as a famous poet once said):

Deep into that darkness peering,
  long he stood there wondering, fearing,
Doubting, dreaming dreams no mortal
  ever dared to dream before.

Micah James stood just like that. He peered, he feared, and he dreamed. The silence was thick as cold butter. But there was no direct attack—nothing happened for minutes and minutes and minutes. Were the Indians waiting until he fell asleep? Finally Micah called out: "All right, you savages! Come in here and get me. But I warn you: I'll fight to the end!" He shouted, and then he listened. Silence there was and nothing more.

Micah was cold and shaking and tired. He stood and he stood and he stood. Then almost without knowing it he stumbled over to his bed and fell down exhausted, and he was not aware of anything until the morning.

Light streamed in the window. A heavy flaw blew through the branches outside. Micah awoke with a start. He looked around. There were no Indians. His house was intact, and it was empty. Micah threw on his clothes. He ran outside. The first person he met told him that she too had heard rattling doors and dishes. It must have been an earthquake, she said shaking her head.

Old Micah James just stood there with wide eyes. I guess so, he said finally. After a bit of thought, he nodded. He felt better; that suited him down to gravel—and in fact that's exactly what he told my great-grandfather. Micah looked down Zane's Trace for a moment. "I guess it must've been an earthquake," he said as he rocked back on the legs of the old wooden chair on a porch by the store one cool summer Zanesville eve of many many years ago.

·5·

The Strangling of Pretty Ruthy Sue

UP IN THE northeast of Ohio there are still some wooden covered bridges, but they're disappearing. It's worse in southern
Ohio—I hear that Ross County doesn't even have a single one
anymore. Ross County's just south of the center of Ohio. It has hills
and valleys and plains, and it's got small streams and large streams
and all these creeks flow into the most important river down there,
the Scioto; once, there were covered bridges over a good many of
those creeks.

Ross County's biggest creek is Paint Creek, and the Paint
Creek valley's got some strange and mysterious regions. Local folk
say that the Paint Creek Valley is the prettiest in the whole state,
but I'd have to say that it's also one of the loneliest. The Paint
Creek valley always makes me think of William Cullen Bryant's
poem:

> The melancholy days are come,
>   the saddest of the year,
> Of wailing winds and naked woods
>   and meadows brown and sere.

And that poem brings Ruthy Sue to mind . . . but I'll get to her in
a moment.

As I've said, Ross County's got some beautiful places. It's got
plenty of black soil and cold creeks and windy, wooded hollows.
Early settlers wrote back to the East Coast about how wonderful
Ross Country was—for instance you've probably heard tell of Abra-
ham Finson, Nathaniel Massie, and Corrie MacBain, famous early
Ohio settlers, and then there was the right Reverend Robert

Wilfred Finley of Bourbon County, Kentucky, who brought a bunch of Presbyterians (or was it Methodists?) to Ross County and founded the city of Chillicothe next to an old Shawnee Indian settlement.

These settlers named the Scioto River and Paint Creek and North Fork, and also Upper Twin, Buckskin, Deer Creek, Salt Creek, and the Kinnikinnick. Paint Creek runs through the entire middle of Ross County and then into the Scioto River; it's a rough and rocky stream and it's got sudden deep spots that surprise you. Spruce Hill is in the Paint Creek valley. Spruce Hill is incredibly steep; you can't miss it because it towers over the other hills nearby. The top of Spruce Hill is actually some kind of old mound with stone walls; maybe it was actually a city on a hill—nowadays people call this and the other mounds around it Mound City.

There's no doubt about it, Paint Creek valley is intriguing. It's old and it's mysterious. Along the Paint Creek River you slip back into an ancient time; it's like looking out into the sky at night. Old-time mound people lived there—they were the ancient people before the Indians. It's interesting that fairly recently the French explorers found some pretty strange people along the Scioto River. The French called them Mesopoles and reported that they were big and hulking. They wore animal skins and they had huge powerful hands—as the Bible says, "There were giants on the earth in those days." If you don't believe me then go down there yourself. There's a place along Paint Creek with two tremendous boulders across from each other, forty-five or fifty feet apart. When the French explorers fired a musket at one of the Mesopoles he jumped the river from boulder to boulder and he escaped upstream. That's why this place is called Giant's Leap. Local folk can point it out to you today—ask Caleb Partridge, if you can still find him.

It's a funny thing, after the French there's nary a remark about the Mesopoles. But when the American settlers began to farm in Ross County they found other strange things—mounds filled with treasures. These mounds weren't like anything the Indians built. In fact, in the pioneer days when the eastern settlers arrived, the local Indians didn't know about the older peoples. The Mound Builders had vanished; they'd filled southern Ohio for about seven hundred years, and then one day they just up and disappeared.

Who knows what those Mound Builders called themselves. Today I've heard college professors call them Adena and Hopewell. But Hopewell is a modern word; it comes from a Ross County man named Mordecai Hopewell. Captain Hopewell had some pretty spectacular mounds on his land, in Union Township on the North Fork branch of Paint Creek. Hopewell's mounds were side-by-side—one was a giant square fifteen acres big and the other was a slanty rectangle one hundred and ten acres big. I've already mentioned Mound City haven't I? That's in Union Township too. Mound City's a big rectangle with rounded corners, and inside the rectangle there are twenty-three littler mounds of all sizes.

White men have been rooting around in these mounds for hundreds of years. They've dug up pearls, stone beads, discs, and copper and silver doodads. They found more than two hundred smoking pipes that are carved in the shapes of bears, beavers, frogs, panthers, rattlesnakes, toads, turtles, and wolves—there are even some with human heads.

These old mounds are like the Mesopole people: they're big and hulking. The mounds don't seem to have been forts, although some of the mounds had big walls that ran straight together for almost a half mile. Were they for ceremonies? Were they living places? Who knows—however from the diggings, you can tell that Mound Builders hunted and that they also gathered woodland food, like fruits, grains, honey, nuts, and roots. The Mound Builders didn't seem to garden or farm much, and they weren't writers either.

Mound Builders were traders. The mounds have obsidian from Yellowstone, copper from the Great Lakes, shark teeth from down near Maryland, grizzly bear teeth from the Rockies, and seashells from Mexico. Mound Builders were also craftsmen; they made animal statues, beads, cloth, handprints, jewelry, and yo-yos, and they buried these things with their dead in the mound cemeteries.

The mound people are gone, but their spirits still wander around Ross County. There are strange stories about them in the back woods. Some of these tales are true, and some are just legends. Some are funny. Some are fantastic. A number of yarns involve the ghost of Ruthy Sue, who still haunts the valley west of Spruce Hill.

I heard about Ruthy Sue from Horace Large. Horace lived back in the hills. He was the pappy of a friend of mine, a Frankfort man named Thomas Warren Large. Horace actually remembered Ruthy Sue. "Ruthy Sue was a young miss of 'ceptional beauty," he told me. "Why, danged if that gal wurn't as purty as a picture on the wall."

Ruthy Sue was fresh and happy and she had many a gentleman friend. She was young. She was pretty, she sparkled, and she was always smiling. She was, as they said in those parts, "as bright as a bell." And Ruthy Sue had a favorite: he was Clem Slatterson. Ruthy Sue and Clem went on picnics together and sometimes they'd take a moonlight ride in Clem's horse and buggy.

Clem, as you may have heard, was a fine young man. His father was a cattle trader who bought animals from farmers thereabouts and sold them to slaughterhouses and to buyers from the East. Clem worked mainly in the stockyard; that's where they stored the cattle. Also, about once a month, Clem would travel out to the backwoods farms looking for animals to buy. He'd inspect the animals and pay cash and then he'd drive them home. Clem was thin and strong and Ruthy Sue thought the world of him; Clem thought the same of her too.

There's a section of the Paint Creek River called the Giant's Leap . . . I've mentioned that already? Well, Horace told me that Ruthy Sue and sturdy Clem were out riding in a buggy one Friday night in May. They stopped in the old covered bridge over Paint Creek to do a little "kissin' and sparkin'." The bridge was along the river just before the Giant's Leap. It was around midnight and suddenly the hounds of the Paint River valley started baying and baying. It seemed as if there was the scent of something floating through the air, but none of those hounds moved, they just sat and howled.

Was it raccoons? Were there a couple a foxes or a wildcat or some slinky skunk? Hounds are the best scenters at night. That's when they hunt, especially for coons—there's something about a raccoon at night that just gets to a hound. I suppose I can't tell you anything you don't already know about raccoons. They live everywhere and there isn't a schoolboy in the whole United States who hasn't had dealings with one. Did you know they live mainly on snakes in the summer? No? Well, they do. They also eat frogs, crawfish, grasshoppers, insects, and even little chickies. In the winter, coons eat acorns and beechnuts and specky corn; but when there's a lot of snow on the ground the coons stay in their hidey holes for weeks, even months, without eating a single bit of food. And you know as well as I do that coons always test their food by feeling it. A coon doesn't sniff like a dog; instead, a coon never tastes anything until it's patted and pulled it with its paws. Those paws are soft and sensitive, like fine leather gloves and . . .

What's that? No, I got side-tracked because it *wasn't* raccoons that night. Horace was certain it wasn't coons that set the hounds a'howlin'—not by a long shot. All the dog noise started in the valley nearest the covered bridge. Then farm dogs from everywhere else took it up, howlin' till dawn. They set the whole of Paint Creek valley near Spruce Hill echoing, and it was a mighty fearful sound.

Daylight came and it was pretty grim out. The sun was too bright. People got together. They were talking real quiet and shaking their heads near the general store at Frankfort. What had started the hounds to howlin'? Everyone knew that it meant no good. Then Ruthy Sue's brother Josh came running down the road. His sister'd been out all night and she hadn't come home yet.

Horace was a boy in those days. He was standing around too, shivering a bit. He told me that Winnifred Wayfield, an old widow lady, stared up at the sky. She shook her head. "Go out a lookin', boys," she said. "But I'm afeered Ruthy Sue is dead." Then every man and boy was out hunting for Ruthy Sue and for sturdy Clem too—and many a shotgun glinted in the morning sun.

How long was it till someone found Ruthy Sue? No one remembers. But find her they did. Her body was crumpled. It lay on the dirt in the covered bridge. Her throat was bruised—she'd been strangled. There were the marks of a giant hand, larger than any man's in the Paint Creek valley. The finger prints were big and purple. Some giant had snuffed out the life of the prettiest girl in all the hills.

And as to Clem? Well Clem was no skinny picket—in fact he was tough as shoe leather. But Clem had plum disappeared. Later that day someone came across Clem's horse and buggy on top of one of the ridges. The buggy was smashed and the horse was dead from a bursted blood vessel—he hadn't been directly hurt or anything; maybe he'd been scared to death. Still, no one saw hide nor hair of Clem. Late in the evening, when they finally gave up and came back, the searchers only shook their heads and held on to their guns more tightly.

Don't ever walk that region at night. Horace said that if the wind is right the ridges near Frankfort moan around about midnight. Sad Ruthy Sue is calling out. Probably she's looking for Clem. That's a savage place, my friend, it's as unholy and enchanted as ever there was beneath a waning moon.

I'd like to show you the exact spot where all this happened but the covered bridge is gone. Horace is long gone too, Caleb Partridge is getting very old, and other people in Frankfort today don't seem to know just where it was that pretty Ruthy Sue and sturdy Clem Slatterson actually went sparkin' on that cold Friday night, deep in the ancient mound country of Ross County, Ohio.

Jemima Who Got the Old-Time Religion

THE SETTLERS BROUGHT old European names to Ohio. One of those names is Jemima, which means dove. You probably think of the dove as a bird of peace, maybe even as a symbol for the Holy Ghost, since European paintings show doves coming out of the mouths of saints at their death. But Ohio's Jemima Coble was not like these Christian doves at all. Jemima was more like a local Ohio dove, which is a bird that fights bitterly with its cousins—Jemima Coble was a tough old pigeon from the backwoods of southern Ohio near the city of Hillsboro.

Hillsboro *could* mean hilly town and Hillsboro's certainly got plenty of hills, but actually the city was named by David Hays in honor of a local citizen, Captain Billy Hill. Hillsboro is the major city in Highland County. Its buildings are made from limestone and sandstone that was quarried over near Greenfield. Around Hillsboro the uplands are pretty bare, but the lower areas have good soil so there are plenty of farms scattered about.

The Hillsboro area used to be wild and woolly. In the pioneer days as a child you'd have heard chilling tales of Shawnee Indians and wild animals. You'd be sitting at night hugging your knees in front of a blazing wood fire in the fireplace and you'd be breathless as Pap told you about wolves and guns and caves and spirits—you shivering there and leaning tight against your mother's leg. Outside it was pitch black. The sky had no moon. An ox cart creaked, the drover shouted: he was working by feel, trying to get his flock of sheep through the mud street. Some of the sheep were probably

strays let loose by crazy old Zeno Wilcox—Zeno learned from the Bible that it was wrong to keep sheep behind fences. And there'd be plenty of distant noises salting the air, real Night Wolves and crickets and owls, and every once in a while someone walked by with a lantern. Otherwise, all was black as coal.

Finally it was time for bed. If you were a girl you'd pat your hope chest before you went to sleep each night. The chest was a wooden box from your grandmother and it was filled with linens and quilts. On weekend nights when you were old enough you'd stay up late and dance the light fantastic in the town hall. You'd have worn a long dress made from pink silk, the kind with a full skirt and tight waist. Pink ribbon streamed down your left shoulder. Your hair had seven braids. . . .

What's that? A housewife? Well suppose you *had* been a housewife—you would've stayed at home all day every day (except for marketing). Housekeeping was more than full-time work. You had to weave and knit and sew. You made quilts, you washed clothes, you gardened, and you cooked. You cleaned the house and the stable. And housewives thereabouts had to follow all the country rules; for example, when you moved into a new house you took only your oldest broom because it was very bad luck to bring a new one, and every housewife kept sun-dried ground-up chicken gizzards: a bit of this powder stirred into a cup of water cured any disease.

If you were a man and if you were musical then you'd have belonged to Hillsboro's First Brass Band. One time, General William Henry Harrison was going to talk in Columbus and the First Brass Band went. Four horses pulled the band wagon, Colonel Armsted Doggett came behind with his log cabin on wheels, and other folk from Highland County followed in their own buggies. It rained all the way and everyone was feeling just as dreary as the weather. Then as you came into Columbus, old Bill Heaton said you'd best play "Hail to the Chief." Well, the Hillsboro band was the only one of the fourteen visiting bands that could play that tune. Ah, you were mighty proud, and even the rain suddenly seemed fine and warm.

Hillsboro had everything in those days. It was the largest town around—the other cities in Highland County were just collections of a few houses. One wild Highland region not far from Hillsboro is called Carmel. In the backwoods of Carmel, people are mixtures of Indians and negroes and white men from Kentucky, Tennessee, and West Virginia. They're a handsome bunch, with tan skins, straight black hair, and fine figures. They live in scattered shacks among the hills. Each shack has a mattress or two set on stones, wood boxes for chairs, and a broken stove; chickens, dogs, cats, and pigs all live indoors with the families.

Many of the Carmel hill people claim to be part Shawnee. Some Shawnee Indians had stayed in the hollows even after the white men had driven out the main tribe; other Shawnee returned from the reservations to hunt or to visit. After all, Ohio was their homeland and there was always good fishing in Ohio streams and the Ohio forests were full of fine berries, roots, nuts, and healing herbs.

In those parts, down south in Highland County, women liked their pipes and their chews. For instance, there was the tobacco-chewing "doctor" woman, Jemima Coble. She was part Shawnee Indian. Is she still alive? I don't know. In her day, Jemima could be found, rain or shine, traipsing the hollows, poking about in the dead leaves with a walking stick for herbs to cure the "gatch" in her stomach.

Miss Coble is quite a character. She walks around mumbling to herself and patting the ground with her tappey stick. Jemima uses a lot of plantain: she calls it "waybread," but it's just the same common weed that you find everywhere. The crushed leaves help ease skin itches, like poison ivy and insect bites, and they also stop nose bleeds, and waybread roots are good for most pains; also, the stems are a laxative. Of course Jemima will tell you that you don't need any plants for hiccoughs. Just sit and close your eyes and take three slow deep breaths—but before you let out the last breath swallow twice *then* breath out—it always works.

As I've said, Jemima Coble is part white and part Indian. I suspect she's a *jessakeed*—an Indian prophet—or at least she's descended from one. Jemima is short and stooped and her face is lined with thousands of wrinkles. She's got wide eyes that are pale blue. She stares at you with a tilted head. She drools a bit of tobacco juice. If you're good to her, she'll let you have a drink of water from her flask; this water came from a spring that the "Jedge man from Hillsboro" once drank from, and that's why the spring is a magical place.

If you stop her on a walk—or if you catch her attention and she stops by herself—Jemima Coble will give you a bit of dried plantain root. Old Jemima begins talking as if you'd just interrupted her in the middle of a story and she supposes you'll know exactly what she's talking about. "Yes this purse is from Cathay," she might be saying, or, "Don't mend your clothes while you're wearin' 'em." Then she'll tell you to be kind to stray dogs and she'll predict that someday you'll die quietly next to a stream.

Miss Coble will shake her head. She'll tell you she's just an old and gentle woman but once upon a time she was "the ornriest, cussedest, guntotin', knife-throwin' woman in Pin Hook Holler, 'count of the guv'ment liquor I got to usin'." In those days she would swear and spit. She'd hit anyone for practically no reason at all. People crossed the street to stay away from her—their stomachs ached just looking at her. She shouted and she yelled and she kicked. Once, in a drunken stupor, she lay in a ditch at night. It was winter. The snow was thick and the ice was slick. She almost froze to death. If you want proof she'll take off her shoes and stockings and show you where part of her heel is gone; that's the place that got the worst frostbite that night.

Jemima will tell you how she finally crawled to her cabin. She locked herself in. She rolled on the dirt floor. She thrashed and called out. She chanted "*hi-le-li-lahl*" (she'd learned this from her grandfather, who was an Indian) over and over, beating on a piece of wood. She hit her legs with a hickory stick and she screamed and called out foul words. She propped her feet up on the bedside like a jinniwink. Finally she was a success: she cast out the devils and she received the genuine old-time religion.

Not everyone believed that Jemima was a new woman. When her neighbor Aunt Tildy Wooten saw Jemima, she shook her head and called out: "You're a fake, Jemmy. You never gone to church in all your live-long life. You're just a devil in disguise. Listen:

> The Devil an' me,
> We plum agree—
> I hates him,
> An' he hates me."

It was just like a couple a school girls. Jemima spit at Aunt Tildy and said:

> I'm Willie Wastle
> In my castle—
> All the dogs in town
> Can't pull me down.

Then Tildy said:

> Whenever there's a house of prayer
> The Devil builds a chapel there,
> An' 'twill be found on 'xamination
> Devil's got the bigger congregation.

Jemima hit the ground with her tappey stick and roared back:

> In the year 1849
> The devil made some swine,
> But by an' by he changed his way
> An' made it into Aunt Tilday.

Tildy shook her head:

> In Pirie's chair you'll sit, I sez,
> The lowest seat of hell;
> If you don't up and mend your ways
> It's there 'at you must dwell.

I'm told this went on and on to no end. Jemima claimed that Tildy was ugly as a mud fence. Tildy said that Jemima (favoring her mother's family) had a face that'd stop a clock. Jemima feuded with Aunt Tildy about which of them really had the "genu-wine" old-time religion. The two women were the talk of the Highland County hollows. One day there was a bit of shooting between them and eventually on one Saturday in June Aunt Tildy Wooten had to call the law to the hollow to settle all the "fightin' and feudin' and such." I guess it worked because there hasn't been much shooting since.

·7·

Three Chips in the Mulberry Tree

LAST WEDNESDAY Herb Grady and me went to visit Wren Caplinger. You always find Wren sitting in a rocking chair that he got from his daddy's house. It doesn't take much to get Wren talking, rambling on about the good old days—but after a long day of work I don't mind listening. I just sit and sip his whiskey and those same old stories wash over me like a warm bath.

Eventually Wren got around to the buried silver story. I've heard it before. It's a true story; his family's been telling it for generations and Wren heard it as a child from his grandmother, Drusilla Minney Caplinger. I think that Hoad Minney used to tell it too—he heard it once from his father, Henry Minney. Maybe you knew Henry? He was ninety-six when he died a couple of years ago. Thornton Minney—known as Pompey—was Henry's father and he was actually *in* the story; he was the one who heard the deathbed confession about the "three wooden chops—the three chips—in the mulberry tree." Here's what Wren said happened.

This all happened down in Ross County—you know, south and west of Columbus. I guess it's just one big valley down there, the Scioto River valley. There's plenty of fine farms, but they get lots of floods—floods wiping out whole farms of corn and wheat in a bad rainy season. The place's got other problems too. Long ago, way before my daddy's time, people down there got the Fever from the swamp lands. Whenever someone got the Fever they vowed to up and leave, but of course they were always too weak while they were sick. Then when they got well again they figured on staying a bit longer since that's where they grew up; I guess not many of them ever left because of swamp Fever after all.

Ross County farms are mainly corn and wheat. Also there are fruit trees—apples and mulberries. These trees spread everywhere by themselves; so, even if you didn't plan on it ahead of time, when fruiting season came you always had more than you needed for yourself. You could sell plenty in the market too, and lots of the apples were sent up north.

Anyways this took place a couple of generations ago. In those days down in Ross County there was this old wood-wagger. He was a loner who'd had gray hair ever since anyone had known him. He had a beard and he was quiet and mysterious. His name was Tillman Peters, and none of his neighbors knew exactly where he'd come from.

Of course there were lots of strange old coots living in the Scioto valley. They were people who wanted to forget something about their past or their family or who wanted to disappear or who just didn't like company. This Tillman Peters was one of those strange loners. He lived his own life, all alone in a log shack far back in a dark hollow at the foot of a high hill along Black Run— nowadays they call the hill Baum's Orchard Hill and they call Tillman Peters's hollow Kendrick's Hollow.

Tillman did a little gardening and a little hunting and a little wood cutting and hauling and he ate lots of mulberries. He even took care of the mulberry trees growing wild up and down in the wetlands by his cabin. Tillman's house was in a mulberry valley. I'm sure he picked that place because it was filled with mulberry trees. Some of those old trees were over seventy feet high; those were red mulberry trees—folks down there called them morals. The mulberries were dark red and purple and they came out late in the spring. And were they sweet? Let me tell you—they were better than strawberries. Some people used mulberry wood for fence posts and furniture and tool handles and Indians wove clothes from young mulberry shoots, but old Tillman just wanted the fruit and he made it clear to everyone that they'd best leave his trees alone.

Tillman wasn't a mean feller, but he wasn't too sociable neither. He didn't try to make enemies, but he didn't have any friends. Tillman liked Thornton Minney and even patted him on the shoulder when he saw him. (Thornton was just a kid in those days.) But Tillman only saw people when he came to town, and he came in about once or twice a month. He never said "Hello," he just nodded. He didn't look around much—he always went into the General Store and bought a few things, and he always had plenty of money with him.

The years rolled by. Seasons came and seasons went. The trees grew larger and older. Tillman kept to himself, but he seemed to get on fine all alone. People said that he was rich. I can tell you that Thornton Minney thought they were right. He'd heard that old man Peters had three chests filled to the top with silver dollars. It certainly was true that he always paid with silver. Lots of people thereabouts had seen these silver dollars when Tillman bought things in town, lots of people figured Tillman had stashed quite a pile of money somewhere, and lots of people wished that they could get their hands on some of that money.

Old Wren Caplinger'd finished his whiskey. He stopped rocking, he nodded to himself, then he poured another drink.

Dogs've got sharp noses. . . . What's that? Why'd I mention

dogs? It's because some people are like dogs: they've got special scentin' abilities. Did you ever hear the old saying: "Money don't smell"? Well, down in Ross County they sure didn't believe that. Old Aunt Myrt claimed she could smell silver and she said that she smelt it in the hollow where Tillman Peters lived. Some folks had done more than smell silver, they'd actually seen the three chests full of silver dollars; that's what people said—but no one remembers the name of those exact people.

Still it was a plain and simple fact: everyone knew Tillman Peters had silver money and he had plenty of it. Tillman got old, but of course the money never got old. Tillman got wrinkled and skinny and scraggly but his money stayed the same. Tillman walked bent over. He was thin and shrunk; he was whiskered and weak. Was he ninety or a hundred? Who knows. He managed to stay pretty healthy but he sure got slow and shaky.

Then one day Tillman suddenly got sick, very sick. It was a Sunday in June. Jon Taskey came by and found the cabin door open. He peeked in. Tillman was lying on his bed. He was sweaty. He was coughing. He was breathing hard. Tillman tried to talk, but all Jon could understand was "Pompey."

Did I mention that Pompey was Thornton Minney's nickname? Well, it was. Jon put a wet rag on Tillman's forehead, then he went for Pompey. Pompey and Jon came back that afternoon. Tillman was still sweating and moaning and even weaker than before. He tried to talk, he rasped, he coughed and coughed and he couldn't catch his breath. Pompey sat close but he could understand only a few words: *chests, silver, buried, three chips,* and *mulberry.* Tillman coughed again and again till he shook. Finally he stopped coughing. He hardly breathed. There was an awful silence. Even the outside was quiet as a thick wool blanket. Then Tillman Peters died.

Tillman Peters had got to be an old broomstick of a man. There was nothing much left in the cabin, a few pots and pans, an old gun, some boots. Things were musty and everything felt as dead as Tillman. Jon and Pompey told their story and everybody figured that Tillman Peters had buried his three chests of silver under a mulberry tree and had marked the tree with three axe marks, three chips cut in the trunk.

Well, people listened and people talked, and, although most folk didn't admit it, everybody was out there looking. They were checking the mulberry trees. On dark nights some folks were digging; there was endless searching and scraping and rooting around. People found broken iron cups and ivory buttons. They found bone needles and bone hoops. They dug up old rags and strange-shaped pieces of wood. There were scraps of cloth, rusty nails, bottles, and pieces of glass. But there was no money; no one found even a hint of a chest or of silver.

Wyle Crawfish the divining man with a whole bushel of hazel water switches came down from Columbus. He crawled around on his hands and knees sniffing but he didn't have any more luck than anyone else. Wyle said that old Tillman must have witched those chests so they couldn't be bothered. And Wyle may have been right; old man Peters must've had money sniffers in mind when he hid his chests of silver. Still it don't seem to matter that nobody's found the money or that some kind of spell was cast on it 'cause folks still go mulberry tree hunting, even today. And has any money at all ever been found? Well if it has I've never heard of it.

Wren had finished his whiskey again. He was rocking gently back and forth. His eyes were closed. We got ourselves up and we didn't say good bye.

I've heard Wren's story a number of times and from different folk, so it must be true. People wouldn't make up something like that; besides everything in the world is connected, from woubits to butterflies. Mysterious things and coincidences and whatnot—they're all tangled together. Recently I heard a new twist to this story. Bill Springer said he'd heard that an earlier Ross County mystery—the mystery of Mine Run—is tied into old man Peters's hidden money.

Mine Run was a galena-lead mine, and one time the silver dollars for a payroll were stolen. I wouldn't be surprised if that's where Tillman got his treasure—but he didn't get it directly. You see most people think that it was this mean-eyed peddler who took the money. He'd been hanging around for a couple of weeks and buying whiskey for some of the miners. Then the payroll got stolen. Later the peddler was murdered. One night he simply disappeared, and a few months later the chewed-on skeleton of his horse was found in a nearby ravine.

How do I know he'd been murdered? Well, years later, Garrett Arsham, a tough old miner living nearby, began to feel "dawnsey," as they said. Then he became feverish and down-right ill. He took to his bed. He didn't eat. One night he sat up suddenly. His family gathered 'round. Old Garrett seemed to be listening. Then he said: "I see my home—I'm comin' home." Everyone was quiet.

He was on his deathbed. Garrett Arsham turned his head toward his son. "I got somethin' to say. I'll rest better if'n I tell you." Once long ago, he said, he'd killed a man, a peddler. He'd thrown the body into an old Indian well. The peddler had a sack of money; it was a pile of silver dollars, and Garrett had buried it next to the well. But Garrett could never bring himself to dig the money up again. He'd tried to forget that day and most times it wasn't anywhere in his mind. But some nights and even some mornings he couldn't get it out of his head. Maybe after he was dead, said Garrett, he could finally forget.

Tillman Peters was a cousin of Garrett, and Tillman had been there just after the deathbed confession. He said the money belonged to the Arsham boys now that their father had paid the price of death for it. So, after the funeral, Tillman led a search. He spread out the boys in the area. They spent a whole day—they met back together at noontime and then for dinner, but no well or body or money seems ever to have been found. Tillman supposed that poor old Garrett may have got a little crazy with sickness. In any case, God and the Devil know all, said Tillman. A few years later Tillman moved off into the mulberry hollow where he stayed alone until he died.

Garrett Arsham's buried in an abandoned graveyard on top of

a hill not far from Mine Run. Some of the tombstones are still standing and if you go there you can find his epitaph.

> Here lies Garrett Arsham,
> Please be quiet and civil:
> God knows the truth of him—
> So also knows the Devil.

I suppose that could be Tillman Peters's epitaph just as well.

Heidi the Hound-Dog Cow

LORAIN COUNTY IS citified nowadays but in earlier times Lorain was filled with dairy farms. There were cattle atop every hill. I suppose you've never heard of Felix Renick. He lived in Chillicothe down in Ross County. Renick built himself a herd of short-horned thoroughbred cattle from Europe; these cows gave mighty good milk and soon all of Ohio had Renick cows, even as far north as Lorain.

As I've said, Lorain was dairy country and it had plenty of cows, but none was as peculiar as Heidi. Can you make a silk purse out of a sow's ear? Maybe not—but you sure as shootin' can make a foxhound out of a Jersey heifer, or so I gather from recollections of old-timers in the farmlands throughout Lorain.

Heidi was a Jersey cow who was the greatest foxhound ever to lead a pack. Her full name was Heidi-ho and she chased coons, foxes, rabbits, and squirrels. She chased rabbits any old time but she only hunted coons and foxes when she was with a pack of hounds. Heidi bellowed when the dogs howled and she sounded like an elephant. At night she could be heard three times as far as any dog and there wasn't much sleeping in Lorain County when Heidi was on the scent.

Here's Heidi's history. When Heidi-ho was a three-day-old calf, her mother died. The farm where Heidi-ho was born belonged to the Burton family—Mr. and Mrs. Starkwood Burton, with five boys (Noah, Aden, Eli, Abraham, and Otis) ranging in age from four to eighteen years, and there was one girl, Henrietta. Also there were eleven hounds and a pile of chickens.

Heidi was an orphan, and she had to be hand fed. Henrietta was a motherly child and she took over the baby-sitting chores.

Heidi had a rough tongue, she would suck on Henrietta's fingers, and she drank milk easily. Soon Heidi became a pet, just like one of the family. She ran free in the yard and the hounds considered her a dog. The boys ran with the hounds, and Heidi-ho ran with the boys. Heidi was quick. All day she ran and ran, and boys and dogs and cow chased squirrels and rabbits. It wasn't long before Heidi could run down a rabbit all by herself. She was fast as lightning—over short distances she could outrun any of the dogs.

Heidi could trail by sight or by scent. She ran with her tail up and with her nose to the ground: I guess she learned this from the dogs. Heidi could pivot and turn like a dancer and I've heard from old-timers who remember seeing her running a fox scent in the light of the moon that it was a wonderful sight to behold. You'd almost forget she was a cow—instead she seemed to be some gigantic horned hound-dog.

Heidi'd chase any little animal; she'd run at top speed, bend down without stopping, grab the little beastie on the run, and shake it like a dustrag. She never ate the animals, but she couldn't resist chasing them. She'd see a squirrel at a distance. She'd stop. She'd slink down and tense up. Suddenly she charged. Heidi would gallop at top speed, following all the shifts and backtracks and skids and skads of the tiny creature till she just scooped it up in her big flat cowy teeth; she shook it and she tossed it; she flipped it into the air, and then she ran off for the next squirrel or rabbit or chipmunk or baby coon.

Old George Washington kept a kennel of foxhounds but he didn't have any fox-hunting cows. His doggies were white with patches of black and they were maybe two feet tall and weighed the same as half a bushel of potatoes. The Burton's foxhounds looked just like George Washington's dogs; they were pretty easygoing and didn't seem to notice that Heidi was different from them. The dogs ran in a pack of ten or twelve and Heidi ran in the middle or at the front. The dogs had speed and endurance and stamina and so did Heidi. The dogs sniffed the trail and howled and so did Heidi. The dogs ran all night and so did Heidi, and in the morning the dogs came back scratched and burred and panting and so did Heidi. Heidi could jump any fence in the hills. Hodge Joshen, whose father'd seen Heidi up close, said she had thin hooves and could climb like a goat and that she once even turned a double somerset—if you can believe it.

Well, Heidi-ho grew up. She ran through the swamps. She climbed the ridges, and she was always skinny and dirty. If you saw her I'm sure you'd say she was pointy like a farm woman—you know the kind, an outdoor woman who'd rather mess around horses, stables, and dogs than dress pretty and go to tea and keep house. Of course Heidi-ho was really a cow, a Jersey. She had a broad face and she had short horns that curved inward. Jerseys come from some little island around England; they don't give as much milk as other breeds but Jersey milk has lots of cream and butterfat. However Heidi was a poor excuse for a Jersey—she was too skinny, she ran around all the time, she didn't eat the right hay, and she gave hardly any milk at all.

Maybe Heidi was a dog in cow's clothing. She sniffed and she dug at the ground with her hooves and she chased rabbits and she hunted coons, especially at night. Once the pack had started out, Heidi'd be with them, and everyone knew it for miles around. Henrietta and her brothers, the Burton boys, were proud of Heidi: who else had a coonhound cow?

When they got out of the yard, the Burton dogs were joined by hounds from neighboring farms. All the doggies around knew Heidi and didn't mind her company; she belonged in the fields and the hills. She took to escaping from the Burton's fences and month after month and night after night she would run with the doggies. By the time that Heidi was three years old every dog in the region ran with Heidi's pack. Heidi became a leader in the land of hunting dogs.

Heidi was a big wild cowy foxhound. She slept all day and she ran all night. She made a strange noise when she ran—it was a howling moo. And Heidi-ho certainly didn't learn any of this from Henrietta Burton. Henrietta was a proper well-behaved child.

Henrietta had been born on a Monday; she was golden haired and fair of face, like the little girl in the nursery rhyme.

> On Monday morn when I awake
> The sky is like a silver snake
> Winding its tail through a cloudy lake
> Trailing white pearls to the far daybreak.
>
> Now Monday's child is fair of face
> So I smile politely at my breakfast place
> With muffin crumbs on my collar lace
> And an extra kerchief, just in case.
>
> Then Monday night I watch the moon
> Afloat in the sky—a white balloon
> Or maybe a marble in a black lagoon
> Where I'll fish it out with my runcible spoon.

This was Henrietta, fair of face and polite—but it certainly wasn't Heidi-ho. Heidi was strange and noisy, hound-doggy, scrawny, pointy, and scratchy. She inspired her packs of hounds to new heights. However, what with all the mooing and the howling and the trampling and the chasing about, the women folks were getting mighty tired. "Shakes and stakes—we'd sure had enough of it," said Daisy Mason. There were just too many sleepless nights, there were too many tired dogs and men, there were too many ruined gardens and broken fences. Everyone had to nap during the day because they were listenin' to Heidi's pack all night long. Too little work was being done: the community was going to the dogs, and it was sliding fast. Of course no one talked of actually getting rid of Heidi—who on earth would even think of giving up a good foxhound?

Now at that time, the local countryside began suffering other hard troubles. Times got bad—very bad. There was no money. No one bought anything at all that they could possibly make. The weather was poor. People saved seed from their food to replant. Even the Burton family was starving, and finally the Burton farm had to be sold. Everything—the tools, the buildings, the animals—all had to go. As the song says:

> There was an old man and he had an old cow
> But he had no fodder to give her,
> So he took up his fiddle and put down his plow,
> Singing: "Listen, old cow, consider;
> You're not any good for milking, so now
> I'll sell you to some old widder."

After the sale the Burtons moved to Texas, and, when they left, unpaid debts were left too. All the furniture and the animals had been sold. Who bought Heidi? I've been unable to find out. Several different men bought the animals—but who would want to keep Heidi as a cow? It's true that most Jerseys are rich cream producers but Heidi was no good as a milker—she gave no milk at all—and by now Heidi was getting old and she was tough and stringy and not even fit for eating.

I'm afraid that Heidi-ho was more of a nuisance than a cow. Finally she wound up on a broken-down farm in the south of Lorain County. One night, a Monday in June, she was left unchained. The hounds howled, the dog packs called, and Heidi followed. She trampled through a barn door, a pond, and two farmyard gates; she jumped three fences and she joined the passing hounds on the scent of a coon.

A couple of days later Heidi was found shot. She was lying next to a large hollow tree. Some hunters had followed the pack of hounds; they were a bunch of city fellers and they'd gone out drunk. Jerseys, as you know, are kind of deerlike cattle. Heidi-ho herself was light brown; she was colored like a fawn with a black muzzle and she had short horns. I'd have to say that for a huntin' cow she was a real honey—but still there was simply no doubt that she was a cow.

I just don't understand it—I guess Heidi must've looked like a deer to the drunken hunters. She sure couldn't be mistaken for a little dog—the hounds were black and white with tan splotches and low built and lean. What was that fool hunter thinking when he saw this black and white hound pack with the light brown Jersey cow? Well whatever he thought, whatever he saw, whatever he imagined, the hunter shot poor Heidi in her tracks as if she were a bear or a deer or a raccoon or something. I've been told that the murderer was a lawyer named Barker from Springfield, but others say that he was a tooth doctor named Elwood from Columbus. He sure weren't a farmer from Lorain.

·9·

Rattlesnake Mound

DID YOU KNOW that eating snake meat will keep you young? It's true—I learned this from my grandmother. Ohio's got enough snakes to keep everyone here young. Our snakes live in hills, but not the high hills: they live in those low scrubby hills you see along the Ohio River. Take Belmont County, for instance—it's alongside the Ohio River and it's very hilly, and once there was a famous Rattlesnake Mound in Belmont County right by the river.

Belmont County's directly across from Wheeling, West Virginia. Coming west, European settlers liked the looks of the area so they stayed and put down roots and set up housekeeping. America's first abolitionist group, the Union Humane Society, was organized in 1815 by a Quaker saddle maker, Benjamin Lundy, in St. Clairsville—that's Belmont's county seat. Benjamin Lundy worked for Charles Osborn's paper the *Philanthropist,* the first journal in the United States to call for freedom for all slaves. After Osborn sold his paper in 1821, Lundy published the *Genius of Universal Emancipation* in Mount Pleasant, north of St. Clairsville; a year or so later, Lundy moved the paper to Tennessee and then to Baltimore.

St. Clairsville is up on a plateau in rich farming country on the National Road. Before the National Road came through the region, it was all wild around there. In 1765, Crile Croghan, who scouted for the Ohio Company, reported huge migrating herds of buffalo crossing the Ohio River near Wheeling. There were great gangs of wapiti elk all over the Ohio valley. In 1766, Otis Gordon wrote about "tremendous herds of buffalo that we observed on the beaches of the river Ohio and islands into which they come for the air and coolness in the heat of the day." In 1778, William Baldwin Hutchins wrote that "the whole Ohio Country abounds in Bears,

Elks, Buffaloe, Deer, Turkies, &c." In those days eagles, mountain lions, and wolves were also plentiful, although soon afterward they disappeared from most of the Ohio country. The big animals are gone, but if you know what you're looking for you can still find traces of buffalo and elk paths through the Ohio hills and heading off toward the salt licks of Kentucky and Illinois.

Disappearing animals was an all-too-common rule. You may not have heard of them, but Paroquets (they're also called Carolina parakeets) were everywhere in Ohio: you could find them up to the shore of Lake Erie. Great Paroquet voleries flocked the salt springs. Later, Paroquets were found only down in the southern states, and today they're gone and vanished entirely, just like the wild passenger pigeons.

In the olden days there were no crows or blackbirds or the usual singing birds in Ohio country—these followed the eastern settlers. I've heard that sandhill cranes, whooping cranes, and great blue herons came with the settlers too, when the easterners and their noisy towns chased away the enemies of these birds. Turkey buzzards were here in the Indian times and early settlers found them in flocks. You can still see a turkey buzzard or two wheeling high over any open Ohio field, keeping an eye out for field mice or just rolling along in the warm air currents. European honeybees came with the white man, as did rats. And there were more opossums and foxes after the area got settled. The white settlers sure changed things.

At one time—and I'm talking about before the Indians and even before the Mound Builders—reptiles, the vasty dinosaurs, roamed the American lands. But that wasn't in Ohio. Ohio was at the bottom of an ocean and so no dinosaur bones have ever been found here. Human days saw only the smaller scaly creatures, like turtles and snakes, in Ohio. Yes, vipers, biters, and other bad serpents slithered through Ohio in the pioneer days.

The white men fought the snakes. In pioneer times, there was this tumulus thing, this small prehistoric mound, up toward Moundsville, that was just filled with snakes. The snakes were all rattlers. The settlers hated them. Snakes looked evil and felt evil, and snakebites could kill you. The settlers wanted to dig the snakes out once and for all, and a group of men with picks and shovels and high leather boots and long leather aprons set out one sunny morning to do just that. But during the digging and shovelling, the men hit bones, human bones, old human bones, and strange pieces of pottery. It was too much. The men leaned back and shook their heads. Did they dare disturb that ancient area? They stood around in a circle—Fibs McCoy, Dalton Blandersill, Emmett Chandler, Carey Stippet, Bill Barringer. They looked at one another. Finally, they decided to leave without a single snakeskin.

This wasn't far from Moundsville, which is a city in West Virginia on the Ohio River about twelve miles south of Wheeling. Near Moundsville at the mouth of Grave Creek is Grave Creek Mound. This old mound is a cone more than three hundred feet wide and seventy feet tall. It's got two burial chambers, which are tombs of ancient mound people. In the upper room there was a single skeleton decorated with beads, copper bracelets, and plates of mica. The lower room was lined with wood and it had two skeletons, one with beads and the other just plain bare.

Some of the early white men had dug into the Grave Creek Mound. They were puzzled. What sort of house or fort or temple was this? It wasn't like anything the Europeans lived in. The American pioneers had round-log cabins with wooden furniture—puncheon tables with sapling legs, wooden benches, and blocks of wood for stools. In those days there were no stoves, only a stone fireplace with a small kettle and sometimes a second, larger kettle as a kind of oven. There was no extra furniture. If company came, the host family just took the door off its hinges to make a big table. Along the wall was a shelf where they kept the dishes and the pewter ware. The rifle hung on two wooden pegs over the door. And these old-time pioneer cabins didn't have closets: you hung your clothes out in full view on wooden pins. Every ceiling beam had nails and pegs and hooks for apples, beans, dried peaches, herbs, pumpkins, roots, seeds, and other dried vegetables. In the corner there was a block of dried hominy on a stump next to the hickory broom and the turkey-wing duster.

These were the houses that the settlers knew. Earthen mounds were strange and mysterious. Grave Creek Mound was a complete puzzle and Rattlesnake Mound made no sense at all—Rattlesnake Mound was some ancient hill with a passel of evil snakes. These snakes hounded the pioneers and haunted the round-log cabins. Snakes lay out in all the sunny spots, and sometimes you found them in your cabin at night. I suppose some people might argue that they were useful critters because they ate rats and mice, but they also ate eggs and chickens. And of course the real problem was that these were vipers, deadly poison to people. The settlers wanted to live in peace. They wanted their children to be able to play in the hillsides. How could anyone make a home thereabouts with rattlesnakes sliding and gliding around in and out and everywhere?

The Ohio settlers called these serpents rattlers. In the South they call them maussasaugas and in the Northwest they call them pit vipers, but they're all the same, with a chain of tough rings on the end of their tail that they shake when they're bothered. Rattlers are lazy and sluggish and if you compare them to water snakes you'd have to say that rattlers aren't especially mean. First thing a rattler will do when bothered is to try to slink away. If it's cornered, a rattler's too lazy to bite right off, so he puffs and shakes his tail chain and hisses. It's only if you touch him or if you move real fast that he'll suddenly jump and bite.

But that bite spells trouble. A rattlesnake bite is terribly painful. The place where you're bit turns red and purple and green and swells. Soon—in less than fifteen minutes—you get weak and have to lie down. You might stagger around and have cold sweats and vomit and your heart will start beating to all get out. Then your eyes open wide and you get crazy. You can die in half a day, but if you're real lucky you might get better all of a sudden.

For snake bites it's best to try and get the poison out of your body fast. Put a strap around your arm or your leg where the bite is—put it between your heart and the bite to keep the bad blood from getting loose. Then make a cut, a slit, in each of the tooth marks and suck out any juices. . . . (What? No, the blood won't hurt your mouth unless you have a scratch on your lip or tongue or something.) You have to keep this up for an hour to get all the poison out. The Indians knew this remedy and doctors still recommend it today. In Ohio, Indians also used some herb medicine, two types of snakeroot—the Seneca snakeroot and the Virginia snakeroot—which you chew up and then tie onto the wound with a bandage.

Snake bites are bad and scary business. People living in the regions near Moundsville shook their heads whenever they talked about rattlers. It was very discouraging. Rattlers were everywhere up and down the Ohio River, but too many of them were tangled in that huge snaky pile in Rattlesnake Mound. The settlers were worried, but they stayed away from the old snaky hillock because the spirits of the dead threatened anyone who dared to dig in the mound.

What could the settlers do? A snake might up and bite you any time. You could be walking and thinking of something else and turn a corner and then—whoosh and scrugg, a snake would be jumping up at you. Children had been bitten, swelled up, and died. Even grown men had been killed by rattlesnakes. Could the people live side-by-side with the Devil's pets? Settlers took to praying. Then one day God whispered in their ear through an eastern doctor passing through Moundsville who told them about pigs.

You see, the doctor told them that pigs can eat rattlers with no problem. You know the saying about how the word *edible* means "good to eat and wholesome to digest, as a worm to a toad, a toad to a snake, a snake to a pig, a pig to a man, and a man to a worm." Well this saying is God's truth—although I don't know if pigs are actually protected from the poison or if they just don't get bit.

In any case, early one summer morning the settlers made a wooden corral around the whole of Rattlesnake Mound. They buried the ends of the boards deep and they trapped all the vipers inside with a tight fence. That afternoon, a Tuesday in July, they let in eight pigs, fat old bristly female sows. It was a hot day; it was a scorcher and a roaster. Emmett Chandler, who owned most of the pigs, leaned over the fence. The other men stood around watching and sweating and wiping their heads with kerchiefs. The pigs grunted and snuffled. They pawed the dirt. It wasn't long before the pigs found the snakes and began to eat them. The pigs chomped and pawed and within two days all the rattlers were gone. The men nodded, quietlike, and then Emmett drove his pigs back home. Rattlesnake Mound was finally safe, and I never did hear of a rattler in that region since.

·10·

The Corpse That Wouldn't Bleed

AT THE BOTTOM west corner of the state, not far from Cincinnati, a strange happening took place. It was eerie and gruesome even for the tough pioneers of the Scioto Valley. This was a kind of murder trial, and I've no doubt that it was the oddest performance of the kind that Ohio's ever seen—in fact the trial made such an impression on all those present that people still talk about it today, a century-and-a-half later.

Sharonville is a little town and you may not have heard of it. It's in Hamilton County, just north of Cincinnati. Now, this whole mess began outside of Sharonville on a Wednesday morning in the year 1818. It was damp and foggy. A hard-bitten mountain man named Crile Williams was coming through the woods south of his home. Williams was angry, angrier than usual. His brother Clayborn had taken a horse from Crile—Clayborn came over when Crile was gone and just plum took it. Over and over again in his mind, Crile saw his brother riding off with that horse. Crile was furious. At the moment he was out hunting rabbits but he couldn't get his mind off that horse. Crile heard a noise, he squinted—why, there was a man ahead, sitting on the ground. It was Clayborn. Crile stopped and tightened his shoulders. Then he lifted his rifle, he bit down on his lip, and he shot his brother through the head.

Crile was about to turn around, when he felt a shiver. He walked closer. The man he'd murdered wasn't Clayborn. It was another tall, dark-bearded man, an inoffensive neighbor named Louis Sartain. Louis had even been sort of a friend of Crile's. Crile swore and backed off. He turned and ran. After a half-mile or so, he stopped. He had to appear calm when he returned. So, Crile hunted up some rabbits, he shot them, and then he walked back home, sweating but quiet. That night Sartain was missed from his farm. His brother went out searching the next day, and late in the afternoon Louis Sartain's body was found lying in the woods with a bullet in his head.

Sartain was buried. There was no question that he'd been murdered in cold blood. Sartain's brother Crawford was furious. The Sharonville constable had no evidence at all, so Crawford and a few friends decided to investigate themselves. Most men thereabouts were honest folk. Crile Williams, however, was disliked by everyone. He was a bad man who kicked animals and who'd stolen things when he was a boy. Crile was a hard character. He was always angry and blaming folk and planning to get back at them for something or another; Crile was mean and loud and he drank a lot of whiskey. Crawford found some footprints near the murder area—these were like the shoes that Williams wore. The bullet dug out of Sartain's head was the type used by Williams. And there was no question that Williams had been out hunting on that fateful day.

But these were all the evidence against Crile Williams; no one had any real proof. Williams heard the charges and he got loud and angry. I don't know what you people are talkin' about, he said. Nobody could say much more. There'd been no trouble between Williams and Sartain. Then again, no one ever had any trouble with Sartain. Sartain had no enemies. He was easygoing. He smiled and had a "howdy" for everyone. Men, women, children, and dogs liked him. What would even Crile Williams have had against Sartain?

Some of the younger men formed a group of amateur detectives. Secretly they watched Williams. But Crile lived his normal life. He walked around in a quiet, unconcerned, everyday sort of way. He discussed the murder with his neighbors. He shook his head. Who could've committed this crime? he asked. Certainly the murderer should be punished, said Crile. Crile knew that other people suspected him but he ignored public opinion. One month passed and then came two. The more people talked and thought, the more that they suspected Crile Williams. But could telltale evidence be produced out of thin air? Well it could, and I'll tell you how.

In the Old Country—especially in Ireland and Scotland—folks believed that a murdered man can identify his killer. If a murderer puts his hands on the dead body of his victim, then the wounds will open and they'll bleed again. Many people in the Scioto Valley came directly from the Old Country and they knew that a vengeful God would watch over them and that justice would prevail. In Sharonville no living person could prove who'd really shot Louis Sartain. Someone said it was a shame that they couldn't resurrect Sartain's body and give God and Louis himself the chance to prove just who'd killed him.

Well people talked and talked and a public meeting was called. It was held in the church, the Baptist Church at the edge of the town of Sharonville. After a bit of chatter around and around, John Sheperd finally got brave and said that they should try the Old Country ways. People nodded. Fig Latham stood up, and he and Case Woods argued for trial by ordeal. Sartain's body should be taken out of the grave. It should be put in some public place. Each man in the town would have to set his hands on the body—if nothing happened this would prove his innocence. The Sartain family was at the meeting; they were still upset and they wanted justice. All right, said Louis's brother Crawford, let's go ahead and do it.

Now this was a mighty dramatic idea. Nobody in Sharonville had ever seen such a trial and no one was quite sure how God would react. The men talked back and forth, and late that night the minister finally gave his approval. The people at the meeting agreed that four elderly men of the church would organize the removal of Sartain's remains from his grave. To be most respectful, the coffin would sit in that very church. There, exposed to public view on a certain day, everyone in the town would be summoned. Each man was to come and to put his hands on the corpse; then the corpse would reveal its murderer—it would bleed when touched by the true criminal.

Poor Louis Sartain—his corpse was stomach wrenching. A vast throng of people gathered at the church. Most stood near the door and couldn't bring themselves to look inside. The murdered man's hair and beard had grown half an inch. His body had slimy grave worms; the smell was gagging and terrible. Children were kept at home, but all of them looked out their windows, even if they lived far away, because they knew that spirits might be abroad anywhere on that day.

It was a Wednesday in July and it was hot. The sun glared and everyone squinted; people were sweating before the sun was over the treetops. Everyone knew about the ghastly ordeal and every man felt that he had to prove his innocence. People had talked and talked all week. They wondered what exactly it would be like to touch a decaying body. There was no question that when Crile Williams put his hands on the corpse, thick black blood would stream out. Perhaps the body would ooze blood as soon as Williams entered the room. The decaying body might even move or groan. Last Sunday the minister had quoted Robert Burton. Burton had been a sixteenth-century English scholar and in his famous book, *The Anatomy of Melancholy,* he wrote: "Carcasses bleed at the sight of the murderer." No one in Sharonville doubted that this would happen.

The minister stood in the doorway of the church. John Sheperd took over—he was the constable. Old John was a large, fat man and he was to be the master of the ceremonies. Sheperd had a speech problem and was difficult to understand; nonetheless he was used to talking in public. He stood by the bench on which lay the open coffin with Sartain's body. Sheperd had a list of the local men and he called each name in turn. Samuel Corwine was the first on the list. Corwine was a barber, and there was no suspicion against him. Sheperd said: "Sabuell Cudwide! Sabuell Cudwide! Cobe up and touch de dead body ob Louis Sartain, who was subbosed t'be shot or murdered."

The crowd was hot, sweaty, and very quiet. Mr. Corwine walked up to the body. He examined it. He slowly placed his hands on the corpse. There was silence. There was no blood. Nothing happened. Corwine relaxed and stepped back.

"Uccle Tede Howa'd! Uccle Tede Howa'd!" shouted Constable Sheperd, who wanted Mr. Cornelius Howard to step forward. "Cobe forrud, Uccle Tede, an touch you' han's to de murdered man's torps." Cornelius "Ted" Howard slowly put a hand on Sartain's shoulder. Nothing happened. There was an inadvertent sigh of relief from some of the other men.

The whole church and even the churchyard began to stink with an awful, sickening smell. One by one in answer to their names the men approached the front bench; the coffin sat opened, unmoving, and gruesome. The men filed in, they touched the corpse, and they stepped aside. As each man passed the ordeal he stood along the wall. Some were pale, but all stayed in order to see the last to be tested.

At last, Crile Williams was called: "Mista Cwile Wiyyams!" said the constable. Crile walked into the room from outside the front door. He had a steady step. He was pale, but he looked calm. He knew what people thought. He knew that this whole trial was aimed at him. He knew that his neighbors believed him guilty of the murder and that everyone expected the worm-eaten body of Louis Sartain to bleed or to rise or to moan. But Crile Williams looked not to the left or to the right only straight ahead as he marched toward the body of Louis Sartain, the victim of an unwitnessed woodland killing.

Williams knew that he was guilty. Did he fear that telltale streams of blood would gush suddenly from the bullet hole in Sartain's head? Did he worry about oozing wounds? I suppose we'll never know. Crile Williams stepped past the other men. He walked slowly, as slow as pond water. When he got to the table, he examined the body all over. He looked at it from head to toe. He put out a hand and he touched the shoulder, just like the other men had touched it. Then he turned, and again, as slow as molasses in

January, he passed out of the hot room and into the glaring sun in the street outside.

Nothing happened—nothing whatsoever. The corpse did not rise, it did not moan, and it did not bleed. The hot sticky silence was stifling and thick. Had the murder test failed? Some said that the body was too long in the grave. Others speculated that Williams had bewitched it. Perhaps, said old Fig, Crile Williams really wasn't guilty after all. Was that the truth, the holy truth? The crowd stood silently; they sweated and they sweltered inside the Baptist Church with a decaying body. The minister bowed his head. Where, he wondered, was God all this time? I wonder too.

·11·

Mannassah Who Even Yelled at God

IRON COUNTRY GROWS iron men. They're strong. They defy nature, and they're stubborn. They're men, as the old-timers say, on whom snow melts. Early in the nineteenth century, southern Ohio and northern Kentucky were iron territory because you had every important ingredient right there. The hills had iron, the streams had limestone and clay, and there was charcoal from the forests and coal in the ground, and then the Ohio River let you ship the iron just about anywhere.

Ohio's iron region is in the middle of the south tip of the state. Here, the Ohio River is rough and rugged and there's an odd-shaped sandstone cliff four hundred feet high jutting out over the river bank; this is called Hanging Rock. Hanging Rock is in Lawrence County. Down in Lawrence County there are high hills—abrupt hills—and the soil is clay. There's only a little bit of farmland, and this lies along the edges of the creeks, streams, and rivers. Mainly, the county's got rocks, especially iron ore. The county seat is even named Ironton. This Ohio iron country has old rusty beliefs, like the ideas of witchcraft and such, and there were many witch trials in those days. No women were ever actually hanged in Lawrence County, but two witches—Bessie Lee Clinton and Broom Mayfield—were convicted and banished from the area.

Out of the rugged iron hill country of southeastern Ohio, in Lawrence County along the Ohio River, came Mannassah Johnson, big and strong and ornery. Mannassah lived alone and he raised pigs and farmed wheat on the clay and rock slopes.

Mannassah Johnson had broad shoulders and hairy arms. His hands were callused and cut and thick. He had a beak of a nose, a curly beard, and bristly eyebrows. His eyes were watery blue. When he was angry, his face turned red. At such times (which were mighty often) you could hear his loud voice cursing God and all mankind and thundering through the hills. Mannassah was stubborn. He swore that no man living or dead or even God Almighty Himself would ever get the better of Mannassah Johnson, and it was almost true. Mannassah had a will of iron and he did pretty well getting the better of his fellow men. But Mannassah had trouble with God. To old Mannassah there was no such thing as an unavoidable act of God. Anything that God Almighty could do, Mannassah thought he could do one better—it was sort of a personal feud.

For example, there was a hay field just past the stream on a hill above Mannassah's house. One summer day Mannassah was cutting hay. Far in the west the sky got dark. The air was heavy. Lightning flashed and thunder rumbled. Most of the hay was cut and lying flat; rain would make it wet and heavy and in the next day's heat it would begin to rot. Mannassah grunted. He worked harder. Sweat drenched his shirt; it soaked his heavy beard. The clouds got black. The sun turned mustard yellow and soon it disappeared behind the thunderheads. Mannassah's face was red and dirty.

The first drops fell heavy and slow. The rain was loud. Mannassah straightened up. He grimaced and he frowned. He glared at the hay, still unprotected in the field. He shook his pitchfork at the black sky. Lightning flickered in the distance. Mannassah shouted: "God Almighty, now what're You doin' to me? Leave me alone; I got enough trouble already." Mannassah was furiously trying to bundle the hay. "Listen here—are You havin' a joke on me? This ain't funny. . . . Well, You might be able to get some of my hay wet, but You won't get it all!"

Mannassah turned. He rammed his pitchfork into a bundle of hay. He slung it over his shoulder and ran down the hill for the barn. Down, down, down the hill he ran, faster and harder. Mannassah was a huge man. His long loping strides hit the little footbridge. His speed and weight were too much for the single plank. The bridge broke, Mannassah tripped, and his hay fell in the creek. Mannassah cursed—God had won that round.

But it wasn't always so. Mannassah raised pigs on his farm. He had spotted mongrels, mainly black with short, lop ears and pointed, straight noses. Mannassah's pigs made fine skittery-skattery bacon. Mannassah's brood sow milked well. Twice a year this fat old lady had litters of six little piglets. Mannassah kept them in a square log shed that faced south. He fed them scraps, potatoes, whey, old meal, and roots from the vegetable garden. Every once in a while he threw in some coal ashes which seemed to fatten them up. He kept a big tub of water inside the fence, because pigs drink even more water than they eat food. Mannassah took care of those pigs and "there in the wood, many piggy-wigs stood," but none had a bone in its nose, its nose. . . .

What? Ah, excuse my rambling—anyways, Mannassah's creek rose in a flash one day. It was a flash flood, mighty common in that section of the country. All of Ohio's Appalachian counties, Jefferson, Belmont, Monroe, Washington, and Lawrence, have more floods than anywhere else in the country—or so I'm told. You probably know that pigs can see the wind. Mannassah's little piggies let out a wild squealing even before the clouds burst and the waters fell. Then suddenly it was a pourdown—it was a cloudburst, it was a toad strangler. Waves surged into the pig pen. There were six little piggies in the new litter and three drowned immediately.

Mannassah was furious. He was so boiling mad that he jumped up and down. He shook his fist at the sky. He picked up the other three piglets and he ran down to the edge of his creek. He sloshed in up to his knees. "God Almighty, what the heck're You doin' to me? You're drown' my pigs!" Mannassah was drenched and he was shouting and he was shaking his head and his shoulders. "Listen here, Your Honor, I'm the master of my own fate. If You can drown some of my pigs, then I'll show You that I can drown the rest!"

And with a swing of his mighty arms Mannassah hurled the three squiggling wriggling piglets into the rushing water.

Yep, Mannassah was a stubborn man. He was an independent man. He relied on himself; no one else helped out and he didn't need any help, thank you. He patched his own clothes and he built his own tools of iron and wood. Mannassah'd invented a coffee boiler, which, but for the inconveniences of traveling in those days and his remote distance from the place where such enterprises were attended to, he would have patented. Mannassah told his neighbors that they'd better not steal the design, but if you'll promise me to keep it a secret, I'll tell you how it was made.

Mannassah hunted up a smooth round stone about six inches in diameter; usually the stone was a polished river stone—maybe it was granite or something, I'm not sure. Anyways, Mannassah set this stone in the fire and heated it very hot. The stone smoked as the dust and water burned off. When the stone was beyond smoking, Mannassah used a flat stick and transferred it to a wooden trough (yes, yes, I said "wood"—please be quiet a moment) containing exactly enough water for three cups of coffee. The water boiled—it boiled fast and it boiled hard. Then Mannassh added the coffee—and it was just plain coffee, too, with no weakeners like egg shells or cream or sugar or anything. When the whole drink was steaming, Mannassah quickly scooped out the stone with his wooden spoon and poured the coffee into an iron cup. . . .

Yep, that's it. So, anyways, let me return to my story.

Mannassah Johnson liked to hunt, as did every man thereabouts. He had his own pack of hound dogs with rough dirty coats and every rib sticking out. When Mannassah went a-huntin' with his gun, the hounds jumped and barked and howled and ran wildly in front of him with their noses to the ground in a big swirling mass. Mannassah hunted foxes, coons, turkeys, and wild rabbits. Rabbits are hard to catch without dogs. I hear that the Indians hunted rabbits by making a circle around a field in the evening when the rabbits were out feeding. The men would walk toward each other, being real quiet; then they began to beat the ground to scare the rabbits toward the center until the little critters had no place to escape.

Rabbits can be tough little beasties to catch. Mannassah went out rabbit hunting, but he was often frustrated, even with the help of his skinny noisy hounds. One time in the summer—it was in July, on a Thursday, I think—Mannassah angrily took off for days after a single rabbit.

This was just a small bunny, the kind that women get so squishy over, you know, soft and light and brown and fluffy. This little thing had been sneaking into Mannassah's vegetable garden at night, nibbling at the lettuce sprouts and turnip greens. Rabbits eat bark and herbs and growing hay, vegetables, grape vines, and young trees and they can just about wipe out a garden if they've a mind to. Well, Mannassah saw this rabbit morning and evening, but he couldn't catch it. Mannassah got madder and madder. No little tiny rabbit, even a creature of the Great God Almighty, could get the better of him, no siree. So one morning Mannassah called his hounds, he loaded his gun, and he started after it.

Mannassah yelled, he called out, he shouted and he strained his throat: "I'll git you, you little varmint!... Stop!... Sure, the good Lord guards His hepless creatures, but you—you ain't so hepless, not by a long shot. You just go and hep yourself to everything in my garden.... Now I'm a-goin' to hep myself to you!"

Mannassah's shoulders tightened; his eyes narrowed. He would protect his garden, and he wouldn't mind the delicacy neither: rabbit meat, fried or stewed, is a mighty fine light dinner. And rabbit fur? Why, that would make good trim for a jacket or a hat or even a baby blanket. So, although Mannassah had no baby bunting, nonetheless he went a-hunting—he went a-hunting to get a little rabbit skin to wrap *some* little baby in... What? All right, all right, I suppose I was gettin' a bit carried away—anyways, Mannassah set off after the little critter.

Through the woods and over the hills they went—the rabbit,

the hounds, and Mannassah. At last the hounds cornered the rabbit in a hole at the top of a good-sized bit of a knoll, an old field of a hill. Now, as I've already said, this rabbit was just a common gray. It's burrow was deep and twisty and filled with gnarly damp rootlets. The dogs barked. One of the hounds pawed and dug and howled, but he couldn't unearth the rabbit. Mannassah was tired and furious. Would he quit now? Certainly not. He could see that rabbit just a-chucklin' away. Mannassah would get that rabbit and no other if it took him till Doomsday to do it. So old Mannassah left the dogs there and went home for a shovel.

Mannassah ran back and he began to dig. First the soil was hard; then it was soft. Mannassah was sweating but he dug on. Finally the earth was wet and squitchy. Mannassah kept digging. He dug and he dug. Days passed, but Mannassah kept on working. He would fall asleep at night. His arms hurt so much that he yelled with every shovelful of dirt. He dug off the entire top of that hill. One afternoon he hit a rock. His arms went numb and felt like cornmush. He was too dry and too weak to yell. He just stopped. Mannassah put down his shovel and he sat on the ground. He'd completely run out of spunk. It wasn't till a week or two later that folks saw him around his farm again. Even today, as you drive along the highway, you can see the hill with its top half dug away. Any native—men like Abel Corwin or Zeb Fields or Evan Pommer— will tell you: "Yep, that's the place—that's where Mannassah Johnson dug for days but never caught the rabbit."

Mannassah's neighbors shook their heads when he declared he was fighting the Almighty God. Cotton Clague coughed and stroked his beard and warned: "You'd best be mighty careful 'bout what you say, Johnson." But Mannassah roared: "Listen here— maybe I'm just goin' to pigs and whistles—but, by God, I'll be goin' there on my own terms, I will!" When the fierce old man finally died (giving the Lord the final victory, I suppose) folks thereabouts all wondered what would happen to him. Would he go to Heaven? And if so, would he go quietly?

The funeral itself was pretty quiet. Old Mannassah was finally laid to rest in the family cemetery, high on a stony hilltop filled with brambles and gnarled apple trees. The epitaph on his tombstone is one he'd heard about and made a special request for.

> Stranger, keep in trust
> This ancient mortal dust:
>
> For bless'd be the man
>   Who spares these stones,
> But a curse on he
>   Who disturbs my bones.

Well, no one seems to have disturbed those stones and bones. You can still see the headstone if you visit the run-down old cemetery. There are a few other weathered tombstones there, not in neat rows but pretty much scattered about. The cemetery is next to a woods and there's one great oak in a corner that spreads its branches over the whole plot. Around the edge is an iron fence, rusted and broken, with an iron gate that has a kind of arch over it. Here lie the Johnsons and their many relatives, who were, I've been told, good folk and a might less ornery than Mannassah.

After his death, people wondered if he would be content to lie there without grumbling and complaining while his soul ascended peacefully to Heaven. Somehow the idea of Mannassah in Heaven didn't seem possible. Would Mannassah be happy in a place where God Almighty always had the last word? Would God even let Mannassah through the Pearly Gates? There was a good deal of doubt about this.

People say that even in the deepest winter snow does not lie easily on hot-tempered Mannassah Johnson's grave. Flakes melt as soon as they hit the tombstone—it doesn't matter how cold the weather or how deep the snow is anywhere else. This is the tale whispered around the hill-country schoolrooms, and the children's eyes, round as wagon wheels, widen in wonder as they retell the story. Why, Mannassah Johnson even yelled at God! they say. The children huddle together. They shiver. Then they pull on their rough coats and their home-knit mitts to trudge up the hill—dark bent little figures against the whiteness; they're afraid, but they have to see for themselves. Is there really snow on ornery Mannassah Johnson's grave? . . . What's that? Well, my friend, all I can say is that you can go there and see for yourself.

·12·

Ru Stones in the Far-Away South Pacific

THERE NEVER WERE any volcanoes in Ohio, so there's no pumice here either. There's plenty of sandstone though—just think of Cuyahoga County. On the surface it's gently rolling territory, and underneath it's shale and sandstone, sandstone, sandstone. Cuyahoga County has the best sandstone quarries in the United States. I probably don't have to tell you about Cuyahoga's Berea quarries: sandstone from Berea covers the faces of fine buildings in Baltimore, Boston, Chicago, Cleveland, New York, Philadelphia, and Canada.

Cuyahoga is the name of a large and twisty river that winds in almost a complete circle as it snakes toward Lake Erie. Along the way it drops hundreds of feet in a few miles through walls of sandstone and old glacial drifts. Cuyahoga is from the Mohawk *Cujahaga* meaning crooked river, and the Cuyahoga River certainly "crookeds" its way as it runs through innumerable valleys, gorges, falls, and rapids into Lake Erie at the edge of Cleveland, the largest city in the state.

Cleveland is in the part of Ohio country known as the Western Reserve. This was land that Connecticut kept its hands on after most of the states gave up their western territories to the federal Congress. In 1795, Connecticut sold the region around Ohio's Cuyahoga River to a group of investors who called themselves the Connecticut Land Company; these men sent out a surveying party led by Moses Cleaveland—and it's after him that the city was eventually named.

In 1825, Cleveland was chosen to be the northern end of the

Ohio Canal—that's how Cleveland got to be one of the world's great steel-producing cities—but in those days Cleveland was small; it had only six hundred and six people and fifty houses. One of the towns just to the east, the town of Chagrin Falls, was already much larger than Cleveland. Chagrin Falls was also founded by Moses Cleaveland. The local story is that he named it Chagrin because he was disappointed that the river he'd come upon—the Chagrin River—still wasn't his ultimate destination, the Cuyahoga River.

Chagrin Falls puts me in mind of stone. (I guess that *everything* seems to put me in mind of stone today.) Anyways, as I've said, stone is the base of Ohio and there are Stone Stories throughout the state. Gray stone, black stone, shale stone, limestone, and sandstone. Ohio doesn't have any of its own granites, all those kinds of rocks were carried here by glaciers. There aren't any pumice stones either, but there *are* Pumice Stories in Ohio. These are stories told about the stone of foreign lands and of far off times, and I'll tell you one of those tales.

It was a Friday in a hot month, perhaps July or August, when I heard this story. I heard it from an old man named Mordant Bissell. Mordant lived in Chagrin Falls but he'd traveled the world over as a merchant marine; once he'd been in the South Pacific, and the natives there had told him about Ru Stones.

Mangaia, said Mordant, is a green, green island covered with gray pumice Ru Stones. Mangaia is one of the Cook Islands, far away in the middle of the Pacific Ocean out past where the granny whales play. There the earth is built of volcanic rock—gray pumice stone—and each pumice island is ringed round with pink and white coral. Everywhere there is the light smell of orchids that grow on rocks and on trees in the soil filling the cracks. Tree orchids are the color of cream with a hint of rose and their leaves are bright squinty green. The tree orchids talk back and forth with the ground orchids, which are blue and white and purple and have roots that are sweet to chew.

Over the island of Mangaia the sky is built of solid clear

bluestone—it's skystone and it's high up and far away. Why is the sky so high and filled with a glowing white golden Bottom-god glow? And why are Mangaia pumice stones in the curious shape of bones? Well here's what I've heard.

The arching skystone is very high and no one can touch it, but once upon a time the sky was low and only a thin space was open between the sky and the earth. The rockworn smell of the sea flowed in a tiny space no taller than a rabbit. The long black hair of the islanders was never ruffled, and people living on Mangaia were cramped and very uncomfortable indeed.

Mangaia's clear bluestone sky rested on the broad green leaves of the teve tree, which grows only a few feet tall. Because the skystone was so low, it flattened the arrowroot plants. All the forests were flat. The leathery leaves with long pointed drip-tips snaked among the vines and crawled through the low narrow space between the ground and the sky. The tree flowers and fruits and pods grew out of the trunks, not from the branches. The bright red sunsets were narrow and short.

People were cramped. They were more than cramped, they were crimped and bent and stooped. Tall people crawled. But the Mangaia islanders made the best of things—there was a saying: "If the sky is low then it's easy to catch parrots."

Underground there was much more room. Many special creatures lived under Mangaia. One of these creatures was an old cave god, Ru, who was half man and half stone. Ru's legs were made of light gray pumice stone: his leg bones were blue-gray volcanic rock with small shiny crystals. You probably know this pumice stone. It's an airy sort of rock filled with holes and lighter than dried bone. Pumice feels like a hollow reed, but actually it's hard and old and magical.

This Ru was a very old god, one of the Bottom-gods. His hair was glorious, shining, and golden, and he had a rainbow around his shoulders. Ru had lived all his long life down in Avaiki, which means "the Shades." Avaiki is a huge hollow and the island of Mangaia floats on top of it. This hollow is the home of most of the Mangaia gods. The Bottom-gods live there, where they marry and have children. They weave their clothes underground, just as they garden, cook, fish, build houses, and swim and sail down there.

One day Ru came climbing up from the caverns of Avaiki and he crawled into this world of ours. He could not stand. He could not straighten up. He looked around. What was this? The sky was a low ceiling. Ru could barely stretch his neck. He watched in amazement as all the people walked about hunched over. Tall people were forced to crawl, the plants could not bend up toward the sunshine, birds could not fly, people could never get the kinks out of their backs, and children could not jump and play.

Ru shook his head. He felt sorry for the islanders so he decided to change things. Ru took some sticks and he propped up the sky. He cut the great wavy wooden wings from tree trunks. He chopped the strange twisty trunk roots from banana, banyan, breadfruit, chestnut, cocoanut, ironwood, and nono, and for decoration Ru left the forest orchids growing along these woody poles. Ru was strong, and he strained and he stroaned and he pushed up the sky and firmly he planted the many stakes right there in the ground at the center of the island of Mangaia.

At last the sky was up and the island was down. Everything seemed wonderful above the ground. The heavens were much higher than a person, now that they were held up on Ru's tent poles. The dawn came early. The red sunset shone late. People could walk standing up, they could bend their necks back, and they could wave their arms. Children could jump.

Ru was cheered. The islanders called him the "Sky-supporter." The schoolmaster wrote this little poem about him

> Raise the skystone,
> Supporter of the sky;
> Open up the air

For the birds to fly
And let the children
Jump up high.

Yes, the world was wider, higher, and airier. People took deep breaths. They smiled and they waved their arms. All the South Pacific creatures opened wide their eyes and looked up, up, up. The large brown tortoises with shiny-ringed shells stretched and stretched their necks; even the fishes popped their eyes out of the sea to look around in wonder.

But not everyone was happy. Maui was the premier young and wild Above-ground godlet. He was always in a hurry; he was quick and thoughtless. Maui was small—small enough to fit under the low sky—but he was strong and he liked running and racing and wrestling. Maui had lived on the upper island for centuries and he felt that he owned the region. Now he frowned. Why hadn't I thought of raising the sky? he asked himself.

Maui was not happy. Why did Ru want to change the natural order of things? Did he plan to become the Above-ground king? And why was this useless old man getting so much attention from the Above-ground people? Any god could have raised the sky if he'd wanted to. It's true that Ru had flowing hair the color of the dawn and craggy eyebrows and vast, rainbow-covered shoulders and his voice was like thunder and he walked with a marching step, a striding step that flowed over hills and canyons and mountains. But Ru was old, and now he was acting as if he were *the* god of all mortal people. When Ru was in the upper world, Maui felt angry every day.

Maui grumbled and he fumed. One sunny morning old Ru stood on a small hill looking over the island. He breathed the warm-cool sea breezes. He closed his eyes and soaked in the vast distant cloud-pillowed skies. Then Maui came by. Rudely he bumped into the old god. "What are you doing here, old man?" asked Maui.

Ru said nothing—he only raised his eyebrows.

"Go back home. Go below ground with the other old-fashioned gods," said Maui. "Your handwork is weak. Soon the weather will worsen and you will be sorry and embarrassed."

Ru raised his bushy eyebrows. He felt a tingling tangling in his toes. His golden glow turned into deep sunset colors. "Whatever are you talking about?" he asked quietly.

"Listen here, old man," answered Maui, "when a hurricane comes, the wind and the rains will rush in. What will happen then? I'll tell you what will happen: lightning and thunder will crash and waterspouts and typhoons will blow up. And then your stakes and poles and trees will be swept into the sea and the sky will fall and all the people will be killed."

Ru did not answer. The world was old and Ru was old, but the morning was crisp and the ocean was clear. It all seemed new and very young. The sun was bright. A light smell of banana blossoms slipped by in the air. For a moment even Maui forgot himself and felt happy.

Ru was one of the first gods. Although his hair was golden and bushy, it was nonetheless old hair. Although his shoulders were strong, they were nonetheless old shoulders. Maui stood and looked up at the old, old god. Maui had never known his own father but he pictured him to be just as Ru was, tall as the tallest tree and old and wise and firm and severe. Maui felt that it was long past time that he himself was grown up and strong and independent too.

Ru stood staring silently for many minutes. Finally he said: "You are a child; you are a silly youngster. Who allowed you to talk like that? Have you no respect? I was here when the world was first made. I saw your grandparents' grandparents. Watch your tongue, young man, or I will throw you out of existence—if I get angry, I will toss you far over the sea with a flip of my wrist."

"Oh? You think that you are so powerful old man?" shouted Maui. "Well I'd like to see you do it then."

Ru was getting very angry. He frowned. He made a quick snatch with his right hand. He seized Maui, who was muscular but small, much smaller than Ru. Ru grunted and then he tossed Maui up, up, up to a great height far above the little green island covered with gray, gray rocks in the middle of the blue Pacific sea.

Maui felt weak and dizzy. He shivered and he shook. He was not as brave as he had thought. He was so high in the sky that he became afraid and he dared not look down. His stomach wriggled by itself, the world swam, his heart beat quickly and his throat felt tight. Would he faint? He could not control his hands, which began to shake and shake and shake.

Nonetheless Maui *was* a godlet. He was magic and he was powerful. He swallowed once and he swallowed twice and then he was in control again. Then Maui used his *mana*—a magic spell that he'd learned when he was little and when he still lived below the earth. How did he actually do this trick? I'm afraid that it's a secret so I cannot tell you the details, but as he fell Maui wiggled his fingers, he waved his hands, and he turned into a bird. Maui became a green-tailed pigeon with red wings and pink eyes. For a moment his name was *Akaotu,* the "Fearless One." Akaotu flew high and he flew low. He ate some fruit from the top of the trees. He ate some berries from the low bushes. He ate some seed from the ground. And then as light as a feather or a ferny leaf Maui Akaotu landed gently on a rock.

Maui landed back on the earth. He gently floated down and he turned into his natural form, the shape of a man. Maui was smart and quick. When he walked he lightly swung his hands at his side, he sang out loud in a beautiful voice, he was handsome and muscular, and he had long, shiny black hair. Maui strode like a peacock, strutting with an orange, brown, yellow, and blue tail, walking back and forth. He muttered things no one else could hear. He was angry and tense. He could not see straight. He felt like a volcano exploding. For a short time Maui felt huge. He was like the old giants who lived before the Great Flood. He said to himself:

> Ru, old man, you used weak sticks
> To raise the cloudy heaven's bricks,
> Nighttime black and blue daysky—

Now you yourself must stand on high
To hold the skystone all alone.

Maui frowned. He was the chief god in the upper world. Maui
had learned to wriggle and to change his shape and to roll and flow
and slip and slide. And although he was small he was as strong as
the strongest whale. He would sneak up on Ru; he would wrestle
and he would knock Ru down or toss him up.

Everywhere inland on Mangaia the forest was dense. The treetops were thick and green and cool and one hundred feet high.
Inside the forest sunshine reached the floor only in the middle of
the day. There were small flecks of sparkling bright white at noon,
like crystals on the ground. Maui sneaked through the black shadows of the underbrush, tiptoeing past the white sparkles. He was
silent as a tiny red-striped blue-tongued lizard. He smelled the great
damp leaves. He tasted the thick spicy forest air. He saw sharp
yellow-green rays of light. He heard the parrots out of sight and far
overhead.

Maui crept up on Ru. He slipped out of the forest as if from
an old heavy cellar door. Maui knew many secret wrestling holds.
Ru stood at the edge of the forest looking toward the sea. Quietly
Maui slipped his head and shoulders under old man Ru's legs. Then
with all his newfound strength Maui jumped and shouted and he
tossed poor Ru up, up, up into the sky to a distant towering far off
height.

Maui had jumped and leaped and pushed, and he tossed the
old, old god. Ru was thrown into the heavens. He pressed up
against the sky, forcing it yet higher and higher. Soon the clear
blue skystone—the color of the finest pale turquoise—was so far
up that it could never fall back again. Ru was a giant god and the
force of his body pushed the sky so far and so high that it remained
lifted forever. There was a great sigh. There were strains and groans
and there was the heavy noise of rocks crashing, and then all the
tickling breezes slipped and slid and flew away into the deep cavern-
ous spaces newly created between the heavens and the earth.

Ru was caught fast. He tingled and tangled all over. His collar-bone was stuck in a crack in the sky and he could not get free. Ru waved his arms. His hands wamfled and his legs flapped but he stuck tight in the star-filled skytides. Poor Ru was held by the cosmic crabs. His head and his shoulders were entangled among the stars, and, although he wriggled and twisted and his fingertips tingled and his toes wiggled, he was twined in the star rays, wrapped by the rooty toe-hairs of an old island sea-tree way high in the blue-black sky.

So Ru who was once a Bottom-god has become a Sky-god, distant, afloat, and disembodied; he is the South Pacific Atlas hold-ing the day on his shoulders and lighting the night with his shining hair. After Maui tossed old Ru high into the heavens, the air became fresher and vaster and more open and the little boats at sea with their skiff-skaff sails bounced on the waves both high and low. The bottom half of Ru was stone—pumice stone bones—and slowly these fell back to earth. From time to time they tumble down and shiver and thunder into countless bits and pieces. Today Ru's bones are scattered over every hill and valley of Mangaia to the very edges of the sea.

Ru's bones are Ru Stones. They are hard and light and holey. The biggest bones made entire island caves; the boinging of fresh water droplets echo and ring as the sea rolls in and out of these caves, and far in the distance there are thunderous waves crashing night and day. All over the stoney boney island of Mangaia, chil-dren find bits and pieces of Ru's bones. These broken pumice stones lie everywhere. They fill the hollows, they pile in the hills, they sleep in the forest deeps, and they whistle lightly in the winds of the tropical rain seas.

That then is the island of Mangaia; it is out in the ocean past where the granny whales play. It is as far away from Chagrin Falls as you can go without getting any closer, said old Mordant Bissell, who told me this story on an Ohio country white-washed sandstone porch one summertime not long ago.

·13·

Chimney Rocks and Canter's Cave

OHIO'S GOT UNCOUNTED lonesome caves and a whole pile of them are in Jackson County. Jackson County's in the middle of the state, almost at the tip. Four thick seams of coal run through the county and there's also plenty of limestone and salt. Jackson's first settlers came from West Virginia and from Pennsylvania; then came the Welsh who built the towns of Jackson, Centerville (now it's called Thurman), and Oak Hill. Jackson has a yearly Welsh song festival called the *Eisteddfod* and Welsh folklore from the Old Country still gets told in Jackson's mountains. For instance, there are stories of witches who ride the cows at night and who hex the next day's milkings. Luckily it's not too hard to "right" a hexed cow. You just drop a snippet of cow's tail, cow's blood, and cow's milk into a hot fire—that's all there is to it. I'd wager you'd only learn than in Jackson County Ohio.

Jackson is a popular name. There're twenty-four Jackson Counties in the United States. Ten American cities are named Jackson—two of them here in Ohio. It gets a bit confusing. Ohio's biggest Jackson city is the one in Jackson County. This Jackson is on a hill and it's the center of Ohio's silvery-iron industry. Jackson's an old settlement—long before the Welsh came, well-worn paths led to the area because buffalo and elk and Indians came there for the salt in the local springs. Daniel Boone himself was forced to boil salt when he was captured by the Indians near Jackson, until he managed to escape during a nighttime thunderstorm.

Did Daniel Boone ever live in a cave? I don't know, but I do know that Jackson has some mighty strange and ancient caves. You've probably heard of Canter's Cave; it's about six miles northwest of the city of Jackson. The cave itself is east of State Route 11.

There's a post by the road and you can stop in a quiet shady spot just beyond; off to the right is a thicket. Walk down to the woods—you'll know you're in the right spot because the trees are unusually tall; they're stretching up for the sun, and the dark trunks of these trees are thin and black and the roots run down, down, down into the ravine.

This is an eerie, haunted spot: it's mighty lonesome. But it's just one of hundreds of deep and rough ravines in southeastern Ohio in Jackson County and also in Hocking County. Hocking County was named for the Hockhocking River. (*Hockhocking* is an Indian word that means bottleneck.) Hocking County's got the most wild and wilsome places in the state. It's got canyons and nighttime cliffs and rocks sticking up and down and out in all directions. There are sharp stones jumping up three or four hundred feet above the rivers and waterfalls—and every single one of those deep ravine creeks runs with lonesome water in and out of the caverns.

Hocking County has the famous Ash Cave; that's where Indians met at night—probably they were Shawnee. Flames of the council fires would leap sixty feet high, licking the black ceiling of the cave. The walls were coated with soot, and on council nights hundreds of red faces solemnly watched the hot coals as the men sat in the centuries of ash.

Not far away, a few miles northeast of the city of South Bloomingville, is Old Man's Cave. Old Man's Cave is a hollowed-out rock with an overhanging roof a hundred feet high. A cold creek splashes in the ravine below. The rock looks like a face: you can see the forehead, eye, nose, mouth, chin, and throat, and the stone front is lined and creased and crevicy. Once upon a time, back in pioneer days, a white man lived in Old Man's Cave. I heard that his name was Pap Jones. However some folk say that it was Zeke Harrowford, and the relatives of Oba Little claim that it was actually Oba—but who really knows the truth nowadays?

Anyways, speaking of recluses—two counties to the south there's Canter's Cave. . . . (What's that? Of course I already mentioned Canter's Cave—that's what this story's all about.) As I was saying, there're two trails to Canter's Cave and the Chimney Rocks. One trail is roundabout and crosses the hill in the woods; it goes by the spot where a hunter once found a partly mummified Indian that had some rotting old clothing still on it. The other trail runs straight down into the ravine.

Frankly it doesn't matter which trail you take, because once they get into the ravine both go along paths that get narrower and narrower and have rocks sticking out from the cliffs along the sides. There are cool hollows on each side and suddenly you'll find yourself in a shady little glenlike place with high walls made of solid rock. Queer forms and fantastic shapes are all around in the stone and the dead trunks. If you're alone, you'll wonder how long it's been since the last human was here. There are strange plants and ferns and mosses growing here and nowhere else because the rocks keep out the wind and the water and they protect growing things from hard times and thundery storms. Finally up ahead there's the cave—or at least one of Canter's entrances. The cave is cool in the summer and its floor is always dry; it's not a bad place for an old hermit.

And who was this hermit, James Milton Canter? Once he was a brave Ohio soldier. Back in 1805, Lieutenant James Canter was a trusted officer in the U. S. Army and everyone knew that he had a brilliant career ahead of him. He was only twenty-one. He was fearless. He was a crack shot and he knew how to live in the wild. Also, Canter had been to school—he could read and write. His superiors could count on him in a tough spot and everyone wanted him in their outfit.

But one fateful day Canter heard of Aaron Burr's plan. Burr was recruiting an army to capture part of Mexico. He wanted to set up a new republic, a state for the common man, where everyone would be free and happy and where levelheaded common sense would rule. The Mexican land was empty and would be given away free to everyone, said Burr. The climate was warm, the weather was mild, and the soil was rich. Burr would give high military positions to any well-trained man who joined. Gold and treasure would be divided among the conquerors. Already there was money for food, arms, and other supplies, provided by Ohio's Harmann Blennerhassett.

Canter listened and his eyes lit up. This was just his opportunity. Canter would be there from the beginning, starting the new republic with other smart, ambitious, and well-intentioned young men. Canter hitched a wagon ride down to the Blennerhassett estate on an island along the southern edge of Ohio. Aaron Burr was on the island with charts and men and plans. Burr patted Canter on the shoulder. You'll be a general, he promised. Canter wrote to his wife, who was thrilled and who told his family. Canter stayed in the cabins on Blennerhassett Island, organizing men, mules, and munitions.

The men who gathered were young. They talked late into the nights; they argued and they planned in front of the red embers of the midnight fires. The East was now a playground for the rich and the wealthy, they agreed; the United States wasn't run by the common folk the way Washington had intended. In Mexico they would set up a government run by the real people. Poor folk would be given free land. There would be large town meetings to decide things. Courts would be run by judges who were not fancy-talking lawyers, but just plain people. Aaron Burr promised to bring in good doctors and dedicated teachers and to set up free schools.

Every day was exciting—until sudden stomach-wrenching news came. President Jefferson declared the Burr expedition to be illegal and un-American. In a trice everything fell apart. Burr was labeled a traitor. American forces were sent into Ohio country to arrest all the participants. The new young officers were put on a list of federal criminals. "General" Canter was officially branded a traitor and a warrant was issued for his arrest.

James Canter couldn't believe it. Everything had evaporated. The world had turned upside down. He had spent all his money. He had no position. He'd failed his country and he'd failed his family. His parents were shamed; his wife was hurt and angry.

Canter felt that God was looking the other way and frowning. Canter was an outcast on an official list of hunted men. Soon he would be discovered and captured and put in jail; undoubtedly he'd be hanged.

While planning the expedition to Mexico, Canter had been living in a cabin on the Blennerhassett's estate. When the loyal American troops arrived and swarmed over the island, Canter jumped into the Ohio River. First he swam underwater; then he paddled quietly to the Ohio shore. He pulled himself up, exhausted. His mind was numb. His head ached. He lay on the rough grass and he closed his eyes.

What could he do now? There was no way to return home. He was a marked man; he had to hide. Also he had to do penance. James Canter was a failure and a disappointment. He shook his head. He sat for long hours on a rock. Then slowly and tiredly he walked north until he came to the rugged land of Jackson County.

It was a Saturday in August, the afternoon of a hot and sweaty day. James Canter set out to hide forever. He couldn't face his friends or his family—he could hardly face himself. Canter walked into the country far from any towns. He walked all afternoon and he walked all night. It was cold and dark and quiet; it was endless and black and empty—but, for a time, Canter surprised himself by feeling light and easy. The road seemed downhill all the way. After a while he walked off the road and through a small clump of oak trees to an open field. James Canter pushed on, beyond a ridge, past a meadow, and into the woods. Deeper and deeper into the woods he went. The trees were tall. The forest was thick and up ahead Canter saw a large pile of craggy rocks.

As he got closer he saw that it was more than just a pile of boulders: Canter had found the rocky opening to a cave. The cave was hidden in a ravine. Had it been the tunnel for an underground river? Had great floods rushed and roared through these hills? Canter held onto an overhanging rock and looked down into the blackness. He heard water and wind; he felt cool ageless stone.

Spinks wafted and floated. They blew lightly in the meadows

and they slipped between the chimney-shaped rocks; then they slid into the cave. James Canter followed the wind spinks. He went into the cave and never once did he consider how in the world he might get out again. The cave's tunnel went straight on for some way, then it dipped suddenly down, so suddenly that Canter had not a moment to think. He stumbled, but the ground was soft; he seemed to have fallen on a heap of sticks and dry leaves and he was not hurt at all.

Canter stood up. He found himself inside a winding tunnel. He looked toward the ceiling, but all was dark overhead. Before him was another long passage and far, far ahead he heard the wind rolling and whooshing swiftly away from him. Canter walked on. It was like a dream. Stones fell from the walls. Water dripped along the right—and a moment later there was the sound of water on the left. Were there demons in the shadows? Reremice and blanktees fluttered along the damp ceiling. The recesses were gloomy. Still, James Canter did not feel afraid: he felt light and weightless. Was he dead? He walked on and on and on. The passage seemed endless.

James Canter kept walking. He walked all afternoon and through the night, down one winding passage and up another. When the cave got small, he crawled. Sometimes he saw light, sometimes he felt his way by hand. The farther he went, the more lost he became. But he didn't panic because there was no place else to go. He found that the cave was more than just a single tunnel: it had side passages and huge cracks in the walls. It even had the skulls of old animals—bison, hyenas, rhinoceros, and stag. It had refuse heaps where ancient tribes had left the bones of reindeer and the antlers of other long-gone animals. There were charcoals and burnt stones on the floors. Stone flakes of arrows and spears were scattered about. The walls had thin sketches of men hunting spiral-tusked mammoths.

Canter had found a cave without end, but he was never far from the out-of-doors because the cave had all manner of openings and cuts and crevices. It had streams and side tunnels. It wound into tight spirals and it sloped up into cracked chimneys. It had dry hollows; it had entrance after entrance and exit after exit. James stood for a while in one small rocky corner with light filtering from rooftop holes that he couldn't see. He looked around and he nodded to himself. It seemed that this was to be his future. Perhaps this was also his past—already he couldn't remember. He sat down, and his mind was blank.

James Canter lived in the cave. He drank lonesome water. And what did he eat? Perhaps he ate roots. Perhaps he ate crawfish. He may have had fish. He must have cooked stew because there were fires many nights. Still he got thin, as thin as a rail with a nose so hooked that he could hang over a tree limb. He wandered that cave for thirty years or forty years or more. He had betrayed his family, his nation, and himself, and now he lived in the shadows of the world.

How did folks know that he was still alive all that time? Smoke from his fires slipped through the crevices in the rocks. Wisps and bits of gray drifting smoke spiraled up and people began to call the rocky towers thereabouts Chimney Rocks. The Chimney Rocks are where strange birds build untidy nests in the treetops and where owls hoot and laugh in the tumbling cliffs; it is, as Tennyson wrote,

> Where there are cooling mosses deep
> And through those mosses ivies creep
> In craggy cliffs where poppies sleep
> And 'bove cold streams the flowers weep.

The Chimney Rocks are tall and thin; they are broken and chinked and their cracks are filled with thin cool plants. Sometimes it still seems like a bit of smoke floats above them. Inside and underneath, there are the caves, little and big, dry and damp. It's here that James Canter took refuge. It's here that James Milton Canter disappeared—it's where he holed up and where he walked barefoot and in rags to his unknown dying day. Ever since, this region in Jackson County has been called Canter's Caves—it's a place where there are shadows around every corner, but where no one is ever seen.

·14·

How the Tha-we-gila *and the* Cha-lah-kaw-tha *Found That They Were Equals*

IN OHIO COUNTRY, the major Indian tribe was Shawnee. Once, very long ago, the Shawnee lived as two related but separate clans in what is now Wisconsin. In those far distant days, the clans parted. One group—the *Cha-lah-kaw-tha*—went north and west into Canada, as far as Alaska, and, some say, across the Bering Strait into Asia. The other group—the *Tha-we-gila*—went south and east into Tennessee, New York, and Florida. Eventually most of the *Tha-we-gila* settled in the Carolinas on the upper Savannah River and there they were called the Sacannah.

This was well before the European invasion. When the Europeans arrived on this continent, the Shawnee, restless wanderers that they were, had reunited in the middle of Ohio country. The combined Shawnee nations fought on the side of the English in the Revolutionary War, and later the eastern settlers forced the Shawnee onto reservations in Oklahoma.

To the Indians and to the first European explorers, Ohio country was much larger than the present state, and it's probably a good idea to think of two Ohios, the old and the new. Old Ohio was the entire central eastern area of the continent. It lay between the Alleghenies, the Mississippi River, and the Great Lakes, all the land drained by the great Ohio River. Indians lived in old Ohio in the valleys of the many Ohio country rivers—the Allegheny,

Beaver, Illinois, Maumee, Miami, Muskingum, Sandusky, Scioto, and Wabash.

Madison County is the center of old Ohio and it was in Madison County that the two Shawnee clans met one another again. As I've said, once upon a time in the olden days, but long after the mysterious Mound Builders had left Ohio country, the *Cha-lah-kaw-tha* lived in a foreign country, far away and across the sea. The *Cha-lah-kaw-tha* lived apart but they were still Shawnee. Their stories remembered the wondrous original Shawnee hunting grounds of their greatest grandparents. Now the *Cha-lah-kaw-tha* began to feel the weather around them growing colder. They were having problems with neighboring tribes. One day their chief, Tall Pine, had a special dream and he decided that the *Cha-lah-kaw-tha* should return east; so the *Cha-lah-kaw-tha* migrated across the ice flows and they reentered the land that we call America.

At that time, in those misty days, there were many little Shawnee clans on the American continent, but the *Tha-we-gila* was the central one. The *Tha-we-gila* had the most revered *Mee-sawmi*. Young Shawnee of other clans spent time as apprentices learning the *Tha-we-gila* ways. The overall chief of the Shawnee nation was always chosen from the *Tha-we-gila*. The *Tha-we-gila* were living along the East Coast, in the area of today's Carolinas. But one day, Ahusaka, the chief of the *Tha-we-gila*, had a special dream. When he awoke he decided that his whole clan must travel west. What was this dream? Ahusaka never told—or if he told, no one remembers.

The *Tha-we-gila* wandered west. They walked slowly, through light green valleys, dark brown hollows, red autumn forests. In those same years the *Cha-lah-kaw-tha* clan was trekking eastward. The land was rocky, cliffy, and broken; there were caves, fissures, and chasms. The *Cha-lah-kaw-tha* came to the end of their continent. The cold ocean stretched out before them. Miles and miles of broken ice lay cracked and cracking in the distance. The *Cha-lah-kaw-tha* walked as far as they could along the ice. Finally they came to the end of the ice. There before them was the open sea, the great grey cold sea rolling out forever.

The *Cha-lah-kaw-tha* chief, Tall Pine, stood before the open coldling sea. He stood silent for many hours. Then he called on each family of his people to name their *Opa-waw-kon-wa* or *Ototeman*. The *Ototemans* were animal guardians of the families. As Tall Pine requested, the totems were named, and of the totems Tall Pine chose the Grizzly Bear and the Turtle, because these animals were most at home in the water.

Tall Pine called and the totems came; they were quiet lumbering grizzlies and giant slow-moving sea turtles. The Shawnee sat upon the animals' backs. The great beasts walked slowly into the sea and paddled off. They swam east. They slid through the seas toward the new continent. In small groups all day long the *Cha-lah-kaw-tha* were ferried across the coldling strait, past the ice flows, through the chill winds, and at night they climbed onto the gray stony beaches of the continent we call America. Then the *Opa-waw-kon-wa* returned to the water, they swam back west, and they disappeared. In this way the *Cha-lah-kaw-tha* clan of Shawnees returned to our continent; they never looked back but only walked on and on, east and south, into warmer lands, toward the old Ohio country.

What was happening at that time deep in Ohio country? The *Tha-we-gila* clan had come over the Allegheny Mountains. They had walked through valleys and along rivers. They were journeying westward. They came slowly. They stopped; they rested. They hunted and fished. They tested the land and the streams and the trees. They watched and looked and nodded, but they moved on. Ever on they went—resting, moving, resting, moving—until one day they reached a small river and they camped for the night. This river was at the center of both the old and the new Ohio territories and today we call this the Little Darby River in Madison County.

The *Tha-we-gila* were traveling with many, many families— when they walked they stopped early each day in order to make a comfortable camp. Late one afternoon they set up camp within sight of Little Darby River. The edge of the river had patches of soft grass; the tree roots were covered with moss. The Shawnee ate, and then they lay on the ground to sleep during the dark hours of the night. The women had better ears than the men. Those nearest the river thought that they heard voices. Were these woodland spirits? It seemed as if the voices spoke in a recognizable language.

But were they really voices? Some sort of sounds or echoes or strange animal noises were coming from the opposite side of the rushing waterbrook. *Tha-we-gila* women woke their mates. Soon the entire clan was awake. The older children sat up with wide eyes. They all listened silently. They raised their eyebrows. Some men gestured. They could not believe that the language floating out of the night was Shawnee. It was spoken in a strange accent and it had unusual words and expressions, and the *Tha-we-gila* stayed awake all night listening in wonder to what seemed to be bits and pieces of Shawnee dream conversation.

Late in that deep dark night the voices across the river stopped. The *Tha-we-gila* thought that they had dreamed strange dreams or that they had heard faint echoes of ancient voices carried forever on the light winds of the treetops. They shook their heads; they fell back asleep. Their chief, Ahusaka, dreamed that he was flying high through the air on the treetop winds. The winds slipped and swooped and Ahusaka slid ever so smoothly into a round cave. He swam under water. He could breath easily, like a whale, and he was as flight strong as an eagle and as powerful as a bear and soon he flowed swiftly out on the far side of the cave through a small hole. He found that he was back in Shawnee home territory, on the East Coast—it was the low sandy grasslands with beach peas and rose hips and scratchy salt air where they had lived many months ago and from which they had begun their walk inland to Ohio. Was the river and the cave nearby? Did it slip and slide underground, deep beneath the mountains? Why had he never noticed this before? Suddenly Ahusaka awoke. He rubbed his eyes. The sun was somewhere past the trees to the east. He stood, and he looked across the river.

It was early in the morning. Shadows were long. The air was cool and the woods were damp. Ahusaka and the other men of the *Tha-we-gila* stood silently on the east side of the river. On the opposite bank, the *Cha-lah-kaw-tha* awoke. They, too, stood with raised eyebrows. Both clans stared across the river. On the far bank, each saw a camp of strangely familiar people. For a time the birds chirped and called out. Then Ahusaka, the *Tha-we-gila* chief, said, "Who are you? You must be strangers to this land, but we have heard in the night that you speak the Shawnee language."

Tall Pine, the *Cha-lah-kaw-tha* chief, called back, "We have come from across the waters; we have passed the ice flows. We lived in a distant land and we have walked a long way. We are Shawnee. You speak our language, so you must be relatives of ours."

Shawnee? From across the ice-flow waters? How could that be? wondered the *Tha-we-gila* clan. Their chief, Ahusaka, frowned and asked, "Have you a *Meesawmi*?"

Tall Pine replied, "Yes, we have."

"What are its powers?" asked Ahusaka.

"It can control sun and sky," answered Tall Pine. "Have you also a *Meesawmi*?"

"Yes, of course—and it, too, can direct sun and sky."

The men on both sides of the bank murmured and shook their heads. Both clans possessed *Meesawmis* of equal power. Was there any difference between these two *Meesawmis*? The *Tha-we-gila* and the *Cha-lah-kaw-tha* clans stared at each other. We must put these

Meesawmis to a test, they decided. The chiefs of each clan would demonstrate their *Meesawmis* the next morning . . . .

What's that—*Meesawmi*? A *Meesawmi* is a gift. It is a symbol and a vessel. It carries both the heavy and the light currents of the universe. It is given freely by the Great Spirit: long ago, the Great Spirit gave one gift, one *Meesawmi,* to each Shawnee clan. The *Meesawmi* is the lifeblood, the inspiration, the underpinning spirit of a clan. It has a physical form but that particular object is only the opening to a cave, a cave of everything elemental. Also, the *Meesawmi* is secret. Its exact form—a bone, a pot, a feather, a carving—is not told to anyone. Only the chief and those few elders who have undergone an initiation ceremony know what actual *Meesawmi* is wrapped in the protective leather covering.

The tribal chief is responsible for the *Meesawmi.* He never keeps the *Meesawmi* inside a house; he never allows it inside a tent. Always it is out-of-doors. Sometimes it is set on top of a pole. Sometimes it is buried. Sometimes it is hung from a nearby tree. The actual *Meesawmi* is wrapped with layers of buckskin and the buckskin is covered with cloth or on occasion it is in a wooden case. Wherever the *Meesawmi* is stored, the ground around it is swept carefully and no weeds are allowed to grow there. The *Meesawmi* is sacred. No one speaks of it outside the Shawnee clan and no one inside the clan (that is, no one but the chief and a few elders) knows its exact identity.

A *Meesawmi* represents the depth and strength and unity with which a clan is woven into the world. It holds the power of a clean rushing stream in the flow of nature. To grow up in a clan with a great *Meesawmi* means to grow up in a calm, orderly world that blankets you like your first mother. The great clans have great *Meesawmis* and such clans must help and lead the other clans. The two ancient Shawnee groups had to face each other's *Meesawmi.* This was the ultimate test. It was a deep and serious check. Were the two clans spiritual brothers and equals? Was one clan more interwoven in the whole cosmic tide than the other? Only through their *Meesawmis* could they know.

The *Meesawmi* tests were set for the following morning, a Sunday. That evening each of the clans camped on a different side of the river. Each of the clans prayed quietly. The dinner meal came, and the dinner meal went. It was September. The night was cool. The next morning, the chiefs met on a grassy spot alongside the river. A carved paddle was spun and it was decided that the *Cha-lah-kaw-tha* would test their *Meesawmi* first.

Tall Pine stood. He bowed toward Ahusaka. He turned and went off into the woods. After a few minutes, Tall Pine returned with a birch stick. He requested a piece of gut string from a companion, and he sat and fashioned a small bow. Tall Pine took an arrow from his pouch. He held it up against the sky. The arrow had a sharp, blackened point. Tall Pine sat silently. He closed his eyes. After almost an hour he stood. He watched the sun—it was now nearing noon. Lightly, Tall Pine shot the arrow upward toward the sun. The arrow disappeared into the treetops. The sun began to darken into a bloody red. Clouds appeared. Shadows danced. Would it rain? Then the dark moment passed and the day brightened once again; the heavens were filled with cottony white clouds. Tall Pine sat down, and all was silent.

Time passed. The Shawnee sat silent and patient. Eventually Ahusaka of the *Tha-we-gila* stood. He would demonstrate his *Meesawmi*. Slowly Ahusaka walked off into the woods. When he returned he carried a smaller birch twig: the birch stick of Tall Pine had been one arm long—the birch twig of Ahusaka was one hand long. Ahusaka nodded at a companion, who handed him a piece of gut string. Ahusaka sat and fashioned a tiny bow—stripping the bark, bending the wood, tying the gut string from end to end. Ahusaka took the bow between two fingers and rubbed the wood. He felt it vibrate ever so lightly. He said a quiet prayer.

Now Ahusaka prepared a basin of water. He took a wooden dish and set it in the center of the circle of men from the two clans.

He reached into his pouch. He removed some powdered bloodroot and he sprinkled it on the surface of the water. (Do you know bloodroots? They're green woodland plants and they're related to poppies. Each plant has only one flower. The flower is shaped like a cup and it has smooth white petals and a yellow orange center. Bloodroot flowers open in the morning sun and they close at night.)

Ahusaka poured bloodroot powder on the surface of the water. It lightly crumbled and swirled and sank. The water was clear, then pink, then red. Ahusaka stood back and recited a prayer. He closed his eyes. He raised his eyebrows. Then he took his tiny new bow and he shot at the reflection of the sun in the basin of bloodrooted water. The arrow stuck into the bottom of the wooden dish. The water turned darker and darker red. It became purple. The sky darkened. Shadows danced in the woods. Small gray clouds floated high and wee. And then the sun came back, the world brightened, and all was as before, with birds singing and breezes blowing and the green grass growing all around.

The tingling calm feeling of nature was running very deeply through both *Meesawmis*. Both *Meesawmis* could control the sun and the sky. Both *Meesawmis* had deep kinship with the color blood red. Both *Meesawmis* took even breaths in rhythm with the black night sky. The chiefs nodded. The people nodded. Children opened their eyes wide and looked up at their parents. For many minutes no words were spoken. The *Cha-lah-kaw-tha* and the *Tha-we-gila* were equals, they were brothers and sisters. They were children of the same ancient clan, a clan of the rich cool woodlands from before time began. The chiefs grasped wrists. Then they stepped back and Tall Pine said, "You are from the same fathers as we are." Ahusaka said, "Yes, this is clearly true."

The men intermingled. They began to talk. They spoke quietly. They nodded and smiled. There were long silences. There were calm times. That evening the elders sat around a large fire and the oldest man of the *Cha-lah-kaw-tha* tapped his drum; he sang the chant of *hi-o-lay-i ta-ra-da*. Men from the *Tha-we-gila* patted the ground in time to the song. An elder from the *Tha-we-gila* proposed that the chiefs of the Shawnee nation should thereafter be chosen alternately from each of these two clans. The elders nodded: it was thus decided and no further decree was necessary.

The two clans were equals and they were bound together by blood, spirit, and power. They would forever be a part of one whole. The next morning, the chiefs talked quietly and alone, sitting on an old chestnut log in the cool forest. They decided to exchange *Meesawmis*. Birds sang. Insects buzzed and chirped. Wind rustled the leaves. Eventually the men walked together back to the camp area. Each chief retrieved his *Meesawmi* and returned to the chestnut log.

The chiefs set their *Meesawmis* on the ground and the men sat without words. They did not think any deep thoughts; they just rested their minds and let the woodlands wash over them. It was sometime later when Ahusaka stood and took the *Meesawmi* of the *Cha-lah-kaw-tha* people. Slowly he carried it back to his campsite. Tall Pine stretched and stood. He picked up the *Meesawmi* of the *Tha-we-gila* people and walked back to his campsite. The *Meesaw-mis* were never unwrapped. They were kept always in their tight buckskin swaddling clouts, on poles outside the chiefs' tents. The two chiefs died without revealing the exact forms of either *Mee-sawmi*. After a time, all the original elders passed on to the Wondrous Hunting Grounds also and to this day neither clan knows what is within the many old and neat layers of rawhide that cover the secret spiritual items of the two Shawnee clans, the *Tha-we-gila* and the *Cha-lah-kaw-tha* of ancient Ohio country.

Hardesty Cheeter Meets an Indian Maiden

LET ME TELL you about Crawford. Crawford means "a shallow place to cross a river, a place where crows wade to eat the fish." It's an old Scottish name and it goes way back farther even than the famous Barons of Crawford of the twelfth century. In the young years of the United States of America, William Harris Crawford was a famous East Coast senator. Later, he was the secretary of war and a candidate for president. Crawford was honest and blunt and short tempered, and he irritated people and they didn't like to listen to him. I've been told that two kinds of peaches—the Early Crawford and the Late Crawford—were named after him.

But not Crawford County—no, the Ohio county was named after a different William Crawford. Have you ever been to Crawford County? It used to be a prairie with wild flowers and good soil—at least in the western parts of the county. And back then, when the area was first explored by the European pioneers, the eastern half of the county had giant trees.

Bucyrus is the county seat of Crawford. The city is on the Sandusky River, which winds through four or five different counties. You can boat all the way up the Sandusky River from Lake Erie to Freemont in Sandusky County—and if you do you'll see that the river has rich soil along the banks, and once upon a time it had plenty of bears, foxes, mountain lions, and wolves. Broken Sword Creek flows into the Sandusky River, and Broken Sword Creek brings us to the particular William Crawford in question, the William Crawford after whom Crawford County was named.

Colonel William Crawford had led a small raiding party from Bucyrus when they attacked a group of Indians. The white settlers were losing the battle. When there was no doubt that the white men were going to be overcome, Crawford took off his sword, he broke it, and he dropped it into a creek to prevent the Indians from using it against him. Poor Crawford was captured and burned to death at the stake. Ever since then, the stream has been Broken Sword Creek, the small nearby town was called Broken Sword, and the county has been Crawford.

In those days, the area around the southern end of the Sandusky River was known as the Sandusky Purchase. Hardesty Cheeter, an old trapper, said that when he first moved into the Sandusky Purchase, in the year 1832, he settled near Fort Findlay.

I roamed all the Crawford County woods in the parts called Findlay (said Hardesty). I could never stay in one place, so it wasn't long before I knew every nook and cranny of the area. I could close my eyes and picture every single bit of land thereabouts. Soon, I was the local land expert. Most every newcomer paid me to give him advice, as a guide, a sort of cicerone, and I could always point out the best lots and the most favorable hill or valley or field or stream for whatever he had in mind.

One time, two land hunters came to my house. They were young men from out East and they wanted to find some good farm acres hereabouts. I was always willing to oblige, and I didn't mind an excuse to talk and to show these boys around. Besides, I liked the idea of having this country settled. Who wants everything to be swamp and wilderness? Land's only valuable if people use it— and good farmers use their land well. They keep their land healthy. And as to those men hardy enough to come out here and try their hands at farming—well, more power to them.

I liked the looks of these two young men. They were smiling and open eyed; they were bright and excited. They couldn't wait to move into these parts of Ohio. How they found me, I don't know, but I was happy to do them a favor. I put on my old hat, I took my sack and my gun, and I walked them to the most desirable section that was still unoccupied in our township. This region had streams and meadows and lay right beside the farm of a neighbor of mine, one Jeremiah Hamper.

Jeremiah grew a little wheat and he had pigs and chickens. He had no family and he didn't need much money—but then he didn't make much either. Still, he worked hard. He was hoping to build up his farm; in fact, he wanted to grow oats on the very land I was showing the boys. I didn't know this because old Jeremiah was waiting while he saved more money; at the moment he'd rather spend his money buying seed for next season and some extra feed for his animals. Jeremiah was trying to be quiet about his plans, and he figured he'd got plenty of time to make the purchase.

The neighboring fields were good farm land. They were high enough not to swamp. They were edged by a stream. There were no big trees and few rocks and stumps. My new young friends walked over the area with me. They liked what they saw, and they smiled and nodded. Together we figured out the lot number for these fields. The boys were in a good mood and they thought they'd meet the neighbors, so I pointed out Jeremiah's farm house. The boys walked down the path and through his fence gate, and I turned and left.

"We've come to purchase that land next door—the meadows with the stream alongside," they said to old Hamper. The boys had expected a friendly welcome. They smiled and stepped back but Jeremiah frowned. He said loudly, "You pirates won't get that land; I'm going to buy it myself!"

The boys were quiet. Then they were angry. After a moment, one of them said that old Jeremiah could very well have the land if he could register it before they did; then they turned around and left. It was getting dark. The young men planned to start off for the Land Office in Bucyrus first thing next morning.

I'd already left the boys and I missed this conversation, but old Jeremiah immediately came to me. Would I loan him a horse? I didn't have one. After considerable inquiry about horses, all of which was to no purpose, Jeremiah told me that he had to buy the land—he needed it. He was too old to make the whole journey before the boys did. Would I go to the Land Office in Bucyrus for him?

Bucyrus was a forty-five mile trip. This was nothing for me to walk in a day. Jeremiah offered me five dollars—a princely sum— and I felt that old man Hamper deserved the land, so I agreed to help and I promised to leave early the next morning.

I remember the day well; it was a beautiful fall Monday in September. I passed through a whole field of runch—that's a mustard plant with yellow flowers that keeps away the tumors if you eat it. I also walked by a lot of farm land. I was quite a strider, and at three o'clock that afternoon I walked into Bucyrus. I went straight to the Land Office and I told the agent the number of the lot. Yes, it's still available, he said. So I gave him the price of the land, which was one dollar and a quarter per acre, and I had him make out the certificate of ownership in the name Jeremiah Hamper. Then I yawned. I was quite tired, so I sat down right there in a corner and rested and ate my bread and sausage.

After a bit, the Land Office became crowded; perhaps it was the time of day, near closing. Everyone was pushing to get to the agent, who was standing behind a kind of barred window. I began to elbow my way to the door. I'd made a little progress, when I noticed my two young friends entering. I stopped and leaned against a wall and listened to the interview. The boys presented their claim to the agent. He looked at his records and told them that the very lot they wanted had just been entered. The agent pointed me out. I smiled and nodded at them. They both stared angrily: clearly they felt I was playing them some kind of trick.

The young men walked over to me. How did I get there? they asked. I told them I'd walked all day. No horse? No, I said. At first they wouldn't believe me. I shrugged. Did you actually register that old man's land? they asked. I did, I replied. You see, I continued, I thought that no one wanted the land when I showed it to you yesterday. Afterward, I learned that Mr. Hamper had had his eye on it for years. The land is right next to his farm and it seemed to me that he should have first chance at buying it. "There's a great deal of land that's just as good," I concluded. "I'll be happy to show it to you—none of it would have been right for old Jeremiah."

The young men looked at each other. One of them offered me twenty dollars to change the registration. I shook my head. They were upset, but there was nothing more to say and this ended our conference.

I walked out the door and took a deep breath—best to put these matters behind me. I thought a walk would clear my mind. Perhaps I could even return home late that night. If I followed an Indian trail, which went along Broken Sword Creek, I'd shorten my trip by more than six miles. Before I left Bucyrus, I bought a side bottle and filled it to the top with molasses rum "brandy."

I was young and I felt that I could walk forever. I did however decide to take a drink to give me a boost of energy. It was already quite late in the day, nonetheless I figured that I could at least get through to some settlement before I quit walking for the night. I walked on and on, and after an hour or so I met an old Indian who could speak English. He told me that I was now in Indian territory and that there were at least a dozen miles of wild woods before I came to any white families. I shrugged my shoulders and pressed on. I was determined not to spend the night in the woods among the Indians—I had met few Indians in my time but by their reputation they were the only things in the woods that I ever feared.

It began to get dark as coal, and somehow I lost the trail; undoubtedly a few of my bolstering drinks contributed to my confusion. I remained hopeful and continued walking. Soon there was no question: I was lost. It was too cold to lie down without a fire, and I didn't dare make a fire for fear of being seen by the Indians, so I wandered on and on.

It got darker. In the gloom there appeared a light. Ah, I thought, a safe haven, a place to eat and sleep. I was certain that I'd passed through the Indian Reserve by then. Suddenly two fierce dogs rushed at me, barking and growling. A tall Indian stepped out of the lit cabin and called the dogs. I was stuck. I walked forward slowly.

The Indian met me at his door. He was muscular and he had long black hair. He stared silently. "Is the white man lost?" he asked finally.

"Yes," I answered.

The man nodded and told me to come in, and I obeyed. There, sitting on the floor, were an older woman and a young woman of tawny skin. The man could speak some English and said to me: "Is the white man hungry?"

I said: "Yes, I am, thank you."

The Indian said something to the older woman, his wife, in a language that I couldn't understand. The woman rose, left the front room, and returned with cornbread and dried meat which the Indians called "jerk." The bread had a very unpleasant smell and I couldn't bring myself to eat it; the meat was delicious, though, and I finished it quickly. There was also a wooden bowl of some sort of plain flat cakes. These were dry, but I ate one or two. The Indians ate alongside me.

I was feeling better and safer. My fears calmed. I was thirsty but my hosts made me no offer of drink. We were sitting silently on the floor of the cabin. I got out my flask and took a sip. The Indian raised his eyebrows, and I offered him a drink. Now it was my turn to raise my eyebrows—like many white men I know, this Indian couldn't just sip liquor. Instead, he drank it like water and then he gave the bottle to his wife who drank with equal ease. They returned the bottle to me; I held it out to the young woman but she shook her head and refused.

Still, we said nothing. It wasn't long before the Indian and his mate wanted another drink—my molasses rum was quite popular. The Indian smiled very broadly when I again presented him my flask. After drinking a second time, he closed his eyes and wagged his head from side to side. He opened his eyes and he stood and came very close to me. He laid his big hand on my head and he breathed heavily in my face; then he said, "Yes, yes—white man is not ugly, the white man looks fine." His wife nodded silently and smiled; then she closed her eyes.

We sat a while. The Indian talked to himself. He hummed. He sang. He hallowed and stared at me. I was unsure as to how this would all turn out. I wished either he or I were somewhere else.

The two old Indians were sitting side by side and swaying. The man reached out toward me. I figured that my bottle was my best protection so I gave them both all the molasses rum that they wanted. In no time they emptied my flask. The old woman lay down; she was fast asleep before I knew it. Not long after, the man nodded off too.

I was left alone with the Indian girl. The old Indians were asleep, and the young woman said a few quiet words. She spoke English and she told me that her name was Hiding Bear. She asked where I was traveling.

I told her I'd been doing some land business in the city of Bucyrus and now I was returning home. She asked if I was married. I said no. I smiled and said I wouldn't mind a beautiful Indian wife like her.

Hiding Bear shook her head. "White men do not like Indian girls with dark faces," she said.

I said that she was wrong. She was more beautiful than most white girls, I continued. This was the truth. Hiding Bear looked away. We stopped talking. Had I offended her? I suppose that I was too bold. I rubbed my hands on my knees. The fire was warm and my eyes were closing. I'd walked more than half a hundred miles that day and I was too tired to think clearly. There was a long pause in the conversation. My head slipped. I was nodding off and falling asleep.

I blinked my eyes to try and stay awake. I looked around the cabin; things seemed warm and blurry. Hiding Bear was quiet. She watched the fire. I hesitated to say more—I wanted to behave honorably. Should I have eaten more of their food? Perhaps, tired as I was, it was time for me to leave, even though it was then the middle of the night. I looked down at my boots. Hiding Bear and I were both silent for a long time.

Suddenly Hiding Bear stood up. "Excuse me for a moment," she said. She disappeared into a back section of the cabin. When she returned she was dressed in a beautiful deerskin robe embroidered with red and black beads. She had a small red hat, a kind of leather turban, around her forehead, and she had soft velvet moccasins on her feet. She was quite fresh and pretty and she made me think of some springtime flower like a bellwind or a new mayapple.

I was silent. Should I say something about her outfit? Would such a comment be impolite? What are the Indian manners? I didn't know and I couldn't think clearly, so I said nothing about her clothes. After a moment we began to talk about little things. We talked about the recent rains, and I told her some more details about Bucyrus. She nodded. Then she asked whether I needed to sleep. I answered that I certainly did.

Hiding Bear brought some furs. She piled them neatly for me in front of the fire and I lay down to rest. Over in the corner she pushed some hides into a bed for herself. We talked idly. She told me that her father had given her a piece of land not far from there. She planned to live on that land when she was married. But I will never marry an Indian, she said. Indians only want to hunt; they think that their wives are slaves and they make the wives carry the game if they come along hunting or raise all the corn and potatoes and children if they stay at home.

Hiding Bear went on and on but I barely heard the end of her speech. I was exhausted. I closed my eyes for just a moment and suddenly I slept the sleep of the dead until morning, when I was awakened by the thirsty Indian who wanted more rum. I took the bottle from under my head. It was empty. Luckily I had a second small flask in my pack with cheaper rum. I handed it to him, recalling:

There's none is as wholesome
As true religion and some old rum.

The Indian gave a groan. His eyes were closed but he emptied my bottle and lay down again. He breathed easily; he was calmed— though I doubt it was true religion that had this effect. As soon as he was asleep, I got to my feet and put my pack on my shoulder and prepared to start on my journey home. Before I left, Hiding Bear, the kind-hearted Indian girl who was pretty as a Crawford peach, gave me some more "jerk," deer meat that had been cut into long strips and dried in the sun. It was probably the fanciest entertainment that she had for a stranger. I thanked her and she smiled.

Hiding Bear stood by the door. She looked down at her feet. She was very shy. After a moment she quietly wished me a prosperous journey. I stood back and gave her a military salute; I think I may even have bowed.

"Then I left," said the old stubbly-bearded hunter. "In the daylight I easily found my way. My path crossed the river at a shallow spot, a ford in Broken Sword Creek where crows waded and pecked at fish. I looked back, but I could no longer see the clearing for Hiding Bear's cabin, and I turned and walked on across the creek.

"And that," concluded Hardesty Cheeter, "closed my brief acquaintance with one of the Indian families who lived in my area of Crawford County, way back in the olden days of Ohio when I was just a young sapling of a man."

·16·

Duyvelscar the Wolflet

THE FORESTS OF Ohio's Columbiana County merge with Pennsylvania, and at one time wolves, bears, and elk crossed the border freely. By elk, I mean the wapiti. Wapiti is an Algonquian word that means pale, light, white. The wapiti are light reddish brown with a black belly, a white rump, and a short tail. They are like European red deer but bigger; in fact, wapiti are the largest of all deer, except for moose.

Wapiti love beautiful country. They love open rolling ranges of hills dotted with patches of woods. In the earliest pioneer days, wapiti were as plentiful as the bison—that was when the Indians were the husbandmen of the American continent. Today, after the European invasion, wapiti are extinct east of the Rockies.

Ohio's white settlers knew the wapiti elk. Annie Meeker had seen many of them from a distance. Annie was a small pioneer woman. She lived in the woods of Columbiana County with her new family. When our story begins, Annie Meeker was feeling uneasy. It was night. She hugged her infant Amanda tightly. Annie's husband, Jacob, had gone to start the yearly log drive downstream on the Allegheny, and he'd left her alone in their round-log cabin.

The Meekers lived back in a hollow in the woods. It was quiet at night. Sometimes they heard the Grand Duke, the great horned owl—but tonight was different. The owl had been drowned out by a pack of hungry wolves howling on the trail of meat. That afternoon a hunter had shot a huge bull elk. He'd hung the meat on a tree too high for the wolves to reach and he'd gone to the town of Bayard to get a horse and sledge to haul his prize to the railroad station.

Even in those early years, wapiti were already disappearing from Ohio. Just around the time of our tale, Jim George Jacques killed what he called the "last elk in Pennsylvania" at Flag Swamp. However, twelve years later, John Decker killed a young stag in the Seven Mountains area, and, three years after this, the *Ebensburg Mountainier* reported that two elk had been seen wandering south across the Black Swamp.

In the Meekers's day, wapiti were rare and the hunter was mighty proud of the large one that he'd killed. The pioneers thereabouts were an honest folk; no one would bother the elk, so he'd strung it high in a tree and had gone off to get something in which to transport it home. Now it was night, and wolves had scented the dead elk, even at a distance. They howled throughout the valleys. They made as much noise as sixty coronets, eerie, mournful, and mysterious. The night wolves were hungry, and they were hunting.

Wolf howls grew louder. They sounded like rising horns; trees shivered and rocks echoed. The wolves galloped into the hollow. They reached the tree where the meat was hanging. The wolves stopped, they growled, they paced, and they jumped. The elk hung behind the Meeker cabin where Annie was huddled inside. She thought there were twenty or thirty or more wolves. Each wolf pack has a leader and the leader of this one was well known in the region. He was called Old Brownie. He was long tailed. He was a fighter, and he weighed well over a hundred and twenty pounds. Old Brownie leaped at the wapiti carcass—once, twice, three times— but each time he missed.

Old Brownie ran back and forth. He ran. He stopped. He ran back. He took a gigantic leap and he locked his teeth in the meat, and suddenly down came the huge carcass under the weight of the king wolf. The other wolves kept their distance for a moment, but they couldn't resist for long. The pack began to rip and tear the meat; soon there were only bones and the six-point antlers left. Finally the wolves were full, and they wanted only to lie down and to sleep.

Poor Annie heard the wolves clearly. They came closer and

closer. The hinges were off the back door and it leaned at an angle—Jacob had planned to repair it when he returned from his logging trip. Annie shivered.

Annie heaped birchwood chunks and dry pine on the open fire because she'd heard that wolves and wildcats stayed away from fires. Smoke and sparks flew up the chimney.

The pack circled the Meeker cabin. It was a warm shelter. It had good smells. The long-tailed king wolf, Old Brownie, sniffed at the back door. He pushed it with his nose. The door moved. Old Brownie slid inside and the pack followed: ten, twenty, thirty wolves slipped into the Meeker cabin, all of them sleepy after their meal.

Annie heard the wolves breaking into the cabin. She climbed up on the top bunk. She huddled under the heavy quilts and haps with her tiny child, Amanda. The wolves were tired. They headed straight for the fireplace—this was the one spot Annie had thought sure they would avoid. Annie stared at the shelf above the fire where Jacob's rifle hung. The gun was loaded and it tempted her, but it was impossible to reach.

When he gets the chance, a wolf eats a huge meal and he eats it quickly. He swallows mouthfuls, hunks of meat that he barely chews. Then he likes nothing better than to sleep. Sometimes a pack fills themselves until they can hardly walk. For this reason, the Indians would hunt wolves using buffalo carcasses: the wolves would eat a vast meal nonstop and lie down and sleep, and then the Indians killed them easily.

In the Meekers's cabin, the pack lay down to sleep. They lay on their sides, spread out on the bear rugs and the deer and wildcat hides on the floor before the fire. The king wolf, Old Brownie, closed his eyes. Then he opened his eyes again. He nibbled at an itch on his paw, he yawned a few times, he closed his eyes, and he fell asleep. The others felt safe and fat and happy and they slept too.

One wolf kept awake, he was the watchdog, the guardian. Annie was silent as a mouse. She could not take her eyes off the floor, covered with heavy-breathing wolves, wolves, wolves. It was like an ocean of wolves with tides of sighs and groans and growls.

Morning came slowly. The cabin windows were covered with deer hides. Weak gray light slipped in through the cabin cracks. The fire had burned down. The king wolf stretched; he stood, he shook himself. He sniffed the room and other wolves raised their heads. They yawned; they wrinkled their noses. They nibbled the fur on their backs and their legs. They switched their tails and they stretched their paws. They stood and shook. Soon all were standing and wagging their tails and pushing their pointed noses at each other and licking ears. Then they trooped out of the house through the back door. The wolf pack milled around the scraps of elk meat and bone, they drank at the spring, then they started out at a trot for their home den in the far hills.

Annie lay absolutely still. It was quiet. An hour passed. Annie got out of the bunk. She left her baby sleeping, wrapped in the quilts, and she slipped on her boots and began to clean up after the wolves. She straightened the hides on the floor. Some had been bunched; others were pushed into piles. Under the last pile Annie saw a bit of fur, a paw, a nose. There was a live little wolf, dark, warm, and wide eyed. When it scrambled to its feet, Annie saw that the wolfling was lame. It hopped and hobbled about; it seemed glad to be away from the rough pack. It rolled on its back and wagged its tail for Annie.

Annie soon saw why the wolfling was lame: she'd been caught in a trap. Luckily she was small and had been able to pull herself out but she had ripped a deep gash in the top of her front leg. The scar had the shape of a head, a devil's head; Annie said to herself in Dutch, the language of her grandparents, "*Duyvelscar*," and this became the little wolfling's name.

Duyvelscar was affectionate. Nonetheless she was a wolf—a wild and wilsome animal, with coarse fur and slanted blue eyes. Annie was careful, but she couldn't help fussing over her little visitor. Annie petted the wolfling, and she fed it table scraps.

When the baby awoke, Duyvelscar licked Amanda's face, and Annie breathed more easily and smiled.

Duyvelscar followed Annie around like a penny dog. It was as if Duyvelscar had been waiting all her young life for a mother, for a family, for a home. She was quiet and obedient. She fit into a comfortable family niche—she made a threesome with Annie and Amanda. Annie cooed to the wolfling as much as to her baby and she called Duyvelscar her "little chickabiddy."

In the afternoon, the elk hunter returned. He had a horse and a wagon. He found the pile of bones, all that remained of his elk, and he cursed the wolves and hit the tree with his axe. Finally, he took the six-point skull and without coming over to the Meeker cabin he turned and headed home through the hollow between the two dark hills behind the Meekers's land. Again it was quiet in the woodland.

Three days later Jacob Meeker came home. It was early afternoon. Jacob poked his head in the door. "Annie," he called, "Annie—I'm home."

Then Jake saw Duyvelscar. He narrowed his eyes. He stepped back. "Annie, what's that thing?" he asked quietly reaching for his gun.

"Hold on a moment Jake," said Annie. "This little wolf is a stray. She's a baby; she needed a home." Then Annie told the whole story to Jacob. He sat down and opened his eyes wide. He creased his forehead, and he listened to the tale from beginning to end.

"Strange, strange," was all he said, shaking his head and rubbing his chin.

Things returned to normal in the Meeker household. Jacob fixed the back door. Duyvelscar was quiet; she was Annie's shadow. She shied away from Jacob for days, but after a while she let him pet her too. Days passed. Weeks came and went, and soon it was years later.

Amanda grew. She laughed and she giggled. She rolled in the leaves. She talked to herself and played with cornhusk dolls. She pushed and pulled Duyvelscar, and the wolfling licked Amanda's face. Amanda jumped behind the wolf, and Duyvelscar jumped too. Amanda ran left and Duyvelscar ran right. Duyvelscar ran back; she jumped and picked up a big leaf and shook it. Amanda chased her, but Duyvelscar stayed just out of reach and when Amanda turned away the wolfling ran up and nudged her hand. Amanda ran, and Duyvelscar ran—then they both fell and rolled in the leaves.

The years continued to pass. Spring came and spring left. Winters, falls, and summers—all flowed in and rolled away. When she was four, Amanda walked in the woods by herself, and Duyvelscar ran ahead and behind. She sniffed and she tracked. She was always in sight of the child, but never at her side. When Amanda turned, Duyvelscar turned. When Amanda headed home, Duyvelscar headed home. When Amanda crossed a brook, Duyvelscar lapped the water. When Amanda sat down to play, Duyvelscar was nearby chewing on a leaf or a stick or an odd-shaped rock.

Now Amanda was five. She hiked every single day. Amanda was fearless and the world was magic. Everything in the woodland was tall and deep and warm and felt like protective parents to her. Duyvelscar always followed Amanda and Annie felt that the child was safe. Duyvelscar had never grown very large; she still had a bit of a limp in the front, but she could dash like a deer and she ran after squirrels and rabbits and chipmunks. Duyvelscar loved the summer sun and the southern wind. She nosed the leaf-dirt. She licked Amanda's chin. She had a gentle wolfen heart, and she slept with Amanda all night.

The Meekers lived in a hollow. It was dark and cool in the summer. It was sheltered from the winds in the winter. The loggers and bark peelers hadn't yet gotten to the ice creek, the limestone spring in that hollow, so the trees were still thick and the Meekers's woods were a park filled with candlestick hemlocks four or five feet in diameter and without branches for forty feet, and the light that slid down those trunks was always tan and green.

Well, that afternoon was as soft as ever. It and warm and

calm—it was a Tuesday in late September. Amanda had been building a stick hut for her doll. She sat working for an hour. Now she stretched and ran. Off she went through the woods with Duyvelscar running alongside, slipping behind the shinhopples, darting out into the spots of sunshine.

Not far to the right, over the creek and past the rockfall, lived an ornery hairy man. Actually he was more than ornery—I have to say it: he was simply bad. His name was Har Eben Ford. He was nicknamed "Wild Har," and he was a slinker and a stealer and a fighter. He lived alone in a falling down cabin, back along the ravine that they now call Wild Har Run.

You still hear about Har in Columbiana County tales. He would skin wild rabbits and eat them like bananas. He was tall and thin and unshaved. He never worked regular, but he earned some money as a part-time woodsman, a logger. That day Har was just back from a job where he'd drunk up all the whiskey he could swallow. He was carrying a fullsquare bottle of the stuff and he'd already drunk quite a bit of that too. Har was wandering toward home. He had to look carefully—he was afraid he might trip over a root or a rock. Wild Har saw movement in the brush ahead. It was Amanda, jumping and talking to herself.

The sky was high. Turnstones wheeled overhead. The day was large and wide and far. The child was tiny and light and bright.

Wild and woolly Har stared out of too-wide eyes. He stared from behind a scraggled beard. The child was alone. Crazed old Har thought he would pick her up. He could hold a hand over her mouth. He could take her home with him.

Har came up to Amanda on unsteady feet. He mumbled some words to her and tipped his head to the side. Amanda seemed friendly. She wasn't afraid. Har stooped down. He reached over to pick her up. I bet she won't even make a sound, thought old Wild Har. Suddenly Duyvelscar appeared out of the brush. The wolf sprang at Har. Har dropped Amanda. Where was a club or a branch when he needed it? The wolf lunged and it growled. It jumped behind Har, trying to chew his legs, to hamstring him, to cut his ankle tendons. Then, like a female wolf always does, Duyvelscar suddenly switched to the front and attacked the man's neck.

Amanda was frightened. She got to her feet. She began to run home. The fight continued. There were howls and yells and growls, snarling and cursing. Meanwhile Annie heard the noise. Was Duyvelscar's wolf heritage breaking through—had the wolfling turned on her daughter? Or had other wild animals attacked? Annie stood stock still.

Whatever the cause, whatever was actually happening, Annie was afraid. A chill ran down her back. She shivered. The small pioneer woman picked up a pitchfork and ran down the path toward the noise. She ran and ran and ran. Then she stopped. Wild Har and Duyvelscar were in a life and death battle. Where was Amanda? Annie had to save Duyvelscar. She ran at Har with the pitchfork. It struck him in the back. Har fell over onto Duyvelscar, and the poor wolfling was killed also.

Wild Har was thin and he was wiry. He'd been tough as a pine knot, but now he was dead. Duyvelscar was dead too. Annie sat there; she cried and cried. After a time, Jacob found them. He brought the wolf back home. That night Jacob and Annie buried the wolfling in the small cemetery beyond the ridge. Her grave can still be seen but you might mistake it for that of a child because it's so small. You'll know it, though, because of the inscription on the tombstone.

> Warm summer sun
>   Shine kindly here
> Warm southern wind
>   Blow softly here,
> Green sod above
>   Lie light, lie light—
> Good night, dear heart,
>   Dear wolf—good night.

·17·

The Headless Horseman of Cherry Hill

I'M SURE I don't have to tell you that ghosts live in all eleven of America's Fayette counties. There's a Fayette County in Alabama—there's also one in Georgia, in Illinois, in Indiana, in Iowa, in Kentucky, in Pennsylvania, in Tennessee, in Texas, and in West Virginia. Each of these places has its own particular ghost. Then there's the Fayette County in Ohio. Our Fayette is in the southwest of the state. Fayette's got a lot of flat land, it's got limestone, and it's not too bad for farming, and of course it's also got a ghost.

In Ohio's Fayette County the seat is called Washington Court House. It's a city where you can find cattle and sheep and stockyards—in fact, the area calls itself the Herefordshire of Ohio. People also know their horses in Fayette.

Now, horses are special animals. In a horse all four limbs are made only for running—and only for running forward: they can hardly move any other way. And their teeth? Why horsey teeth are just perfect for grazing in the plains and open flat grasslands. All over this great land of ours, there've been horses since time immemorial. Once upon a time the horses were teeny tiny and were called Eohippus. Eohippus were smaller than dogs and they had lots of toes. Next came horses the size of a big dog, like a collie—these had three toes. Horses today have only one large toe on each foot.

Why do I tell you about toes? Well—why not? You ought to know something about toes if you're going to be an educated person. Anyways, as I was saying, wild one-toed horses used to be

·124·

everywhere, in central and western Asia and on the plains of North and South America. Native Americans had their own fine horses, but when the white men arrived they brought horses from Europe. Soon the white settlers developed American horses. There are the small Morgan horses of Vermont, there are slow draught horses of Lancaster County, Pennsylvania, called Conestogas, and in Virginia, Kentucky, and the eastern South you have the old-type sleek thoroughbreds. In Texas, California, and Mexico there are mustangs. And in Fayette Ohio? Well, you've got your just plain horses.

This brings me back to Fayette's ghost. In Fayette County, on dark moonless nights, the Headless Horseman of Cherry Hill rides a Virginia thoroughbred across the ridges and then down through the cut alongside Cherry Hill. He goes fast and then he stops; he seems to be searching, looking for his stolen bags of gold, at least that's what they say in Fayette County.

Cherry Hill—the very name makes children shiver in southern Ohio. That's where it all happened. People tell all manner of tales about Cherry Hill. It's hard to avoid the place because going from one city to another you have to pass through Cherry Hill's natural cut, which is a kind of valley along the edge of the huge hill. People are forced to take the Cherry Hill road, but it's been getting spookier recently and it's where the headless horseman rides. Not long ago a local man, Tad Bolwell, was coming down the road. It was evening. Tad thought he saw someone riding a horse far ahead. The horseman disappeared around a corner, and as Tad rounded the corner he saw a body lying in the road. Tad couldn't see any trace of the horse; perhaps, he thought, the man is drunk or hurt.

Tad Bolwell stopped his horse. He got down from his wagon and he went over to the man and tried to pick him up. He put his hands down and lifted, but his hands passed right through the body. Tad shivered and stepped back. Then he noticed that there was a hat but no head on the body. Tad jumped. He ran back to his wagon, he leaped on board, and he started driving. But Tad had to drive forward—it was the only way to get home. When he came to the spot on the road, Tad could feel the body as the wheels rolled over it. Tad shivered and shuddered and shook, but he kept on going—and he still gets weak every time he tells about it.

Who was this headless body that galloped and galloped and galloped about whenever the wind was high? Everyone thereabouts knows full well: it's the ghost of Stephen Oliver Decker. Stephen Decker had come west from Virginia and he planned to buy a farm in Ohio country. Stephen had grown up on a rolling meadowy horse farm. When his father died, Stephen sold the farm and packed his saddlebags and headed west. His buckskin bags were filled with gold coins and covered with blankets. He had food for weeks. He was young and strong and he set out early one fine summer morning for the land of golden promise in the Northwest Territory.

Decker was thin. His hair was long and black. He was a romantic. The soft hills of the East Coast were in his blood and he had black loamy soils and black loamy smells all about him. Stephen's father had been a gentleman farmer, so Stephen had grown up with packs of dogs and with herds of thoroughbred horses. He loved the soil. He liked the feel of black dirt. He dreamed of owning his own farm. Stephen could see the endless fences, the meadows rolling out forever, the skies that were blue and dusted with clouds. He wanted to be in the new empty western territory. He would clear the fields all by himself, the streams would be cold crystals, the trees would be tall and straight and filled with raccoons. Stephen Decker would start his own tradition and there would be generations of handsome young Decker children growing up wild and strong in Ohio.

Stephen wanted a piece of bottom land, near a creek that ran back to the hills. Or maybe he'd find a grass hill with horse meadows running out and on beyond forever. He would build a round-log cabin with a creek-stone fireplace and puncheon floors. He could see it all clearly; he could picture the house, the fences, the barn, the stable. Soon he would have a rolling estate and he would return home, back to his childhood home, and he would ask Virginia Winston to marry him. Virginia was shy and pretty and she loved horses and dogs and children.

Stephen had never felt so free—it was like being the wind. He rode across the hills. He followed the Zane Trace, and eventually he found himself on the trail to the village of Chillicothe, Ohio. Chillicothe is on a meadowy plain along the Scioto River. To get into the city, Decker rode through amazing endless green hills—wonderful farming country. He stopped over and over again, just to look and to dream. Clearly he was near his final destination. Why, this empty land was just begging to be filled with horses and dogs and children.

Decker rode into Chillicothe outfitted like a typical country man. He had a hat and a coat and britches and boots. His future mother-in-law had made the clothes. The pants were tanned, tight-fitting deerskin and the vest was deerskin with the fur left on. His boots were a real treasure. They were hard leather and in the beginning they had rubbed his feet raw. (One pair of boots a year was all anyone got, so lots of men just wore old rags tied on their feet to save their boots. Sundays, a man would carry his boots until he got near to the Meeting House where he'd put them on, and after the Sunday service he took them off again. That's what Johnny Chapman did—but there's another story.)

Stephen Decker rode into Chillicothe, Ohio, in Ross County on the west bank of the Scioto River. Nearby are mysterious hollows haunted by ancient voices and several prehistoric mounds, but Stephen Decker felt no mysteries as he rode into town that October. Stephen felt no past and no history—there was only the wonderful limitless future rolling away from him like the meadowy hills. The wind was cool. The evening was coming. Stephen found a tavern, an inn about a mile north of the center of town. He tied his horse, he carried in his saddlebags, and he sat at an oak table where he ate roast goose and bread and drank cider. Two men sat down next to him; their names are not recorded but it's known that they were drummers—wholesalers and salesmen—for patent medicine and that they'd traveled from Philadelphia to try selling things throughout Ohio country.

How about a packet of tea? asked one of the medicine drummers. It's made from wormwood and it heals the aching stomach. Decker raised his eyebrows. Also, continued the salesman, I've some fine dried sweet Annie—indispensable for fevers, bronchitis, dysentery, and diarrhea; then there's still a few ragweed poultices for stopping bleeding and for healing sore eyes. Decker shook his head.

The first drummer looked at the second. Well, he said, we've got root pulp from wild yams; this makes a tincture for stomach problems and for the arthritis. Decker thanked them but said he'd best save his money at the moment. What for? asked the second drummer. Listen, said Decker, I have all my life savings in gold. I'm going to start a horse ranch out here in Ohio. After a few years, you should stop back—I plan to get married, and there's no doubt that my family will need a bit of those medicines.

The salesmen nodded. Decker bought them drinks and they began to laugh together. Stephen told them all about his home ranch and his future wife and the foxhounds he would raise and how the land here was empty and clear and refreshing, clean and wide and open. The medicine drummers looked at one another and ordered more drinks all around.

It was a midweek day, a Wednesday. The next morning, the inn hearth fire happened to be out. The innkeeper sent the stableboy to get some live coals from the farm next door. Later the stableboy reported that Stephen Decker had been up and eating breakfast even before he'd left for the coals. The two medicine traders skipped their breakfast and left immediately after Decker.

Decker set out west from Chillicothe. Soon he was in Fayette, the next county over. He stopped his horse on a hilltop. The countryside rolled away from him. There was green everywhere and there were streams in the valley and thick woodlands in a vast wave to the left. He nodded; he could build a cabin on the ridge. Stephen could see the sleek brown horses running along the open meadowlands beyond.

Stephen didn't know it but he was on Cherry Hill and the road that ran through it—the cut in the beautiful up-and-down countryside—was the very one that was used by all the farmers passing through. Stephen smiled and walked his horse higher along the hill above the road. He set his horse to grazing and he built a fire for supper. What did he eat that fateful night? I'm told that it was a regular feast of bubble-and-squeak—dried beef and cabbage fried together—with a pot of chicory coffee and with corn muffins for dessert.

The sky was black. The stars were out, and frogs chirped. Late at night the ashes grew cold. Decker fell asleep, happy to be in the great wide new land. He was free and young and brave—he hadn't even bothered to make a hidey hole for his gold. Decker slept and the night life cricked and cracked and slipped and wriggled and crawled around beside him. Two dark figures crept up to where Decker lay rolled in his blanket. With an axe, the taller of the two chopped down on the sleeping man and the other dark figure picked up the saddlebags filled with gold.

Early the next day, Ezer Craddock was on his way to Chillicothe to register some land with the local agent. He took the Cherry Hill route and he went through the cut. It was a bit darker there. Ezer saw a horse grazing up on the hillside. There were the remains of a fire nearby. Ezer led his horse slowly up to the campsite. He dismounted. There was a blanket sleeping roll, there was the shape of a man, and there was an incredible amount of blood.

Ezer stepped back; then he turned. He ran and jumped onto his horse and he beat the poor animal to a lather as he rode to the tavern where Stephen Decker had stayed the night before. A group of men got together and four of them, including Wilford Stemps, returned to the grisly scene. Decker's horse was still grazing on the hill. The saddlebags were gone. The campfire was cold, and

Stephen Oliver Decker's blanket was rolled neatly around his body—the body was there, but Stephen Decker's head had disappeared.

Stephen Oliver Decker, the young and hopeful rancher from Virginia, had been dismantled. The men shivered and buried the body. But somehow the good Lord seems to have resurrected him. To this day, a headless horseman can be seen riding past Cherry Hill on moonless nights, searching, searching, searching. He rides and gallops and canters about. He trots silent as the wind and black as the sky. In the vasty night he roams alone, hunting for his stolen saddlebags and also for his lost and lonely head.

·18·

Waupee White Hawk and His Family

NOTHING MAKES YOU want to fly more than seeing a great gliding hawk. Red-tails are Ohio's largest hawks. They soar high on broad wings over open fields and wide meadows; most of the time they're looking for field mice for dinner. Ohio also has harriers, like the marsh hawk—these hawks fly low, gently rocking back and forth, cradled like a baby in the winds. I suppose from its name you'd guess that marsh hawks like marshy areas—well, you're right. They like open wet grasslands and big damp meadows. The males are gray underneath, so the white settlers called the marsh hawks Gray Ghosts—but the harriers' bottoms are white, and the Shawnee Indians called them White Hawks.

One of the old Shawnee legends tells of a hunter in Ohio country named Waupee, meaning White Hawk. Waupee had been a skilled hunter and the son of a chief, but one day he disappeared forever—this is his story.

Even when he was young, Waupee lived by himself in a remote part of the forest. He rarely visited his home village. Waupee grew tall and strong all alone. He was thin and handsome. He was quick and quiet. He easily slipped through the deepest forest and he could follow the smallest track.

One fine morning, Waupee was out in the wilderness, past all the usual trails. He had been hunting for days, and he was far, far afield; he was wandering beyond range of Indian calls and Indian drums. Waupee White Hawk was traveling through an open forest, through patches of pine and oaks and tulip trees. Waupee stepped evenly, in a smooth light pace; he kept a gentle rocking rhythm that tapped in his mind.

Waupee could feel the trees. The nearby ones tingled and tangled—the far off ones hummed. Waupee's feet were like shiny green oak leaves. His arms were like strong young branches. His field of vision narrowed and he could see far, far away. All was smooth and warm and cool at the same time. He slid along on gliding feet, almost soaring on the wind. Hours passed. He thought no thoughts. Everywhere there were bits of brightness, of shininess, through the high foliage. The light dappled the forest floor; it spotted the wintergreen berries and the mayapple leaves. But now things were a bit brighter. Was he coming to the border of the forest? Before he actually saw it, Waupee knew that an open field lay ahead.

Waupee White Hawk stepped out into the sunshine. He was in a meadow, an open fieldland, a wide grassy range. Waupee walked into a plain covered with all manner of grasses and flowers; there were asters, goldenrod, Indian blanket, orange hawkweed, wild carrots, and wild roses, and along the edges were blackberry brambles, jewelweed, and violets. Waupee wandered into the meadow and he came to a ring worn in the grass. What had trampled the grass, the leaves, the flowers, the mints? Did animals run round and round there at night? Waupee's grandmother had told him about these places, calling them fairy rings. Sometimes small white mushrooms ringed the edges. Waupee studied the area: there was no path leading *to* the circle and there was no path leading *from* the circle.

Waupee looked closely at the grass. He raised his eyebrows. He looked up at the sky. Then he stepped back and found a tall thick bush. Waupee sat. He took two breaths; he relaxed his toes, his legs, his stomach, his chest. He tightened his fists and then slowly he relaxed them. Again he took two breaths. Waupee was patient, and he prepared to wait.

The sun slid along the hills of the sky. The clouds came and the clouds went. Waupee waited. Eventually Waupee heard a drum tapping lightly. He looked up. Something was coming down from the sky. It was a basket, a huge woven basket, and it was filled with young women; there were twelve beautiful sisters, the daughters of the Star Chief. The basket rocked from side to side as it was lowered from a clear blue window high in the heavens.

Lightly the basket touched the ground. The twelve girls leaped out. They jumped through the grass, laughing, and from some mysterious place, a drum continued to tap. The young women ran around. They tossed a shining ball. They threw wooden hoops wound with hide. They sat and teased each other and braided their long black hair; they acted out little plays and imitated animals and people. When they called to each other, Waupee was surprised to hear that the girls spoke Shawnee. He listened closely and found that the youngest was called Morning Junco. She was pretty and gentle. Waupee could not take his eyes from her. What was the strange story of her life? Waupee stood up and called out. The girls were startled; they seemed terrified. They jumped back into the basket, which quickly floated up along the winds and slipped back into the blue window high in the heavens.

Waupee watched them with his mouth open. He thought, "Amazing. Those girls are beautiful—but now they're gone, and I suppose I'll never see them again."

Waupee camped not far from that spot. The next day he came back to the trampled ring in the meadow. He had decided to stay there in disguise. Waupee White Hawk made himself seem small and he put on the skin of an opossum. In the sky there were five white clouds floating far and wee. After midday the basket again came down from the blue window in the heavens. The girls stood along the edge and watched everything—they were entranced because, although they lived in a wondrous land, there were no rough grass meadows in Star Land. As soon as the basket touched the ground, the girls jumped out. They were careful, however, because they were afraid of the man that they had seen yesterday. Waupee stayed silent next to a bush; he was in his opossum disguise. The girls were playing and shouting. Waupee crept closer. The girls looked at him. They had never seen an opossum before, and the girls froze—then they ran and jumped into the basket and quick as a wink it was whisked back up through the clear blue window in the sky.

Waupee sighed and took on the shape of the strong young warrior that he was. Waupee was the son of a Shawnee chief. His hair glowed in the afternoon sun. He felt at ease with his strong arms and his powerful legs. His fingers moved smoothly on their own. He stretched and walked like a mountain lion. Still, he felt uneasy in his chest.

Waupee returned to his campsite in a hollow in the woods. The ground was cool; the leaves on the wintergreen and the may-apples were warm. There was a gentle glow on the tree roots as the sun set. The night seemed long and Waupee did not sleep well.

The next morning, Waupee White Hawk washed in the stream, he stretched and he ran; then he stopped, sat, and emptied his mind of all thoughts. Waupee absorbed the sounds of the woods. The tingle of the world washed over him. After many, many minutes he opened his eyes and he took two deep breaths. Then he stood and he went out into the open fieldland. On the way he saw a gray mouse run into an old stump. The mouse was small and harmless; it would not surprise or scare even the young girls in the basket. So Waupee turned himself into a tiny field mouse with long whiskers and a long tail. He sat in the grass at the edge of the trampled ring in the field. He waited and sniffed the air and he wiggled his nose and peered out of big bright black eyes.

After midday, the basket appeared like a speck high in the sky. It slipped and it slid. It rode the wind. It floated down, down, down. The sisters sat inside laughing and teasing each other and playing with their long black hair. Finally the basket bumped down in the center of the fairy ring in the field. Out jumped the twelve sisters and they began to run in the grass.

"Look—by that bush over there," shouted Morning Junco. "It's a tiny mouse."

The girls ran over and gathered around the mouse. They bent down; their long black braids tickled the grass tops. They put out their hands to pet it. Waupee ran back into the taller grass. Morning Junco ran after him. Suddenly the basket started to move. The other eleven sisters looked back surprised and they ran and jumped in, and quickly the basket floated up and disappeared into the blue window in the sky. Morning Junco was too far to reach the basket. She ran to the center of the circle and watched it go up and off into the golden blue heavens.

Morning Junco started to cry. Waupee turned back into his normal form, a strong young hunter with long black hair. He came over and gave Morning Junco a hug. "Don't worry," he said, "I'll take care of you." Morning Junco took his hand, and sadly she followed him from the meadow.

Waupee walked with the young woman back to his home village. Morning Junco was greeted warmly. Soon Waupee married her. Morning Junco remained a very quiet person. Waupee brought her soft hides and fine food. Waupee's family welcomed Morning Junco into their meetings. The women asked Morning Junco's counsel. Children listened quietly to her stories of the many animals in the sky and the adventures of the Star people and the little gossipy tales of the will-o'-the-wisps.

Fall came and fall went. Winter passed. Then there was the summer. Late one summer day a baby boy was born to Morning Junco and Waupee White Hawk. The couple named him Chipping Sparrow. Morning Junco was happier—she sang in the mornings and she smiled in the evenings. But Morning Junco missed her sisters, her mother, her golden land in the heavens, and her father, Star Chief.

More years passed. Chipping Sparrow grew. He became as fast and as silent as his father and he took to slipping soft little tufts of hair from the backs of sleeping wolves. Morning Junco settled into a routine. Still, she often thought about her family. What were they doing now? How did they look and sound? She felt that her old life was a dream that was slipping away from her. She wrinkled her forehead and tried to remember long and hard. She had heard her father and her mother reciting many magic incantations. Was there one that would allow her to fly? Was there a spell or a prayer that would carry her as high as the highest bird? One day Morning Junco remembered something that she had heard. It was a charm used by her grandmother. Morning Junco smiled. She knew that these words would carry her home. She would sing the song, and then she would visit for one day and return.

Morning Junco knew that Waupee would be upset, so she did not dare to say good-bye—she could not face him. Early in the morning, Waupee went out hunting. Morning Junco worked quickly. She made a basket just large enough for her and Chipping Sparrow. She put some dried meat and four corn pancakes in a rawhide sack. She put the sack over her shoulder, she told Chipping Sparrow to follow, and she carried the basket out into an open field. Morning Junco wrapped little Chipping Sparrow in a blanket, and she began to chant. She chanted and then she sang. The words came to her from her tiny childhood; they had been etched deep inside her by her grandmother.

From faraway the leaves in the trees rustled and a wind came. It lifted the basket. The basket floated up, higher and higher. It swung gently; it rocked from side to side. Morning Junco sang louder and louder in order to raise the basket. Her voice was carried by the wind, and Waupee, hunting far away, heard Morning Junco singing. He looked into the sky and he saw the basket floating above the clouds. He started to run toward the fairy circle in the open meadow. But now the basket was just a speck—it could have been a high-flying bird—and at last the basket vanished through the blue window in the sky.

Waupee looked until the clouds washed away his vision. Then he stared down at the ground. He could do nothing and he could think nothing. His wife was gone. Little Chipping Sparrow was gone. It was too sad to think about.

The basket floated up, up, up. Morning Junco sang more quietly. The basket slowed. It slowed, and it settled gently on a cloud.

Morning Junco had reached her home in the stars. The endless depths of the cosmic tides overwhelmed her. How could she have forgotten the tingling feelings of the great endless reaches of time and space? For a moment Morning Junco barely remembered that she had left a husband on earth. She looked down at Chipping Sparrow; then she sighed. Morning Junco was not as happy as she had imagined she would be.

Morning Junco's eleven sisters and her mother and her father were crowding around her. They walked so closely that they practically carried her back to her home tent. They all talked at once and told her stories and fed her cream and honey. Fabulous things had happened since Morning Junco had left and each person was bursting with "and then she said . . ." and "he carved the . . ." and "before they knew it, he had . . ." and on and on. Her sisters braided her hair. They gave toys to Chipping Sparrow and they also gave him soft leather shirts and golden moccasins and finely beaded headbands.

Morning Junco had planned to stay for one day only. But how could she skip tomorrow's special evening meal? And then, before she knew it, family life slipped back over Morning Junco and time passed. Morning Junco was happy and she was sad. Her father, the old Star Chief, watched and he shook his head. One day he said to his daughter: "Go back, little girl, and take your son. Get in your basket and go down to the earth, to Chipping Sparrow's father. Ask him to come up here and to live with us."

Morning Junco's eyes widened. She took in a deep breath and shivered. No mortal had ever come into the endless cosmic hills. She was cold and warm at once. She shivered again; Morning Junco was scared and she was also happy.

"Waupee White Hawk is a hunter," continued Star Chief. "Undoubtedly he is out hunting at this very moment." Star Chief nodded to himself. "Tell Waupee that if he is to visit us, he must bring potlatch—he must bring presents—one present of each bird and animal that he catches in his forests. He will know what to bring."

Morning Junco smiled and then she laughed. She ran out of their teepee. She took her little boy and the two of them hopped into the basket. Morning Junco waved and sang and Star Chief waved his old bronzed arms and the basket began to descend. Down, down, down it went, jimping and jumping through the cosmic breezes and the white clouds and slipping along the mountain passes of the timeless skies of long, long ago.

It was a Thursday in the fall, a crisp early October day—or so I hear tell. Waupee was sitting sad and quiet in the enchanted prairie. The flowers were gone. The thistles were brown. The tips of the cattails were fluffed and shredding. Waupee crossed his legs. He rested his hands on his knees in the center of the fairy circle in the open field lands where Morning Junco had first come down to earth. How long had he been there, eyes closed, lightly chanting? Waupee did not know and neither do I. The breeze tickled his ears and then, from far, far above, Waupee heard a voice singing. It was Morning Junco; she was coming back down in her basket.

Waupee opened his eyes wide; he looked and stood unbelieving. The basket floated down to earth. Out jumped Morning Junco. She hugged Waupee and Waupee hugged her. Chipping Sparrow ran around in the grass and laughed and fell down and laughed again.

Morning Junco stepped back. "Listen . . ." she said, and she relayed to Waupee her father's message. Waupee nodded. Immediately he set out on a hunt. He was deep in Ohio country. For the animals, Waupee caught bear, bison, chipmunk, coyote, deer, field mouse, gray wolf, groundhog, fox, opossum, rabbit, raccoon, skunk, squirrel, wapiti elk, and weasel; for the birds, Waupee caught bald eagle, blue jay, cardinal, chickadee, crow, duck, goldfinch, junco, kingfisher, owl, red-tailed hawk, robin, rock dove, sparrow, turkey, turkey vulture, white hawk, and woodpecker; he also found blacksnakes, fish, frogs, toads, and turtles. Waupee caught all these wild beasts. He began to put them in his soft leather sack but very quickly it was filled to the brim. Waupee frowned. In order to carry them all to the heavens, up to Star

Chief's realm, Waupee decided to save only a token of each, a fin, a foot, a tail, or a wing. All told, it took five full days of hunting. When he had everything ready, Waupee and his wife and his son went to the fairy circle in the meadow. They climbed into the basket, and they floated up into the cosmic reaches—and then two times beyond.

This was like a dream to Waupee. Up and down and as far off as he could see everything was clouded and beautiful and white and blue. There were strange deep streams that ran cool and fast and rocky. The distances went on and on. There were endless mountains and falls and pine forests. There were hints of the far tides of stardust and moon mist. And then the basket descended among the mountainous clouds and rainy breezes and sun-dappled leaves, rocking like a child in the arms of the Great Mother.

Morning Junco's mother and sisters stood together waiting. The little family of Waupee, Morning Junco, and Chipping Sparrow were hugged and then they were taken to a great feast. There was corn and pumpkin. There were meats and creams and honeys. There were maple treats and sugar canes. There was bread of the lightest golden texture. Polished wooden mugs were filled with juice from raspberries and blackberries.

Star Chief sat on a smooth oaken log. He smiled and he nodded. He ate lightly from a dish of seeds and ground corn cakes. After the meal, Star Chief asked Waupee to distribute the tokens of his hunt. Each of the guests received a foot or a wing or a tail or a paw or a feather or a bone or a fin. Each person bowed and took that wild beast as his totem. Star Chief recited a chant and now each guest could turn into his own creature by holding the token that he had received from Waupee.

Before giving tokens to any of the others, Waupee had reached into his soft leather bag. He took out a long, white tail feather from a white hawk. The feather had fine gentle ridges and it had brown lines on its spine. He stuck the point in the back of his hair. Next he gave Morning Junco the feather of a slate-colored dark-eyed junco, a little bird with a trill like a Chipping Sparrow. To his son,

Waupee gave one of the brown-gray forked tail feathers of the little Chipping Sparrow itself, a tiny bit of a bird with a chestnut brown head and white eyebrows.

All the guests went home and slept. In the early sunshine of the next day, Waupee, Morning Junco, and Chipping Sparrow turned into their totem animals and flew off into the clouds. They soared high. They circled the treetops. Gently they dropped down, down, down, rocking on the updrafts and floating into the center of a fairy circle in the open field land below and then rising up again to fly off into the cosmic land of Star Chief where they live still to this very day, light and happy for ever after.

·19·

The Giant Bones
of Geauga County

IN THE STATE of Indiana, there was once a steer named Ben or Big Ben or Old Ben or something like that. It was near Kokomo, I think. This Ben was a Hereford and he weighed two-and-a-half tons and was eighteen feet long and more than six feet tall. Of course that's nothing compared to Paul Bunyan's cows—well let me be a bit more scientific, Paul had Giant Oxen, animals of the species *Bos taurus giganticus*.

Paul, as you know, lived up north most of the time, but it wasn't only northern lumber camps that can lay claim to Paul Bunyan—he had ties to Ohio too. One time they dug up one of Paul Bunyan's giant oxen in northern Ohio. You've never heard about this? Well here's the story as it was told to me. I heard it from Rachel Stacklee, whose best friend was Cadie Dimmick, whose father had actually dug up the bones in Geauga County.

It all began in the north—in Minnesota or Wisconsin or upper Michigan or some such wild place. Paul Bunyan logged and he raised cattle there. Paul's oxen were so big that he could hardly keep more than two or three of them on his farm at a time. Every spring he sent the young calves away to all parts of the country. One little baby ox, Reba, was shipped down here to Ohio. Reba was a daughter of Benny, who was the son of the famous Babe, and Cadie Dimmick said that her father may have dug up Reba's bones.

Reba's father, Benny, was called the Little Blue Ox. It's true that his hair was dark blue, but Benny certainly wasn't little. When he was a youngster he grew two feet every time Paul looked at him. One morning, the ox barn was gone. Later Paul found it on Benny's back: the Little Blue Ox had grown out of it overnight.

Another morning, with all his growing during the night, Little Benny was hungrier than usual. He felt starving; he was famished. He kept pawing and bellowing and mooing for more food. He ate all the hay that had been stored, so the cook started feeding Benny pancakes. But this Little Blue Ox just couldn't get enough. He demanded food, food, food, until there were two hundred men at the cook-shanty stove trying to keep him fed. About lunch time, Benny's stomach began a-growlin' again. He broke loose, he tore down the cook shanty, and he ate all the pancakes piled up for the loggers' midday meal. It was then that Benny made his mistake. Benny looked around and saw that there were still more pancakes on the stove. With a giant roar he tore over to the stove and he swallowed it whole, coals and all—and I'm afraid that finished him off.

Paul Bunyan's most famous ox was Babe. No one knew her exact size. Reliable men said that she was forty-two pick-handle lengths long and that she was seven derby hats wide between the eyes. And strong? Why that ox could pull anything. One time down in Texas, Paul's men were drilling an oil well—that was near Breckenridge, in Stephens County, if I recall rightly. It wasn't much of a hole, just sixteen inches in diameter, but they drilled and they drilled and they went down as far as they could. Nothing came up except dry dust. The foreman was an old hand who knew what he was talking about; he shook his head and said they should just give it up as a far-an'-away dry hole because there was absolutely no oil ever goin' to be found.

Paul was mad, and he was no quitter. Paul Bunyan wouldn't give up for nothing or for nobody. He yelled and he swore. He paced around for two or three days. One afternoon he actually smashed the derrick into kindling wood with his bare hands. Then he saw an advertisement in the paper by some rancher out on the dry plains. This fellow wanted to get a whole passel of postholes dug in the hardscrabble earth around his huge farm. Paul went over to inspect. Normal digging was out of the question: it was much too difficult on that land. Paul asked whether the man would like to buy some postholes that were already dug. Certainly, said the fellow, I'll take ten thousand post-holes, each three feet long.

Paul smiled. He was in a good mood. He hitched a chain around his empty duster hole, the one under the smashed derrick. Then Paul hooked up Babe and pulled fifteen thousand feet of the hole out of the ground. Ah, but Paul got mad again because the hole broke off and this left half of it in the ground. Anyways, Paul said that there was no use of a posthole being a full sixteen inches across—so he just quartered the hole and then he sawed it up into the right lengths. Now he had enough, and he bundled the holes onto a cart and sold the lot to the man who owned the rock hard prairie land, and Paul made quite a nice pile of money on the deal too.

As you can tell, Paul had a bit of a temper. He'd get mad at anything, living or not—his goat was got by men, moose, and marshes. One time he was logging on what was known as the Whistlin' River. The river got its name because every single morning, right on the dot at nineteen minutes after five, and then again every night, right on the dot at ten minutes past six, the river reared up in a big wave. This wave was two hundred and seventy-three feet high. Then, when the wave slapped back down, it let out a squeal that sounded like a whistle and could be heard for six hundred and two miles in any direction.

Whistling was mighty strange, but this river was famous for more than its whistling. The Whistlin' River was known as the orneriest river that ever ran between two banks. It took a fiendish delight in tying whole rafts of good saw logs into more plain and fancy knots than forty-three old sailors ever knew the name of— yep, this wild river was an old "side winder" for fair. The Whistlin' River was mean and crooked and kinky; it was rocky and tricky. Unfortunately it was the only route of transportation in that part of the state, so it was the sheer devil to take logs downstream. Each time Paul had to float a raft of logs on the old Whistlin' he got mad and ornery, and finally he got to thinking that the only practical solution was to tame this river once and for all.

Paul looked at his big ox. He knew what to do: he'd hitch Babe, the Giant Blue Ox, to the Whistlin' River. Old Babe would yank it straight or die trying. Babe was so strong that she could pull mighty near anything that could be hitched to her. Paul's problem was just how to hitch Babe to the river. Babe's chain wouldn't hold water, so Paul had to wait till winter when the river froze. Paul was just itchy with impatience—but I'm told that somehow he waited until the cold month of January. Of course he had other problems— but, listen to me, I'm gettin' carried away: I'd meant to tell you about things that happened closer to home, here in Ohio.

Let me return to Cadie, who told the story to Rachel; Cadie was the daughter of Royal Dimmick. The Dimmicks lived in Montville, a little town in Geauga County. Mr. Dimmick wanted a watering pond for his cattle. So he hired five men to help him dig out a hollow beside his stream, but on the second day he had twice as many men and free help to boot and this is the reason why.

On Friday, August fourth, 1871, Corey Stepnick and four other workmen began to dig. They were about a mile-and-a-quarter east of the center of town. It was a low gnarly marsh spot on the edge of the Dimmick property. The diggers tore out the roots and pulled up the black muck. Then they came to a layer of blue clay. By noon they'd cleared three feet of clay. Suddenly they struck something hard; it seemed to be a round stick of wood packed way down in the clay.

Corey Stepnick was a strong man. He took an axe and hit the thing and broke off a piece nearly a foot in length and pulled it out. It was hard and light, but it wasn't wood—it seemed to be a piece of a giant bone. The thing had a hard smooth surface, it had a crust about a quarter inch thick, and it had chalk inside. Royal held it up and looked closely. On the inside there was a tiny fencing, a criss-cross spongy-looking stuff.

This was bone all right, and it was huge. It was immense. It was from some giant animal. Corey and the other men dug wildly, flinging clay every which way. Now they were in a hole six feet deep and soon they'd uncovered the whole fragment, and it looked like a tusk. This animal must have died there an awful long time ago, said Corey. Other bones were struck by the picks and shovels. These were gigantic too. Were they from one of Paul Bunyan's huge oxen? (What's that? Tusks on an ox? Well, maybe it was one of Paul Bunyan's giant wild boars—I can't explain all the beasts of natural history. Just be patient and I'll tell you what I know.)

That afternoon and all during the next day, more bones were found. The tusk was long but broken. At first they got about three feet of it; then they found still another piece—the whole thing had probably been six or eight feet long when the animal was living. How could the beast have held up its head? This tusk was twelve inches around at its wide end. The workmen washed it. The outside was smooth and light; it looked like soapstone. It was pretty much hollow and it seemed to be a giant tooth that had stuck out of the animal's mouth and that came to a point way past the creature's nose.

That tusk was a shocker. The men took to digging all around. They found more giant bones nearby. Nine round joints of the backbone lay in a row. Twenty ribs each bigger than the next stuck out of the mud like a huge curvy comb—the largest rib was five feet long and four inches wide. There was a bit of skull too and it had large holes in the bone. The men dug until it got dark. They could barely make out the clay at their feet. Finally they quit. The air was cool, the shadows were gone, the men were still sweating. They shook their heads and rode back in the wagon to their homes to tell their wives a most amazing story.

The next day the men were there bright and early. Extra sons and neighbors had showed up too. The ground was damp and the sun was still low and shiny and yellow. The first diggers quickly found a leg bone, a foreleg below the knee. At the knee end, the bone was nineteen inches around, and it was cracked in three places. Pete Fordesty picked it up and saw that the inside was crisscrossed with tiny spaces: it looked like a hard sponge.

Royal Dimmick stood back while the workmen dug. They piled the bones on the ground. One man washed off the pieces. It was a powerful big skeleton, huge and thick and heavy. Its neck was short. Its backbone was eight or ten inches wide. The lowest ribs, those near the hips, were broken off and lost, so no one knew how long they actually were. On the other hand, the upper ribs were in perfect shape. Now, you may never have seen a skeleton of a pig or a cow or a dog, but these men had. They knew there was something strange about these old ribs. Most animals have ribs with the flat side out, next to the hide—but this old creature had the *edge* of the ribs facing out. Also, the men couldn't find any hint of a collar bone—and that's just like cows, who don't have any collar bones either.

The clay they were digging in was blue clay and it was more than four feet deep where the massive beast was dug up. There were teeth marks on the bones. Royal said that some other animals, like bears or wolves or some such, must have chewed on the carcass after it died.

The hip bones were massive, wider than a child is tall, nearly four feet from one edge to the other. They never found all the animal's bones. The men dug up what they could and they laid out the pieces along the ground. All four legs were thick as tree trunks and the upper leg bones were much longer than the lower leg bones. Was this an ox? If so, it was gigantic and strange shaped and it had tusks. Perhaps it was some kind of wild boar or even an elephant; maybe it was one of those mastodon things. No one's ever reported seeing wild elephants in Ohio (if you don't count the crazy tales of Sleepy Stepson) and elephants don't show up in any Indian stories. The only huge animals I ever heard of were Paul Bunyan's ox Reba, the one who'd been shipped down the Great Lakes to a farm in Ohio country.

Some of the local men thought that this giant animal was even older than Paul Bunyan's days. A professor from the Western Reserve Teacher's Seminary said that, once upon a time in the old cold days in Ohio country, wild elephants and giant beavers lived hereabouts. I've also heard tell of great gray ground sloths and mighty beavers and huge boars and tiny horses. . . . What's that? Dinosaurs? No, there's no question that Royal Dimmick hadn't dug up either a dinosaur or a rumpscuttle. And in case you're wondering this wasn't one of those large fishies from before Noah's Great Flood.

> Atop the wavelets tipply low
> Passing through the undertow
> Two mushrooms cap the urchin roe
> And snapping shells which thickly grow
> On Chinese crabs of the cloud-dark reach;
> Then skittering scattering up the beach
> They chimp and champ in calico,
> In gingham dress and starchy bow. . . .

What? Well, *I* don't know why I told you that poem—it just suddenly came to mind. Anyways, there are no dinosaur bones in Ohio, only bones of fish and of hairy animals like wild elephants and ancient oxen. Oxen are pretty old, you know. Hebrews and Hindus wrote about them and you can see them on Egyptian monuments—and that's from three or four thousand years ago. You can even find bits and pieces of cattle bones in Europe alongside those old stone tools and hunting things that they dig up in caves.

Today all our cattle and oxen came from herds across the ocean out of the Old Country of Africa and Asia, but I hear that long, long ago in Ohio country there were wild cattle too. They ran around on the open plains in large herds—that was before any people, probably even before the Mound Builders. Some kin of those old wild cattle eventually became bison and buffalo and musk oxen. By the time of the Indian days, buffalo and bison lived everywhere across the land, from the Atlantic to the Pacific. Their shaggy cousins, the musk oxen, are still around but they live only in cold places—Canada, Greenland, and such like.

Cows and oxen and bison were the largest animals that home-spun Ohioans knew, so Royal Dimmick thought he'd dug up some ancient ox with tusks—perhaps it'd been a relative of the famed oxen of Paul Bunyan, said Royal, maybe it'd been Reba herself. Nowadays all those giant oxen have been herded away just like the mighty bison. The other giant animals—the mastodons and giant sloths and huge hairy beavers—they're hiding in mysterious, wild, dank lands—I guess they're off in the deep swamp country. Those giant hairy animals go far back, way back into the dark past of men. We tell stories about them but who can really get a handle on that distant history? Does anyone remember back through the ages? Who recalls the days when giants roamed the American con-tinent? I'm afraid we only see those days in our dreams. It's only in the dark, in the late black hours—that's when we can stare out into the vasty cosmic depths. That's when we come into that huge ancient church—it's in the night and we're just tiny, tiny little people specks. It's only then that we ever really go back that mighty far ways into our grandaddy's firstest home, among the giants of the night.

·20·

The Ghost Town of Fallsville

DO YOU REMEMBER the children's riddle: What goes and goes and goes, yet never moves its toes? The answer is: a water-wheel for a gristmill. . . . You've never seen an actual waterwheel? After a spring flood it's a sight to behold—you can't take your eyes off it, what with all the rushing and flowing and the water roaring and rolling and pouring off the end and the wheel cricking and cracking and splashing in the sun.

Speaking of waterwheels—there's a poem called "When You and I Were Young, Maggie" by George Washington Johnson, with the verse:

> I wandered today to the hill, Maggie,
> To see the scene below,
> And I watched the creek and the mill, Maggie,
> As we used to a long time ago.

I had that exact same feeling when I visited the town of Fallsville in Highland County. Highland County is a pile of hills between the Scioto River and the Little Miami River. There's a bit of flatland and a tad of rolling fields, but farming is hard work. After a long day of spring plowing, even the strongest Highland man was all wore out; his team would be flecked white with salty sweat and they'd stop to take a long loud drink at the creek on the way home to supper. In Highland County, people lived where they could farm, so folks were spread out in the fields and the hollows. And those old-time Highlanders were all individuals: they wore bandan-nas and cut-up coffee sacks, and most came from a mix of Shawnee Indians, negroes, and rough white settlers.

I've told you about the city of Hillsboro before. It's the county seat and it's right on the dividing line between the Scioto and the Miami rivers—that's about sixty miles south of Columbus. Hillsboro was laid out in 1807 on land owned by Benjamin Ellicott of Baltimore, and, like the Rome of old, Hillsboro stands on hills, seven hundred and fifty feet above the level of the waters of the Ohio River.

James B. Finley didn't live in Hillsboro but he did stay in Highland County after leaving Kentucky. Finley was a famous Methodist minister, charismatic and wild. He moved to New Market Village with his bride, Phoebe. . . . You don't know about Reverend Finley? Well I'll leave his story to another time. Let's see— where was I? Oh yes, Highland County has Fort Hill, a strange earthen thing; it's some sort of construction of the mysterious mound-building peoples and it has dirt walls that are more than twenty feet tall.

When the Eastern settlers came, there were no Mound Builders; there weren't even many Indians. Easterners and southerners just settled here and there and the county was built helter-skelter. Roads followed old Indian paths and travelers were constantly upset by stumps and mud holes and boulders and washouts. Most of the time you had to wade across the streams, and even the largest roads led only to piles of rocks set to keep your feet dry crossing the rivers. Bridges were rare: Thomas Timothy Flint wrote home to Boston that when he finally found his first bridge in Highland, Ohio, it was "nothing more than two long trees thrown over the stream, about eight feet apart, with round logs laid across them side by side."

Highland County once had a town called Fallsville. You won't find Fallsville on any modern map—it's one of Ohio's ghost towns. Once upon a time, though, it was an official city. Fallsville was founded on Thursday, April twentieth of the year 1848, by John Timberlake, who named it for the local falls. There was already a wide road to the falls and this became Main Street. The falls is six miles north of Hillsboro, and here's exactly how you get there. Drive a mile-and-a-half on State Route 73 to a fork. Take Carey-town Road (that's the right branch). Go four miles to the second township road on the left and take this road about a half-mile. You'll see a Fallsville Falls sign—that's the ghost town.

Originally, the land north of Hillsboro had been part of a grant. Ours was a big wide country in those days and the federal Congress gave out land grants right and left to men from the army. This particular land grant went to Jonathan Bayhan, who'd been a lieutenant during the Revolutionary War. Bayhan sold some of the land to Captain James Trimble, some to John Timberlake, some to Clyther Haughton, and some to Bay Boardsman. Trimble willed his parcel to his son William Trimble. William had a son named Allen. . . .

What? Ghosts? Certainly not—the Trimbles were a very real family: William was a U.S. Senator, and Allen was Ohio's third governor. Allen Trimble sold his land in parcels. In 1825 he sold two hundred and six acres to Simon Cyrus Clouser. Simon Clouser also bought some adjacent land from John Timberlake, including a gray stone house and a gristmill along the waterfall.

Simon Cyrus Clouser was a bit of a mystery. Clouser was new to the area. He was a quiet man and no one knew exactly where he'd come from. People assumed that he was a widower. In 1826 he moved into the Timberlake house with his two small daughters, Jane and Joeline; they came trundling in from the East with a wagonload of furniture and a scruffy dog.

In those days you didn't just come into some new place and look around and nod and set up shop as a farmer. It took two, three, or even four seasons of hard work. You had to clear the land. You had to fence. You had to get the crops growing. Sometimes you had to build a cabin. Clouser was lucky to get a house and a business ready-built.

Most new settlers started off farming and they began with Indian corn. You could eat Indian corn fresh or dried. You could make cornmeal mush, johnnycake, and corn bread, and the pigs and the chickens would eat corn too. The corncakes were a favorite of the children—one of my old uncles from southern Ohio used to tell me how, when he was little, he'd steal slabs of johnnycake when his mother wasn't looking. Uncle Clete hid the corncakes between logs at the back of the house, and he ate them when he was hungry during long afternoons; Uncle Clete said johnnycake was never as good as when it had aged awhile in the logs.

To make all those pioneer corn foods, you had to grind or pound dried corn into a coarse meal. Mostly this was done by hand—Indians used a hollowed log or two flat stones. When someone finally got the energy to set up a stone gristmill, it was a welcome relief to an area; so, people came to Fallsville from all around in order to have their corn and wheat ground into meal and flour. When he moved in, Simon Clouser took over from John Timberlake and became Fallsville's miller. His gray stone house had a long white picket fence with a gate on Main Street, and right behind the house was the gristmill alongside the river where the water fell forty feet over three shelves of limestone.

Inside Clouser's mill were two four-foot grindstones and outside the mill there was a gated wooden trough that guided the water over the waterwheel. The waterwheel was directly attached to the top grindstone. Fallsville's grindstones were sandstone, quarried in Berea, a little town in northern Ohio, and they'd been carted down by ox wagon. Both grindstones had slits and grooves cut in their faces. The bottom stone was fixed in place; the top stone was supported on a wooden spindle stuck through the bottom stone, and it was the top stone that was moved by the waterwheel.

Every day, Simon Clouser poured grain through holes in the top stone. Water turned the stones and flour was pushed out to the edges. The two Clouser girls used brooms to sweep the flour into wooden troughs; then Simon sieved the flour to separate out the debris, which was bits of sticks and pebbles and unground grain.

When Fallsville became a formal town in 1848 it had three streets, Main Street, Mill Street, and Cross Street, and it had eight houses. The first families came from North Carolina—they were James Underwood, Moses Smith, Conestoga Johnson, Johnnie Holmes, Isaac Woodmansie, and the Carey, the Edwards, and the Clouser families. Fallsville was a Methodist settlement; in 1830 the Auburn Methodist Church was built. This church is gone now, but the cemetery is there and that's where the Clousers are buried.

People north of Hillsboro still recall a few odd details about Fallsville. Jemmie Crawlins says that sometime around 1850 the Highland County Literary Society had a talk one evening by Charles Edwards. The Highland County Literary Society was the meetin' place of young educated men who came to eat dinner once each week. The members dressed fancy, they talked fast, and they had debates, orations, and lectures. Charles Edwards called his speech "Fallsville, as it will be 50 years hence." That evening, Edwards—a Fallsville resident—looked into the future. Fallsville, he said, would become the leading town of Highland County. Trains would connect it with all the big cities in the East. Limestone quarrying and grain milling would be its major industries. Edwards was cheered by his friends: they clapped, they patted him on the back, and they shook his hand.

Colored people were a rarity in those parts so most of them are remembered. Fell Evans recalls hearing that, even before the Civil War, several free Negroes lived in the area. One of them, Andrew Lux Payton, bought several lots in the 1860s; he lived there till his death in 1893, when he was Fallsville's last official resident. Another Fallsville Negro was Whitewash Sam Johnson. Sam Johnson got his nickname because he whitewashed fences, barns, and houses. He made his own whitewash solution from the local limestone by crushing the rock, heating it in a kind of outdoor oven for two or three days, cooling it, powdering it, and mixing it with water.

The residents of Fallsville feared witches, and they sprinkled salt in the footsteps of strangers to counteract any evil that might have come into the village with them. Many a traveler passing through the town left with puzzling memories of the Clouser sisters, Jane and Joeline—skinny as toothpicks—haunting his tracks with a salt shaker.

Was gold and treasure buried there by Indians? Well that's what they said in Fallsville. The Clouser sisters called in water witches, men who could sniff out more than just water. With a hazel stick in front of them, they walked along slowly in a trance sniffing the air. When their stick passed over something unusual, like water or minerals or buried treasure, the stick began to shiver and to jiggle and it pointed down toward whatever strange thing was underground. I don't know if anything was actually found; if it was, the Clouser sisters never told.

Over the years the town emptied. Clete Lightman said that strange people began to wander around. On the night just before Shrove Tuesday a ragged boy would knock on the Clouser's front door and chant:

> I'm hungry with a stomach-ache
> Give me now a muffin cake
>   And I'll bother you no more.
> But if you haven't time to bake,
> A gray and jagged stone I'll take
>   And throw it at your door.

Every Christmas Eve, an Indian chief came to the Clouser's gate. He wore deerskins and feathers and moccasins. He didn't say a thing; instead he made hand signs. He would point and wave, trying to tell the two old women where Indian gold and treasure were hidden. One Christmas an Indian expert, Mr. Eben Rhodes from Hillsboro, was hired to come and to interpret the signs, however the Indian failed to appear that year.

As the Clouser sisters grew older, people said that they had buried all their valuables. They were supposed to have described the hiding places in secret wills to each other and then sealed the wills with drops of their own blood. But where are the wills and what happened to the treasure? No one knows.

After the Civil War, Fallsville began to slip away—it got smaller and quieter and dustier. No railroad came up the valley. People went to the larger gristmills in Hillsboro. Fallsville families died out or moved.

I went down there to see Fallsville for myself. It was a cold Saturday in November not long ago. I found the edges of the Clouser's gray stone house. There was also a section of stone wall along the stream bank. A broken wooden wheel lay half in the water and the wood had holes like the eye sockets of a skull—"the water that drives the mill decays it too," as they say. Wheat fields have taken up the rest of the village. Farms have spread. Fences cross old roads. Occasionally, local farmers plow up broken pieces of dishes in the springtime. Much of the original fencing is gone, but the gate in front of the mill is still there and it hangs open and askew.

21

Theodocia Saved from the Night Wolves

YOU'VE ALREADY HEARD about Geauga County, just south of Lake Erie in the northeastern corner of the state. Up there the land is gently rolling and filled with sugar maples. The Geauga County forests have plenty of other trees too—there are ash, basswood, beech, black walnut, cherry, chestnut, oak, and whitewood. These forests had plenty of animals in the old days. You could see bear and deer, wildcats and wolves, and also bats, beavers, chipmunks, coyotes, fox, mice, opossums, rabbits, raccoons, river otters, skunks, squirrels, weasels, and woodchucks. At one time there were even rattlesnakes—in fact the early settlers of the town of Chester were overrun by rattlesnakes. Some of the snakes were longer than a man is tall. The rattlers lived in Sand Hill, and they were more than a nuisance—they were downright dangerous. Finally one morning a group of twelve men came to Sand Hill wearing heavy boots and leather aprons. They killed thirty-two snakes, all they could find, and ever since that day the area's been free of those evil reptiles.

Way up in the northeastern corner of Geauga County and only ten miles from Lake Erie is the town of Thompson. Thompson's cemetery has six generations of the Patterson family. Even on the oldest tombstones you can still read some of the inscriptions, such as the one for Theodocia's little sister Emilia.

Here a pretty baby lies
Sung asleep with lullabies;

Pray be silent and don't stir
The gentle earth that covers her.

Emilia died just after the beginning of the new century, in 1800.

When Europeans first came to the Geauga County area, they met the last of the Erie Indians. The Eries, who called themselves the Cat Nation after the local wildcats, lived near the lake. Their villages were along the winding Cuyahoga River and the various smaller rivers and streams—such as the Chagrin River, Conneaut Creek, Doan's Creek, and the Grand River.

The Eries were of Iroquois stock: long, long ago the two tribes had come from the same ancestors. However, in the years of the white man's first settlements, the Eries, along with the Huron Indians, had been at war with the Iroquois. The Eries fought with bows and poisoned arrows. When the Iroquois got hold of guns from the Europeans, they suddenly became the better fighting force and, in 1653, the Eries were completely wiped out.

Theodocia Patterson came later. She was born in Massachusetts in 1791 and she grew up in Thompson in Geauga County.

Her father and mother, Joseph and Kate Patterson, had come to Ohio country from Southhampton Massachusetts. In Theodocia's day there were no Indians in Geauga County, but people still blamed strange happenings on the Indians. Indians were supposed to be hiding in the deep woodlands along the steep river gorges where wolves, bears, and wildcats could be seen.

When Theodocia was seventeen, she rode alone to the city of Mentor in order to deliver some blankets to her cousins. Mentor is in Lake County, fifteen miles west of Thompson. Theodocia packed the blankets, a roll of home-woven flannel, and a dinner of dried meat and cheese, and she tied these neatly and tightly onto her saddle. She kissed her mother, she got onto her horse, and she left home before noon. Theodocia planned to reach her cousins' house by nightfall.

Theodocia was smart, tough, and independent. She'd been born on a Saturday—and Saturday's child works hard for a living.

On Saturday morn the great daybreak
Has sparkling rays like gold snowflakes,
It tickles the sleepy clouds awake
And puffs them out like fat cupcakes.

I fill the day with the work that I find
Setting my toys in a neat straight line,
Then I draw little dogs (the children's kind)
And practice new letters I've just designed.

Saturday night brings Autumn to mind
The ceiling shadows is a pumpkin vine
With orange-yellow squashes and beans entwined
All curled round my bed in the cool starshine.

Like the rhyme, Theodocia was a serious but imaginative and hard-working Saturday child. In another year she would be attending the Western Reserve Teachers' Seminary. This school met on the top floor of the old Mormon Temple in the town of Kirtland in Geauga County. It was opened only a few years after the first teachers' college in the United States had been established in Lexington, Massachusetts. The Western Reserve Teachers' Seminary had high standards and it turned out sought-after teachers. Its most famous pupil was Thomas W. Harvey, who went on to write *Harvey's Grammar*.

But at the time of my story, Theodocia was still betwixt and between schools; she'd finished the children's school and now she was working at home before going on to the Teachers' Seminary. On that fateful autumn day the sky was clear. A few high white clouds floated without moving. It was warm, it was a Sunday, it was early in November. The leaves had fallen—they were a brown and red ocean with slips of yellow, and they hid the path. Theodocia followed the blazed trees, the triple chip marks on the trunks along the trail to Mentor. Theodocia was bored. Her mind wandered. Her horse followed the best footing. They crossed a stream, they tramped up a hill, they avoided roots and rabbit holes—and soon they were lost.

Theodocia looked around. She opened her eyes wide; she shivered. There were no chip marks on any of the trees. There was no trail. She stopped the horse. Everything looked the same in all directions. Brown, red, and yellow fall trees flowed off evenly every way she looked.

Theodocia sighed. There was nothing else to do but to search in an orderly manner. Theodocia had the horse walk forward, then to the right, then to the left. She passed open patches and creeks. She and her horse wandered through thickets of jewelweed. They tramped through piles of queen-of-the-meadow—what the Indians called gravel root and what we now call joel-pye weed. (Joel-pye weed? It was named after Joe Pye, a white man who said that he was an Indian and who used this particular weed to cure fevers.

Towerin' and purple-flowered old Joe Pye
He stood taller 'n the whole wide sky,

And he looked right down with his long leafy eye
On little tiny chil'ren, just like I.)

Soon the afternoon clouded and darkened. Nightfall was coming. The town of Mentor was nowhere in sight. People were far away—they seemed to have disappeared from the face of the earth. Theodocia felt she was in some ancient time. There was an endless silence of wind. There was the swish of horse feet through the brown leaves. Theodocia would be spending the night in the woods. Was she near her home? Was she near *any* home? Were there Indians in the woods? Were wolves lurking in the brush?

The young woman from Thompson took a deep breath. She had to work hard to keep from thinking of frightful things. She had to keep the night spirits at a distance and behind the trees. She took another deep breath and tightened her fists; she'd have to remain calm and face facts. There was a tree with a low branch. Theodocia stopped her horse. She climbed down. She hung her bonnet from the branch. If something *did* happen to her then this would be a signal to whomever followed her out here in the wilderness.

Theodocia frowned. She'd have to be a grownup. She looked around; then she walked over to a pile of thick underbrush. She tugged at the fallen branches and she dragged logs. Carefully she set the largest ones against the tree trunk and she made a little hut. Then she tied the horse's reins to one of the logs so that the horse stood like a guard directly in front of her doorway. Theodocia sat and folded her arms. Then she unfolded her arms. She smoothed her skirt. She stared out into the darkening woods. Theodocia could think of no better plan—she would just wait out the night.

After a while, Theodocia got up. She went over to her horse and unpacked her dinner. She ate the dried meat and the cheese; she drank some water from her leather flask. It was getting darker and darker, and Theodocia tried to settle down and to sleep. The world seemed unreal. She felt that she was in a bedroom larger than any other in the world and that it was filled with all the strange and shadowy things that were normally kept out of the bedrooms of the young and the innocent. God will protect me, she thought, shivering.

Finally Theodocia dozed off. Then she awoke suddenly—had she been asleep for minutes or for hours? It was pitch black. There was a noise, a trumpeting or the blasting of horns. Perhaps a search was in progress. Theodocia opened her eyes wide. She sat up. All was silent. There was only the cricking and cracking of insects and branches. Then she heard the noise again. It was howling—it was wolves. Somewhere not far away night wolves were hunting in a pack and they howled like a dreadful orchestra of horns. Leaves crackled. Twigs broke. There was panting and low growls, and Theodocia felt very cold and she could not stop shivering.

European settlers feared wolves and everyone had heard wolf stories. The fear was old and it had been brought over from Europe. Actually no wolf had ever harmed a person in Ohio, but this made no difference—fear doesn't come only from experience, it comes from somewhere deep inside a person. And the wolves *were* real— the settlers called them the night wolves.

During the daytime you rarely saw a wolf. Wolves rest in the day and they stay away from people, from cabins, from villages. However at night wolves feel bold. Wolves hunt at night. After nightfall, packs of wolves may even prowl around a hunter's camp and howl at the fireside. At night they steal sheep and calves. Wolves sneak in under cover of shadow, and that's why the Ojibway Indians called them *Mahengun*, hungry sneaks. At night, wolves will even steal up close to men. I've heard of hunters who fell asleep drunk in the snow and the next morning they found rings of wolf tracks round and round their blanket piles.

The night wolves had come to Theodocia. But shiver and shake as she did, she remained safe. The wolves sniffed and coughed and growled. The horse snorted and neighed; it sneezed and it sighed. The dry leaves crackled. Branches snapped. The wind blew. But He who had created that boundless wild land room had also set a protective hand over Theodocia. The girl prayed.

She promised that she would trust and serve God always if He, in His infinite goodness, would keep her safe. She prayed so hard that she could not hear the wild animals outside. After a while her head nodded, and Theodocia fell fast asleep.

And then all of a sudden it was morning. It was a bright, quiet, brown-leafed morning in the fall. Theodocia's skin was tight and dusty and at the same time damp. She was achy. She moved her head and her hands slowly. She peeked out of her little branch hut. There was her horse, standing quietly outside. The leaves had been trampled, but there was no one and nothing in sight. The night wolves must have been there, but now they were gone. Theodocia reached up and untied her bonnet from the tree branch. She climbed onto the back of her horse. She closed her eyes and she slapped the horse on its flank. Slowly the horse began to walk.

Where were they going? Theodocia didn't know, but she felt safe. God had protected her. He had saved her from the night wolves and He would lead her home again. The horse tramped through the woods; he felt warm and big and safe to Theodocia. The horse crossed streams, it squdged through the mud, it side-stepped the raccoon berries, it brushed the leaves. Then, through the goodness of the unseen Agent, blazes appeared on the trees. Was she heading home or was she heading toward Mentor? She was still a bit dazed and she couldn't decide. Theodocia and her horse walked for one hour and then for another hour. And what was this? Suddenly she was home. Theodocia had come home for breakfast, and now she was exhausted.

Theodocia had come home. She closed her eyes. She pictured the inside of the cabin, the cool pantry, the warm kitchen. Soup and stew and bread would be cooking. The house was quiet and safe; why, they had never even heard, let alone *seen*, a wolf there. Theodocia felt a warm glow. She felt fine as frog's hair. She had made a promise to God and the world was good and new and wonderful. When Theodocia walked in the back door, her mother raised her eyebrows and opened her mouth. Theodocia sat and told her mother the whole story, and the two women talked and talked with Mrs. Patterson shaking her head, saying over and over, "Only the good Lord knows."

Theodocia kept her promise from that day on. She was now a tried-by-fire Christian—she had faced the night wolves and she had lived them down. Theodocia Patterson went to the Teachers' Seminary the next year. She studied seriously; she stayed up late at night, writing slowly and neatly and reading everything twice by candlelight. In a few years she graduated and became a teacher. Then one October she married Seth Hulbert. All told they had three sons and four daughters, and Theodocia and Seth were one of the first eleven families who founded the Congregational Church of Thompson, Ohio. Poor Seth got the tumors thirty years later and he died of them in 1843.

In the Lord's year 1847, Theodocia married Warren Corning of Mentor. When Warren died, Theodocia married Roger Murray of Concord; that was in May of 1856. Five years later, Roger disappeared. In 1863 Theodocia married Lemuel Baldwin—formerly of Concord. Unfortunately in 1867 Lemuel became insane. It was thought best for the two of them to live apart and Lemuel went to Iowa with his son, Silas, from an earlier marriage; Lemuel lingered weakly for more than a year and died without ever becoming rational.

Theodocia Patterson Hulbert Corning Murray Baldwin survived a passel of husbands. She lived to be eighty-one years old but she never actually *saw* a live wolf in her life. At the end of her life, Theodocia suffered. She had stomach pains and bowel problems. She was always sore in her middle. She treated her cramps and her aches with tansy leaf tea but still she hurt every morning. She lived until December 1872, and she died in the house of her daughter, Mrs. Clarinda Garis, in Thompson, Ohio. Theodocia's last words to her grandchildren were: "See in what peace a Christian can die."

Theodocia Patterson had been born in Massachusetts and she was buried in Ohio, in the Thompson cemetery, a small and ancient park where raccoon berries grow in the wet spots along the wall in the autumn. Do you know the old saying: "The last one out closes the gate"? Well, no more of Theodocia's Pattersons are left in Thompson, and the gate on the cemetery fence now swings wide open in the breeze.

22

Some Recollections of an Ohio Wolf Hunter

I ONCE KNEW an old man who'd been a wolf hunter back in Ohio's early days. I was just a young'un when I met up with him; at that time, he was bent and white and deaf, and this is a bit of what I recall of his ramblings.

Most of my life, said the old hunter, I lived in Hancock County, over in the northwest of the state. That's where I met Hettie Burke; she was one of the first white settlers to come here from Pennsylvania. Hettie was like me—she had a high regard for wild animals. Hettie and I weren't like the farmers in Hancock County: they thought most wild animals were just pests and nuisances and threats. The farmers didn't mind deer and ducks and the like because these were food, but they gave no thanks for the rabbits that ate gardens and the squirrels that stole corn and they hated wolves that ate sheep and chickens and small calves and piglets and even dogs.

There are almost no wolves around now, and there are mighty few foxes. People say that without wolves and foxes, squirrel populations have shot up, that they've grown all to get out. Well that isn't right and those folks just don't remember the old days. Squirrels've always filled the woods in these parts. Before my time, the state lawmakers even passed an act—that was in 1807—requiring every man of military age to present one hundred squirrel scalps to his township officer each year. A man was charged three cents for each scalp he was missing and he was given three cents for each scalp over a hundred that he brought in, and because of this law there were these roundups where fellers killed ten and twenty thousand squirrels at a time, and they earned a pretty penny at it too.

In my day, folks felt that wolves were just no-good evil. The state voted to pay out money for wolf pelts. There was always wrangling and they changed the laws a lot but most of the time the bounty was about three dollars for the scalp of each full-grown wolf and two dollars for the young. It didn't seem to put much of a dent in the wolf packs, though: in one county (Franklin County, where Columbus is), there were only thirty or so scalps turned in each year after the law got passed.

Well I doubt whether it was because of that law, but you can hardly see wolves nowadays. In the beginning, though, they were all over Ohio. I grew up in Geauga County and, back in the summer of 1800, I hear that there was this visiting lawyer, a Mr. Woolham Woodruff, who'd come to Geauga from Boston to see his uncle's family. He wanted a trophy; so, he shot a wolf that'd already been trapped by Eli Fowler and Ephraim Clark. (These were pretty low-down fellers, I must say—they knew wolves were harmless to humans. Clark and Fowler caught the wolf, strapped his feet together, and carried him back to the town square where this lawyer feller just outright shot him.)

If you said "wolf" to an Ohio farmer, you were saying "killer." Wolves meant nighttime death. In the dark hours wolves came in low swifty packs and quickly killed sheep and calves and goats and dogs. But wolves weren't any threat to people—it was the farm animals who suffered. In Geauga County, old Daniel Dayton brought his eastern sheep flock when he homesteaded to Burton in February of 1805. One or two nights later wolves attacked. It was maybe two or three o'clock in the morning, Daniel heard the noise, and he and his dog came running out. Sure the wolves lunged at him, but it was all show and bluster. Daniel and his dog stood their ground by the log fence and the wolves dragged off two sheep as they slunk away.

Did you ever hear of Horace Cook? He was an old-timer, born

on Friday, September twenty-seventh, 1811. Why do I tell you this? I don't know—I guess his birthdate isn't important but I mention Horace because he had an old dog named Tom. Tom was a brave one, he was. He used to drive the wolves back into the woods all by himself. Of course, then the pack would follow old Tom back to the sheep fold, sticking to the shadows. These wolves had made a runway at the foot of the hill toward the town. . . . (What? Oh I forgot to tell you—this was also in Burton in Geauga County.) Wolves were often seen crossing the road. On their way to school the boys used to find plenty of wolf tracks and the young'uns also found a place where the wild beasts had rolled in the snow like dogs. The boys hurried by that place—they'd heard that a person who saw a wolf before the wolf saw him lost his tongue and couldn't talk for a time. Those boys ran past the wolf crossing, just like in that poem.

> The pass was steep and rugged
> The wolves they howled and whined,
> But he ran like a whirlwind up the pass
> And he left the wolves behind. . . .

What? Now, now, just be patient, I'm comin' to my story, said the hunter sipping from his cup of coffee. As I said, he continued, I lived in Hancock County in my green years—that's quite a ways west of Geauga and quite a ways wilder too. Now one day, when there was a nice snow on the ground, I started in pursuit of deer, there in Hancock County; this was sometime in the early 1830s. Soon I discovered a fresh track that was marked with blood. There were human footprints and I knew that someone else was after the deer so I wouldn't let my dog, whose name was Lead, follow him. We had a kind of a code, you see, and the deer was someone else's.

I was stopped and was standing there. I looked off toward where the deer came from. There was a large white dog—no, danged if it weren't a wolf. Well wolves are always stealing goats and sheep from the farms and they're fair game for anyone. My dog was growling. "Get 'im!" I said to Lead. Lead jumped out. The wolf crouched and attacked; it was fast and strong, and much as I respected wolves, I liked my dog better, so I loaded my gun. The wolf saw that I was moving toward him and he did something that was just like a wolf: whenever a human moves toward a wolf, the wolf retreats, so this animal growled, it turned, and it ran off.

I followed with Lead at my side. Soon we came across the other hunter, the one on the trail of the deer. This feller also had a dog; it was a large furry black and brown thing. We had a few words and we decided to team up so we sent our two dogs after the wolf. Together those dogs kept the wolf busy. They rushed at it from each side and they took turns jumping toward its legs. The wolf kept back; it was growling and angry. Finally the other hunter shot it. I took the wolf hide and the other feller took the wolf scalp. We nodded, not having much more to say, and each of us went our own way.

I've been a wolf hunter for years, and I respect them. Wolves're mighty independent critters. They're wild animals—not just big dogs. Have you ever seen a live wolf? It's got slanty blue eyes and it's cool and ferocious. Few dogs can hold off a wolf attack. A wolf's got a large head, it has strong jaws and large teeth. Wolves run like the wind. And as to strength? Why a single wolf can catch a buck deer and kill it and then eat the entire thing. Wolves are meat eaters, you know: mostly they eat smaller animals, but sometimes they catch a big deer or even an elk.

I learned a lot about wolves from old Hettie Burke. Hettie actually raised up a young wolf cub, an orphaned female. I saw that wolf any number of times. Dogs usually smell things or hear things but wolves are watchers, and this little wolf had amazing eyesight. She could recognize Hettie from far off, even when she was dressed all in new clothes.

Now that I think on it, I suppose that there must be some dogs with wolfie eyes since wolves are ancestors of dogs. People made wolves into dogs. Long time ago, hunters picked certain wolf pups and raised them up and kept choosing and choosing and after a while you had dogs. Dogs are *parts* of wolves—it's kind of like you've just taken a chunk of wolf and made it into a whole animal. If you've ever see a real wolf then you'll find that even in the wildest of them there's kind of a hint of a family pet. If you get a little girl-wolf you can raise it into a real trustworthy pal. And I've got to say it again: wild wolves just don't attack men. Why a wolf wouldn't even attack a baby—he'd be too afraid of being hit by the rattle. As Hettie said: "Anybody who claims he was et by a wolf is a danged liar!"

Of course there's no denying the other side of the matter: wolves are bloodthirsty toward other animals—they're mighty fine killers. Still, they keep good family relations among themselves. They take care of their own, they fight side by side, and they eat in packs. They nose each other and they lick muzzles. They watch over their brothers and sisters. Wolves always collect in groups. In the evenings they plan their hunts; they have a pow-wow before going out at night, they roil around, they growl, and they howl. Then off they go. When they're tracking a deer, one wolf makes straight for the target and the others circle around quietlike. They move quick and low and they hardly make a noise till after the dinner's killed.

But that's for other *beasts*; it's for critters that aren't people. Hettie always said: "Wolves're just plain 'fraid of people." She's right too. I've been well acquainted with wolves for over thirty years and I've never known them to run after a man unless he had a dog they wanted. Wolves've followed my dogs when the mongrels had been away from me, but, when they came to where I was, the wolves would growl and turn and slink off and even run in the other direction.

After the sun's down and night's come with all the shadows and the like, things're different. Wolves come close. They howl. They make a frightening noise that'll put a chill in the air. If you're ever in a camp surrounded by howling wolves, you'd feel they were after you. And if you made it through the night alive—as I've no doubt you would—you'd thank Heaven in the morning that divine intervention protected you. But, truth is, the wolves howl to build up their spirits and they'd never attack a person.

Little wolfies are mighty cute. They're fluffy and soft with kinkled fur. I've seen plenty of 'em for a rather strange reason. Now I'm sure you've heard that even scaredy little animals will fight when their babies are threatened. But this isn't true of wolves. Mama wolves won't attack people even if their babies are being picked up or bothered. We've gone into many a den and taken out the little babies with the mothers right there. Sometimes the older wolves come close and howl, but they never touched us. I learned this from an old trapper I knew—but I don't know what danged fool first dared to try this trick, it certainly wouldn't have been me.

When we were hunting wolves we'd go out into the woods in the evening and set up a howl like a wolf. Some mother wolf would answer and this way we'd find the direction of the den; then we'd wait till daylight and howl again. If the answer came from the same place, we'd find it pretty easy. Or maybe we'd already be close enough to search for tracks. In the winter you'd find footprints from the grownups and in the summer you'd find scraggly, winding trails in the grass from the young'uns. You can also find animal left-overs—bones, feathers, skins, bits of deer horn—scattered 'round-abouts the dens, and if you look close you might see some blood trails from the food dragged in by the males.

Mama wolves take care of their babies in the den that they've made. Sometimes it's a hollow tree, or it could be a hole in the rocks. Sometimes it's a cave they've dug under a pile of logs. Wolves always manage to surround themselves with branches, logs, rocks, or dirt. The father wolf stays out of the den when the little pups are born—but still and all these *are* pretty much family animals. If a mama wolf is killed and the pups are old enough to get along without milk then the father takes over. He'll move the whole crew to a new den if the old one's disturbed and he'll be sure to get plenty of food for the young'uns. He goes out and eats a huge meal and then he comes back home. The little wolfies lick his mouth and he pops out the food again from his stomach. When the mother's around, the father might drag some meat back to some-place near the dens and store it there.

As I've said, although it's hard to believe—and it certainly can be a mite scary the first time—a person can walk right into one of these gnarly wolf holes completely safe. Oh the wolves'll growl and show their teeth, but they'll never ever fight a man. Even when a wolf's caught in a trap a person can go up to it and tie it and take it home alive. . . . Oh, yes—this is the absolute truth; I can swear to it since I've done it many times myself.

I remember one early winter day; it was a Monday in December. I was comin' home from a deer hunt but I'd sat out the day before because it was the Lord's Sunday. It was slushy in the woods. The leaves were wet and black so I walked slowly and I slipped plenty. Late in the morning I came on an empty wolf trap. There were tracks and broken branches around. Soon I caught up to a man with a live wolf tied up on his back. The feller was old and stooped and had a snarled beard. His clothes were dirty. His eyes were wet and yellow. I said hello and what was he goin' to do with the wolf. Oh, he says, I got two dogs at my camp; they need training. I'm goin' to take this here wolf back and teach my dogs a thing or two. "Come'on with me," he said. "I'll feed you a bit of grub."

He was going my way so I shrugged my shoulders and followed. We reached his camp in less than a half hour. One dog saw the wolf and ran right off into the woods barking. The old man swore and dropped the wolf. The other dog was kind of scraggled and white and black. It barked and jumped and wanted to fight. The old man untied the wolf. It crouched and was pretty wary and it growled. It's ears went back. It showed its teeth but it didn't attack. So the old feller yelled and threw sticks. He threw a rock and finally the wolf got mad. The dog ran up. The wolf lashed out with its teeth and it grabbed the dog's neck and shook him like a rag. The wolf was faster than greased lightning and strong as an ox but somehow the dog twisted free and ran off into the woods with the wolf on its heels. I was standin' by a tulip tree and I wasn't happy.

I never liked animal fightin' and Hettie Burke'd taught me to respect wolves, so I turned and left and said not one more word to that old man.

·23·

Sandy McGuffey, Sam Brady's Indian Scout

YOU'RE TOO YOUNG to have learned your ABC's from a *McGuffey Reader* but at one time that's how every child started reading. The author, editor, and compiler was William Holmes McGuffey, an Ohioan—in fact he was president of Ohio University—but that was well after Mad Anthony Wayne. And why do I mention Mad Anthony? It's because of Sandy McGuffey, who was a relative of Bill McGuffey—he was his uncle I think.

Anthony Wayne lived from 1745 to 1796. He was a Scotch-Irish Pennsylvanian. It was the British who called him Mad Anthony; the Americans considered him a hero—he was like General John.

> General John was a soldier tried,
> A chief of warrior dons:
> A haughty stride and a withering pride—
> Those were General John's.

Mad Anthony was born on New Year's Day in 1745. By the age of thirty-four he was already a brigadier general. During the Revolutionary War his capture of Stony Point on the Hudson was daring and brilliant, and it won him a gold medal from Congress. But powerful men value power the most, and Wayne was more proud of his new appointment—by President Washington—as military commander of the Ohio region. General Wayne had five thousand men under him in an army known as the Legion of the United

States. Among his lieutenants was young Duncan MacArthur, the companion of Alexander McGuffey. . . . What's that? Who was Alexander McGuffey? I've already said, he was William Holmes McGuffey's uncle.

To get a bit more orderly about this story, let's begin with the spring of 1790. In those days Ohio was the western frontier of the United States. Along the frontier border there were constant small battles and raids and angry meetings between the U. S. Army and the Indians, the Shawnees and the Wyandots. In 1780, Mad Anthony's deputy, Captain Samuel Brady, with seven men, raided a Wyandot village in western Pennsylvania. (Brady killed some of the Indians and he burned their houses.) Captain Sam Brady then remained there as an Indian fighter with headquarters at Wheeling, West Virginia.

Sandy (Alexander) McGuffey and his best friend, Duncan MacArthur, were Sam Brady's chief scouts. Duncan was three years younger than Sandy. He was smart and quiet and self-assured, and later he became governor of Ohio. Sandy and Duncan were wild-country boys. They'd been taught by the wagoners of the Alleghenies. The Allegheny wagoners were men more rude, more profane, and more selfish than sailors, boatmen, and snake hunters all put together. Wagoners made their own laws. They walked around drunk and mean. They claimed the mountain trails as theirs and theirs alone, and they were the pirates of the frontier.

Wagoners led the lines of pack horses carrying gunpowder, iron, kettles, pots, rum, and salt to the frontier. They were masters of the mountain passes. Traveling settlers met the wagoners, who also drove great herds of cattle and swine, the animals shaggy as wolves, and the drivers looking wilder than the animals. You stood aside when you saw the wagoners coming—you looked away or down at your boots.

From the wagoners, Sandy'd got a mongrel dog named Jock and Duncan had a wild dog named Meggie. Jock was a round bouncy thing with short legs and with black and white hair like a skunk's. His tail was bushy and curled and it was tipped with white. Jock had wide eyes, his ears pointed forward, and even when he slept, his hair bristled at any sound. His body was solid as a groundhog. No question, he looked mighty strange, but it made Sandy furious if anyone laughed at his dog. Sandy said Jock was the smartest dog in Wash County and the best trained, excepting of course for Duncan's Meggie. These two dogs stayed right at the young men's heels, and they never ever barked in the woods.

Sandy didn't get to bury Jock; Sandy never even saw him die. Dogs live fast and hard and they die young. Many dog owners can't understand a dying dog. Dogs know when they're about to die. When the time comes, the old thing leaves home and walks as far as his tired body will go. Then he crawls under a bush, a log, or a rock, anywhere he can hide and sleep. He closes his eyes and he dies peacefully—usually curled up, as if asleep. So, I suppose, it was with Jock.

But I meant to tell you another story, from the days after Jock, in the cool spring of 1790. Sandy and Duncan were pretty much on their own most of the time; they roamed the whole of Ohio country alone. Oh, they checked back with the troops every now and then, but their job was to keep an eye on that vast area between Fort Pitt—which is now the city of Pittsburgh—and Fort Washington—which is now Cincinnati. They camped in the woods and the hollows; they slept in caves as far north as Lake Erie and as far west as the Wabash River. Together, Sandy and Duncan walked the forests. They chomped on cattail roots and in the late summer on blackberries. They ate coon and squirrel and rabbit. Sometimes they caught a deer. They slashed through jewelweed thickets and rabbit's foot and brambles. They waded snaggy streams and they made rafts of logs tied together with wild grape vines for the rivers. The days went as the urge moved them and the two young men wandered chatting, daydreaming, and idling through the empty Ohio Country in those wild and woody days of long, long ago.

From friendly Indians, Sandy and Duncan learned medicine. They used yarrow roots as an anesthetic and milkweed as an anti-septic. They made cough medicine from sap of the solomon's seal and also from red clover syrup mixed with the juice of roasted onions. They drank hot chokecherry juice for diarrhea. They took willow bark tea for fevers. They rubbed wild mint sap and black walnut bark tea on their faces to keep off the mosquitoes. They brushed their teeth with strawberries.

Sandy and Duncan traveled throughout the wide and varied Ohio country on military errands. During the spring of 1790, Brady sent Sandy and Duncan across the Ohio River as scouts and advi-sors for a young eastern military man: this was Captain John Horace Boggs. Boggs had just come to the frontier from Maryland, where his father was some sort of bigwig. Boggs brought a troop of ten men with him. They rode stiffly into Wheeling on horseback; they had come to deal with troublemaking Indians.

Sam Brady shook his head. "Watch over Boggs," he told Sandy and Duncan. The two young scouts went on ahead. Captain Boggs and his men followed. Boggs's fine white horse was neatly brushed; his saddle was soft Virginia leather. The men reached the banks of Little Captina Creek. Nary an Indian was in sight. Captain Boggs frowned. He led his men to a high campsite. Then for days the men rode up and down Big and Little Captina creeks. On the fifth morning they found fresh footprints on the fringes of the camp— Indians had been watching them as they slept. Were Indians in the nearby woods at that very moment?

Captain Boggs was angry. He was insulted. The Indians had often attacked settlers in this region. And what was the provoca-tion? Indians seemed to think that they owned the land hereabouts. Captain Boggs shook his head. Let them come out in the open; then we'll see who can fight, he said.

The two Captina creeks were well known to Sandy and Duncan. Indians used the region as a camping area and as a water route into the Ohio River. Earlier, this had been the site of an attack by white men on the Indians. The West Virginians across the river had heard war rumors and they feared that the Shawnee were planning a raid. Captain Michael Cresap was a trader headquartered at Wheeling and he volunteered to head a protective militia. Under his direction, the settlers met and decided on a preemptive attack. Cresap and six others shot and killed two Indian canoe men on the Ohio River near the mouth of the Wheeling Creek. A few days later, the white men attacked an encampment of Shawnees on Captina Creek. One Indian was killed, and the Shawnees vowed revenge.

This was the recent history. Sandy was worried. "I think we should spread out quietly and crawl into the woods," he said to the Captain.

"What?" said John Horace Boggs. "You want me to sneak around as if I were afraid of some savages? No—never. We'll ride in as a group." Captain Boggs ordered the soldiers to untether their horses and mount. Ten young men tightened their saddles. Ten young men jumped up and sat high and proud. The horses' manes were cut short. Their hair was brown and scratchy. Boggs spoke loudly. He had his men canter in parade style. He led the way himself, and the soldiers followed, riding up and down the thickly wooded banks of Little Captina Creek. Sandy and Duncan, on foot, their fingers twitching on their cocked guns, crept in and out of the undergrowth—watching, searching, listening.

Suddenly a gun fired from the bushes. The captain groaned. He fell forward and slid from his saddle, dead. His horse shied and whinnied. There was splashing in the creek. There was the crackling of branches in the woods. There was more gunfire.

Sandy and Duncan jumped and ran. They reached a big sycamore that was at least eighty feet tall and four feet in diameter, at the edge of an open area. The two white men crouched behind the tree; then they fired into the bushes. Sandy fired eight times. The

Indians fired back. One of the bullets knocked some sycamore bark into Duncan's face. Duncan reloaded, nodded, and said to Sandy: "That Indian gave a mighty fine shot for sure."

Meanwhile the ten soldiers panicked. Four had come galloping up behind their captain. Three of those fell from their horses wounded. Indians rushed out from their ambush. Six more soldiers came riding up. Their horses thrashed and rashed in the stream. The Indians shot at the soldiers; some of the white men fell, others jumped down, four or five ran noisily through the wet and slippery slonk.

A crowd of red men rushed the scouts. Two Indians chased Duncan down the creek, through a marsh, and over a small ravine. Sandy ran up a hill. Three Indians were right behind him. Sandy hit the top of the hill. There were tall pines all around. He wheeled suddenly. His gun was empty but he pointed it at them and shouted: "Kiee-yah!" The Indians dove into the brush and Sandy tore away down the other side of the hill. He tripped over a root and a rock. He scrambled up and ran, ran, ran. One of the Indians ran after Sandy. It was a foot race down the hill and over branches, logs, and rocks. Sandy pulled ahead. He was breathing hard but he kept going and soon the Indian disappeared behind. Sandy reached the base settlement half an hour before Duncan, who turned up as if from a fresh country walk and with hardly a scratch. The two men raised their eyebrows and saluted each other; then they went off for a meal.

Sergeant Heaton took over and, later that afternoon, a group of soldiers went back to the creek. The Indians had vanished. The crumpled body of Captain Boggs lay where he had fallen, with five bullet holes in him. His men dug a grave and buried him on the spot. Today, people tell of the bloody Battle of the Captinas where the gallant Captain John Horace Boggs rode ahead of his men; Captain Boggs, they say, would not give an inch and he himself received the first charge of a massive Indian attack, protecting his men like a living shield.

Sandy and Duncan tried to find the Indian raiding party. Quietly they haunted the area. A few days later, in a thicket upstream by the creek, Sandy discovered traces of old blood. Sandy and Duncan hunted on their hands and knees. They found broken twigs and scraping marks in the soil. Past a small rock pile, they discovered freshly buried bodies of three Indians wrapped in their buffalo robes and smelling of the powdered chokecherry bark and berries that the Indians used to treat bleeding wounds. There were bullet holes in the bodies. Were these Indians whom Sandy and Duncan had shot from behind the sycamore? That was all the scouts ever found.

Time passed. The weathers came and went. It was years later, and Ohio's Indian wars were over. One cold Sunday in December, Sandy was in Wheeling, West Virginia. After Colonel Ebenezer Zane had set up a city there, a strong oak-timbered stockade fort was built at the top of Main Street hill; Zane called the stockade Fort Henry in honor of Patrick Henry. Sandy McGuffey was now the senior military advisor at Fort Henry.

On this cold clear Sunday, McGuffey strode down Wheeling's Main Street. A big Indian came up to him. "I am Orange Hawkweed," he said. Sandy tilted his head; he didn't recognize the name. Orange Hawkweed said, "It was many years ago. I was at Chokecherry Creek—you call it Captinas. It was during the Boggs raid." McGuffey stood back. The Indian continued, "There were almost forty red men." After a moment of silence Orange Hawkweed said, "I was one of the three who chased you up the hill that morning."

Sandy raised his eyebrows. Well, he thought—could this really be? He looked carefully at the Indian. Orange Hawkweed put out his hand. Sandy nodded and solemnly shook the hand. Then he squinted at Orange Hawkweed and rubbed his chin. "Would you dare to race me again?" asked Sandy. The Indian smiled. "I am an old man," he said. "I am too," said Sandy.

Orange Hawkweed pointed to a tree. Sandy McGuffey nodded. The men bent slightly—and then they were off. Orange Hawkweed was still quick as a cricket, but Sandy was faster. They ran and panted and Sandy slapped the tree trunk first. The two men were out of breath. Again they shook hands. Then the Scottish settler, Alexander McGuffey, and the Shawnee Indian, Orange Hawkweed, walked back to the road, and they turned and parted ways, never to meet again.

·24·

The Gloomy Valley
Near Steubenville

EARLY EUROPEAN SETTLERS didn't have the luxury of developing their own new crafts in America. The strange valleys, the wide plains, the winding rivers absorbed all their energies—there was a raw and disconcerting mystery in the new land, and it kept the Eastern settlers off balance. For a long time, American know-how remained European know-how—in farming, in weaving, in industry, in science, in politics, in the arts, and in the military. For example, do you remember America's General Baron Frederick William August Henry Ferdinand Steuben? He was an American military instructor but he was German born, bred, and trained.

Steuben was the son of a soldier and at the age of fourteen he became a soldier himself. Soon he was made a lieutenant, he fought in the Seven Years' War, and then he was adjutant-general of the Free Austrian Corps, where he was a personal military aide to Frederick the Great.

Steuben was bright and tough and serious. He was a canon of the cathedral of Havelberg. He was grand-marshal to the prince of Hohenzollern-Hechingen. In 1777, his friend, the Count St. Germain—then the French Minister of War—told Frederick that the American military badly needed discipline and instruction. Steuben left Europe, and he arrived in Portsmouth, New Hampshire, in December of 1777. Steuben was warmly received, and later that winter he began drilling the inexperienced soldiers at Valley Forge.

In May of 1778, Baron Steuben was made inspector-general of the U. S. Army. Steuben was a methodical organizer from top to bottom, and he wrote the standard military text *Regulations for the Order and Discipline of the Troops of the United States.* New York, Pennsylvania, and New Jersey gave him grants of land for his services, Fort Steuben was built in Jefferson County, Ohio, in 1789, and the U. S. Congress voted him a formal commendation, giving him a gold-hilted sword and a lifetime yearly pension of $2,400.

Steubenville in Ohio was named for Baron Steuben. The city is in Jefferson County, a place filled with valleys—some pretty, some dreary, and all of them eerie and strange. Hills climb too steeply from the very edge of the Ohio River. Ravines drop off unexpectedly. In the early pioneer days of the Ohio country, a young woman wrote about one of the Steubenville valleys in Jefferson County. This woman was Susannah Darnell, the daughter of Ebenezer and Amanda Hanniford Darnell. A bit of her writing, set down in her old age, has been preserved by the Mingo Bottom Historical Society.

Dankish days always remind me of Mingo Bottom (wrote Susannah). Mingo Bottom is by Steubenville; it is far from Mount Pleasant, where I was born. Soon after we moved, I had a curious experience that I cannot account for simply by fantasies of my mind. It is a small matter, but it still puzzles me, even in my old age. There is a little valley near Steubenville, to the southwest of the town, and in it I found a low clear-cut that I used for travel. It was by far the easiest route from Mingo Bottom to Steubenville: it saved miles. I would use this shortcut whenever I went marketing or whenever I needed to go into town. This valley was always empty. It cast shadows even at noon—as the Bible says, it was "as the shadows of great rocks in a weary land . . . and, when the sun sets, the shadows appear more long and terrible yet."

In those days we were farmers, and on our farm we kept pigs and a few biddies. My father's name was Ebenezer, and he loved the pigs. We had a breed called Magie. Magie pigs are friendly. They are easy to raise and will eat almost anything. Daddy said pigs are the Lord's way of changing farm leftovers into people's food and into leather for saddles, bristles for brushes, and fat for lard, for oil, for soap, and for candles. The piggies ate our leftovers and they also foraged on their own, and we gave the young animals extra grain, fruits, grass, weeds, and food scraps.

The people who lived nearby in Mingo Bottom thought that I was brave and tough like my mother. They called me a tomboy and a weedy-sprout and a "right-strong" girl. From those days, I remember the silly poem about Nate Sanger and his cousin Billy Cameron of Mingo Bottom.

> His toes around awrung along
> Sanger skritched the cricket song
> And Cameron sipped his smally bowl
> With warmling soup and a steamy hole.
> It's a cool wind-day past the stable door
> On a rough-edge stair and a wooden floor,
> So he lightly slides his feet discrete—
> No shiny shoes on the strawed concrete.

It comes back to me so clearly even decades later. Now, do not ask me what that verse actually meant because I do not know—but people used to say it about them and about me too. Anyways, I would take out after our farm animals and I would not let them give me any guff in return. I seemed strong, but actually I was not such a tough girl. When I walked through the strange valley to or from Steubenville, I became shaky and weak and I knew that I was really only a scared child after all. Did others know that too? I would wager that some of them must have seen me as small and weak—that was the real me, unmasked and revealed.

It was that dismal valley that showed the true me. Was the valley haunted? Even from the beginning I knew that it was a strange place. The first time I went there was when we moved and I had to drive our biggest pig for some distance, because it was my job to get the large pigs, one-by-one, from farm to farm.

The pig was pretty well out of young piggiehood: it had

reached that indefinable stage of swine life when you call a pig a shoat. I put a rope leash on its hind leg just above the knuckle, and I pulled. Sometimes the pig would stop dead in his tracks. Everyone knows that at this point, to get a pig to move, you have to get behind it—if you are in the front, you will get nowhere. I used a stick to poke the pig from behind. I kept hold of the pig with the foot leash, but the local style of gnarly fencing—Virginia fences they were called—was my dread. The piggy ran under every single stake he came to, through the holes and the corners and 'round the tangly weeds—and I would have to let go of the rope and pass it under the stake and into my other hand, all of this done carefully so he could not escape.

I am told that a foot leash is the Irish way of leading a pig—certainly it is not the most enjoyable way to walk along by the side of an American stake-and-rider fence. The pig was stubborn and ornery and ran into and out of every single pole and twig, and I said a few expressions not befitting of a young girl. This did not make the pig and I any better friends.

All the pigs of that day were pretty wild. They were black spotted mongrels different from anything we have now. The olden day pigs were active and enterprising; they were self-reliant: all they asked was a free range of the woods, to run every which way snuffling and snorting and rooting about. But of course even the wildest pigs could always be tamed by food.

Pigs eat a lot—five, six, or seven pounds of food a day. They drink even more water than they eat food. Our pigs were always hungry and they ate everything in sight. You could make them stand on their hind legs and twirl around for pieces of apple. They ate vegetables. They ate young chicks and ducks and lambs, and our biddies clucked and flapped and kept well away from the pigs. The pigs ate rats and snakes. On a few occasions the older pigs ate young piglets. It is not that we did not feed them enough; it was just that pigs are eaters. In fact, it is piggy stomachs that get pigs into most of the tight places where they are ever stuck.

In the summers the pigs ate acorns and nuts all day long. In the cold weather we fed them corn. We had a hut for the animals, made of logs, to protect them against the winds and cold rains and snows. We fed them there too, and they quickly learned to collect at home in a noisy herd in the evenings. In the summer, the pigs took to the wet spots during the day; they lay in the mud in the shade on their sides, panting and dozing and flipping their curly tails.

The young pigs got marked with notches on the ear, and each farmer had his own code. In those days pigs were never fattened to weigh anything like the hogs of nowadays. Everybody said the meat is sweeter when pigs are not fed so much. Probably this is true because our thin pigs were near to the taste of wild boar, which is absolutely delicious. The old-time animals were small—they never weighed even a hundred pounds. They had scratchy skins and tightly curled tails, sharp brown hooves, and noses that they were always sticking and rubbing everywhere.

We got some of our pigs by wagon from the East, and the eastern farmers got them from Europe. There were also some wild boars loose hereabouts—maybe these just escaped from herds brought over on European boats; I do not know for certain. Daddy and I kept our pigs betwixt and between—half domestic and half wild—and the pigs had the run of a fenced-in bit of the woods. Looking back, I would say that our pigs were rather respectable. They were social and faithful and clean and, if well fed, they were well behaved. They slept piled and packed together. At night they alternated nose and tail, grunting and squirming, and if it was cold and rainy the question as to which pig should sleep undermost occupied the entire night with squealing and rooting about.

The country where we lived was very hilly and rough. Our land was stony and stump filled and poor for growing things. The woods had oak, with a bit of maple along the creek bottoms. One valley, the fateful ravine through which I was forced to walk when going to Steubenville, was filled with Osage orange trees, which are somehow related to the mulberry. Osage has hard wood that is bright and yellow and has whorls all through it. Its fruit is bumpy and green, like a large green orange, and its branches are spiny.

American Indians made Osage root tea to wash sore eyes. I have seen horses eat Osage oranges but people do not eat the fruit. If you cut up the oranges the pieces will keep insects away. I have a few Osage oranges in the corners at home: my grandmother, Hattie Hanniford, taught me that a dried Osage orange in the back of a drawer not only smells good, it also scares off spiders. The Osage orange trees in my dreaded valley seemed to scare off spiders, and every other possible creature—maybe they scared me too.

This place was my valley of doom. Nothing actually happened to me there, but whenever I walked through the clear-cut, I felt dejected and low and weak. In order to drive our large pig to the new farm, I had to walk through the valley, and I remember that first walk quite clearly. It was a midweek day, a Wednesday in January. It was cloudy and damp. The snow was wet; the branches were dripping. The air was heavy and I was afraid—but of what? There were no animals and no people.

The pig walked very, very slowly. The crossing route through this dreary area was a little less than two miles. In the spring it would be silent and damp and filled with low green plants with big flat leaves; it would have clumps of nettle and jewelweed and marshwort. There would be little wet boggy places. That winter day it took less than half an hour to cross. Always and everywhere there was a light dismal fog. The air was thick.

The pig's feet made squishing sounds. There were no birds or insects, only clammy shadows, shadows of some unseen power that lay heavily in the low regions. I felt that something was following us—but what was it and where? When finally we climbed out the far side I was sweating and weak and breathing heavily; my heart was beating fast, my chest was tight, and there were tears in my eyes. When I returned home I felt badly for the whole afternoon and I had nightmares in the deep hours of the night.

This happened every single time I walked the valley. In my

whole life this was the only place that ever affected me so strongly. Was it haunted? After walking that valley I always felt thin and weak and tiny, no bigger than a cake of soap after a week's washing. I would take a sup of hot tea in the cool weather (lady's slipper tea was the universal cure for depression in those parts), but no amount of honeyed tea ever seemed to cheer me. No cakes, no gentle breads could pull my spirits from the lowlands of that desolate valley.

Recently, long, long after my childhood days, I have heard that a pioneer family once lived in that valley and then disappeared suddenly and entirely, without a trace. Perhaps that was the cause of my feelings. I just do not know, and nowadays, far from that time and place, who can ever say what made the daughter of a Steubenville pig farmer so chilled, weak, and uncomfortable in that old gloomy valley?

·25·

Marion Jamson's Two Iron Kettles

ROSS COUNTY IS a place of hidden things. It's a land of treasures, mysteries, bones, and mountains. Folks say that way back when—once upon a time and a long, long time ago—Ross County was in the middle of the ocean, a warm salty sea that was shallow and stretched between the Piedmont Plateau and the Rocky Mountains. Ross County was underwater and the mountains came later. By mountains, I mean the recent mountains—the mounds built by some unknown prehistoric people. There were at least three tribes of these people—today, we call them the Hopewell, the Adena, and the Fort Ancients.

All these people were earthworkers and Mound Builders. They lived in Ohio sometime before the Indians. The Fort Ancient people clearly were farmers. They stored corn and roots in subterranean cellars, along with beans, plums, and nuts. What else do we know about these folks? Well, they fished—their hooks were made from the wing bones of birds—they worked with leather—their awls were made from wild turkey bones and from the front leg bones of deer and elk—and they sewed—thin bone needles have been found in all their mounds.

South of the city of Columbus, in Ross County, are three famous places where the Fort Ancient peoples lived. I think I've already told you about Spruce Hill. It's in Twin Township, near Bourneville on the bank of Paint Creek. Spruce Hill is a mound in the shape of a triangle. You can still tell that huge fires were once built within the walls along the top edge of the mound. Today, the walls are crumbled and you have to close your eyes to imagine how they looked long ago, strong and majestic, safe and secure. Did they have guard towers or statues or tall decorations? I suppose we'll never know outside of our dreams.

Another mound down there is called Gartner Works. Gartner Works is in Green Township, about six miles north of Chillicothe on the east side of the Scioto River. The mound is seventy feet wide but only seven-and-a-half feet high. After the Mound Builders, the Indians came and lived there, and dribs and drabs of Indian pottery are all over the outer earth of the mound.

Then there's Baum Village, also in Twin Township, across the Paint Creek from Bourneville. Baum Village is the biggest prehistoric village that's been found anywhere in Ohio; just the village itself took up more than eighteen acres. There are old foundations and walls and tunnels and cellars. In addition, there's a square mound a hundred and twenty feet long and fifteen feet high. Diggers found pottery all around the edges of the mound and they found skeletons in the middle; there were more than seventeen human skeletons laid out together like a cemetery. Just north of the skeletons were holes and timbers—maybe that was the foundation of a house. This "house" was oval. It was twenty feet long and twelve feet wide with twenty-one upright posts. There was a fireplace in the center. The floor was smooth dirt and it was covered with polishing stones, broken pottery, and hammer stones; also, there was a large stone mortar and many animal bones, including bear, deer, raccoon, and wild turkey.

The burial sites were just south of this houselike structure. In the cemetery, each body had a pottery bowl near the head. The bowls each contained a single bone awl made from the shoulder blade of a deer; a few pots had copper beads and shells too. In a place not far from the human burial ground, there were the bones of dogs. I spoke to Lem Ostler, who found these dog bones. He told me that Professor Stampling of Ohio University put some the animal skeletons together, and he found that these old dogs had a short face and that they were about the size and shape of bull terriers.

One day, the old Mound Builders just slipped away. No one knows why they left. Maybe they got itchy to see new areas. Perhaps they were killed off by disease. Or they could have mixed with the early American Indian tribes. For whatever reason, they just up and left—now the Mound Builders are gone but the mounds remain. Many a buried treasure's hidden in these mounds. There's gold, there's silver, and there's jewelry. There're statues and skeletons. Magic amulets and strange carvings guard old wooden chests and bandaged-up piles of goods. Of course no one tells when they dig up something valuable, some real treasure—people just report the everyday things they've found. No one tells about the gold necklaces and the coins: they just show off the bits of silver and amber and turquoise fragments and the copper beads and broken pottery and bone tools.

The mound land of Ross County encourages diggers and it encourages buriers. In pioneer days, Marion Jamson buried a large amount of money there—people say it was in two iron kettles. Marion Jamson died alone. He had no relatives. No one knew where he'd been born. No one remembered whether he'd come into the Ohio country from somewhere else or whether his parents were Ohioans. All they knew was that, for as long as anyone remembered, old Marion had lived on a farm deep in mound territory, in Twin Township, Ross County, Ohio.

Marion had money—and he had a lot of it. Where had it come from? Was it an inheritance? Had he saved it? Had he stolen it? People talked, but no one knew the answer. Anytime that old man Jamson needed something, he bought it with cash. He never used credit and he never traded; no matter what the price, Marion Jamson always paid cash. Lindy Butler said that each month the old farmer would walk into her store with a fistful of bills that were torn and greasy. Usually he had greenbacks, currency that'd just been introduced in those days. The value of the greenback went up and down, but Marion seemed to have an unlimited supply. Sometimes he also used gold coins. He picked up his sugar and coffee and salt pork and beans and he laid the money right on the counter. He put his goods in a sack and the leftover money in his pocket and without a thanks or a good-bye he turned and walked on home.

The years passed quickly, and they also passed slowly. Old man Jamson got older. He was wrinkled. He was deaf. His hair was like thin cotton. Marion limped and groaned and grumbled. One fall day he came into Lindy's store and bought two big iron kettles. Marion bought the best—they were well-made iron boiling pots with spouts and handles. These were expensive. What could he want with one kettle let alone two? They were huge kettles. They were too big for coffee or tea; why, you could brew a week's worth of coffee in one of those kettles and still have room for stew.

One snowy windy day in January, Marion Jamson came down with pneumonia. He ached and he coughed. He dragged himself from his bed and he started the fire. He stirred up some herbs in his crusty old pot. Perhaps boneset tea would cure him. Marion coughed and coughed. He was dizzy and dulled and weak. Finally the water boiled. Boneset tea has a gingery tingle to it; old man Jamson added lots of sugar. Nothing appealed to him, but he forced himself to drink a whole cup. The tea had no effect. He drank two more cups. He felt faint. His face was red. He was sick in his stomach with cramps, terrible pains, and belly machinations. He had a high fever. The old man crawled back into bed and he closed his eyes. That evening Marion Jamson died.

A neighbor discovered the body. Two men from town came and buried old Marion on a corner of his farm. The sheriff took charge of the farm; later, the township sold it to a new young couple. Meanwhile people came at night. Where were Marion's kettles? Marion must have buried his money in them. The cabin had a stove, some small pots, a cup, and three spoons; there were two old jackets, a broken clock, and a Bible. The dried food—flour and beans and coffee—went to the county jailhouse. The sheriff took Marion's gun. And that was it. People searched under floorboards in the cabin and under the porch. They looked in the garden. They emptied Jamson's shed of its tools; dried animal skins still hung on the walls of the shed, but there was absolutely nothing else of value inside. In the garden, someone found bits of Indian pottery. Someone else found a broken clay pipe. But no one found even one kettle anywhere.

Over the years people continued to dig through Marion's garden. Meanwhile the land changed hands. Several families, the Brantons, the Kimmelwaites, and the Kanes, have lived on the farm since Marion's day. Each family had unusual experiences. Each family heard the story and hunted for the kettles. Today the Pottingers live there. My grandmother knew them. The Pottingers had a difficult time clearing the land and tearing down Jamson's old tool shed.

When the Pottingers bought the farm, there was no place to live. There'd been a fire and the main cabin had burned down a few years before, so the Pottingers had to build a house. In those days, Ohio cabins were made of round logs with the bark left on. The chimney was stone and clay and it was on the outside of the cabin at the far end. The rest of the house was made of wood, with few nails and little iron anywhere. The better cabins had a wooden floor. The ceiling was just four or five rafters running lengthwise, and often there were no windows—the cracks in the roof and between the logs let plenty of light in.

You could put together a round-log cabin in just one long day. This was what Ephastus Pottinger set out to do, so he organized a community cabin raising. Neighbors came from six, eight, even ten miles away—Ned, Jeb, and William Postlethee came in from way over by Elmgrove. Everybody arrived early in the morning. Mrs. Pottinger and the other womenfolk had already got pancakes on the campfire griddles. Each man had a job. Seth was built like an ox: he hunted corner stones while the first logs were cut. Two men with axes worked on each tree. Another man with an ox, a lizard, and a chain dragged the logs over to the house. (Lizard? It's just a strong forked log that you can chain other logs to when you drag them.) Two men stood by the foundations with axes, saws, froes, and wedges; they made the clapboards and also the puncheons for the floor.

To make the corners, it took skilled axmen. Cross-cut sawyers cut the door space and the chimney holes right there in the growing house. Strong young men laid out the rafters and then the roof logs. A mason set the hearth stones and fit together the chimney from Seth's collection of rocks and boulders. As the morning warmed, Mr. Pottinger stepped back and wiped his forehead with his kerchief. He looked at the progress and he nodded.

The cabin grew fast, like a young tree. Inside, in one corner six feet from the back wall and four feet from the side, the finisher (that would've been Ned) bored a hole in the wooden floor. He had an oak branch with a fork at the top. He smoothed it and pounded it into the hole in the floor till it fit snug. This was the main bed post. Ned laid twelve straight sticks—hickory poles—from the fork onto a ledge on the side wall. The poles fanned out and they made the bottom of the bed. Later, Mrs. Pottinger set a straw mattress on the poles, and, with a couple of thick blankets, she had the cosiest bed any woman could want.

Late in the day, with the air cooling, the men aching, and the women sitting more than standing, the front door was hung on its wooden hinges. Ned had moved from bed building to planking outside the cabin. He'd pieced together a door that looked like the top of a long table. The wood was heavy, rough, and splintery. Ned measured and trimmed, and he took pride in the fact that when it was hung it fit just right—well, almost just right, because they had to take it down again for one last trimming. A wooden latch held it fast on the inside. If you pulled the latch string in, no one could open it from the outside. The door was thick and heavy—no light wind kittling the lintels would open that door, I reckon.

They worked without a break all day and into the evening. Women kept a table filled with hotcakes and tea. In the afternoon, some of the men tried to tear down Jamson's old wood shed. Apparently various strange things had always kept the previous owners from completely getting rid of this old building. The Kanes, for instance, who'd lived there before, got rained and stormed on the whole week they were trying to knock down the shed. Later the Kanes had gotten burned out and decided to move. Sam Kane told the Pottingers that no one'd ever get this shed down. "It's haunted—there's som'pin not right about it," said Sam.

Ephastus Pottinger frowned. "We own this land now," he said. "I don't want any old ramshackle huts here." He looked at the men helping him build his house. "I don't want no old legends and I don't want no ghosts. I'm clearin' everything out—I'm not going to put up with no skeezicks. We're goin' to start fresh and clean."

The workmen dug down and under the foundations of the shed. They pushed their shovels into the ground. Everywhere it was wet with rotting leaves. Frogs and insects ran into holes along-side the roots. The shovels clanged in the earth, like they were striking a hollow pot, and the men dug deeper but they never found rock, metal, or kettle. The old timbers seemed to go down forever, and eventually the men gave up.

Over the years, weather rotted the wood of the shed, the walls crumbled completely, insects ate the boards, and the old shack just fell apart by itself, slowly, year after year after year. I guess you'd have to say that by now the shed is finally gone. You'd be hard pressed to find any trace of it, unless I pointed out a few stones and old rotting timbers to you.

However the cabin itself's become haunted by the ghost of old man Jamson—he just moved in to the Pottinger's place without a hello or a howdy-do. My grandmother told me about the house. One night she stayed with the Pottingers. You see, Carey Pottinger was grandma's age and they'd become friends in school. Carey invited grandma for a visit after the holidays in winter.

It was a typical Ross County January winter, dry and cold. Grandma got out of bed. The air was bitter and icy, and grandma felt like something the cat's dragged in. She dressed. She held her breath and splashed cold water on her face. The house spiders were still as stone in the corners.

Breakfast was mint tea from the root cellar and hot oatmeal and honey. Grandma told Carey and her mother about strange noises she'd heard the night before, clankings like metal hitting metal. Grandma hadn't slept well and the morning was right welcome. She was achy and stiff.

Mrs. Pottinger listened to grandma's tale of night noises; then she nodded sadly. "Have some more tea," she said. She sat down at the table with the girls and told my grandma about old man Jamson and the money and the shed. Carey was quiet. Grandma shivered. Grandma was very happy to ride home that afternoon in the straw wagon, and she never visited the Pottinger's again. As far as anybody knows, the two kettles still haven't been found. I suppose that they remain hidden, buried somewhere in mound country—they're "the unsunn'd heaps of miser's treasure," as the old men of Ross County would say.

·26·

The Quaker Tribe

IT WAS THE morning—or was it the evening? At the moment I forget. But I do remember that it was cool and rainy; the sun was out, shining somewhere. . . . Oh yes, my friend, that can happen. In fact, two rainbows glowed for a moment against the gray clouds. We sat quiet in the old house of an even older man. He talked to us in a chant—he was an Indian named John Whitefeather, and this is is what he said.

From our Iroquoi brethren we have always called the largest river to the south, the Ohio. White men use the Indian name for the whole country west of the river. The white men who came here and settled the Ohio country are a mixed lot, and they have quite a few different views about spirits.

For instance, there are the Congregationalists. Among white tribes Congregationalists consider themselves special—"elect," they call it. Congregationalists say that they keep the true religious spirit of the first white settlers.

Do you know Eef Coker? She is a white woman of another sect, the Presbyterians; Presbyterians have a council, a central ruling body, called a Presbytery. Then there are also the Baptists, who initiate members by immersing them for a moment under water—as do the Campbellites. The Methodists follow the dictates of two religious leaders, John and Charles Wesley, who decided that the main religious tribe in their country of England was too easygoing, so they set up a more methodical observance of the religious rules of behavior—others nicknamed them the Holy Club and the Methodists.

For most tribes the Sabbath is the white man's day of rest and prayer. The Seventh-Day Adventists (such as my friends Lem and Sadie Harrowford) do not consider Sunday as the Sabbath day; instead, their Sabbath is on Saturday. Then there are the Episcopalians, mainly upper-class aristocrats of white man's society.

Here in Ohio country each of the tribes from Europe has its own particular cults. The Germans have groups called Dunkards, Mennonites, and Amish—all of these are religious cults with special rules. Some do not allow buttons on clothing. Some require beards. And each allows only simple decorations on their persons and in their homes.

I should also mention the Shakers. These are an industrious people who live together in their own closed communities. Shakers trade in seeds and herbs. Shaker fields are evenly plowed and neatly weeded. Their mills are spotless, and they are careful craftsmen. Their shops are filled with trim and simple handmade brooms, smooth utensils, and precisely built furniture. I am told that the name of the tribe comes from some ritual dance of theirs—they have trances and visions with hopping and jumping and dancing about. Shakers believe in remaining apart and unmarried, and the number of members of their tribe can only increase when they convince others to convert. An important Shaker settlement is north of here, near the winding river, the Cuyahoga.

Also there are the Quakers. Many Quakers live in the Ohio counties of Columbiana and Jefferson. Quakers have plain gray clothes. They are a plain gray serious tribe. They have formal old-fashioned ways of speaking and they use *thee* and *thou* for the word *you*. The Quaker tribe is well known for its kindness and its courtesy.

I knew a young white man named Jimson Smythe who lived in the area of Mount Pleasant just west of the Ohio River. Jimson was a Quaker. He had grown up on a hillside farm. He wore plain brown clothes with a broad-brimmed hat. His wife wore a full-skirted dress, a bonnet, and a shawl. Twice a week, Jimson went to a prayer ceremony in a local Meeting House; he went on first day, which is Sunday, and on fourth day, which is Wednesday. Jimson was the first Quaker whom I had known personally.

Quakers originated in the white man's home country of England. The first Quaker chief was George Fox; I am told that his father was a weaver. George Fox became a clergyman. His followers called themselves Friends but others called them Quakers because of Fox's lecture to Judge Bennet of Derby—Fox told the Judge he had best "quake and tremble at the Word of the Lord."

In the beginning of the white man's invasion of this land, there were few Quakers and those who came were considered to be heretics. Early on, two women Quakers, Mary Fisher and Ann Austin, arrived in the city of Boston. Their books were taken and burned. They were called witches and they were imprisoned for five weeks. Finally they were sent away.

The early Quakers were a bit obstinate. After the poor treatment of the Fisher and Austin women, other Quakers purposely moved into Boston. The courts banished them, and three men and one woman were actually hanged. Early American Quakers irritated the other tribes. They mocked the traditional church and the court and the government, they interrupted public worship, and they carried on their own ways with a certain fanaticism. Things degenerated and the Quaker tribe left the coast for Carolina and Ohio. William Penn founded a Quaker colony in Pennsylvania, where he forbade any police or military power and where he set up an honest relationship with other tribes, including the local Indians.

Now what exactly are the ways of these Quakers? They were always strong and enthusiastic, but over the years they became quieter and soon the Quakers settled into an orderly community that is quiet and prudent. Nowadays they live a peaceful life of hard work and charity toward others. The Quakers do not like fads and fashions, complex doodads, or shenanigans. They dress simply. They speak traditionally—and Quakers make their speech follow their beliefs: All men are equal. No one is entitled to special verbal adornments; so, in England, they addressed the white man's king simply as George.

The Friends, as the Quakers call themselves, do not take oaths. When testifying in court a Friend just affirms that he is giving the facts. "Friends," they say, "are like lanterns: we bear our lights within ourselves. We do not need to swear out loud an external oath." The Friends do not believe in war or military forces, and they would rather have their property be confiscated than willingly pay the government for any of its hurtful behaviors.

As we know from sad experience, the white man is arrogant. He comes from a warlike species. Fortunately a few white tribes, such as the Quakers, are pacifists. They will not join the military. They are against slavery: two famous Quakers, Benjamin Lay and John Woolman, preached loudly against the evil of holding slaves. In some ways, however, Quakers are like other white men. The early Quakers did fight on occasion. And Quakers have always taken firm stands on the correct principles of dress and manners. Then, too, Quakers speak out in no uncertain terms against the evils of liquor.

The usual white man's trappings of religion do not sit well with Quakers. For example they do not have formal, hired priests. Quakers claim that only God can give out titles and badges and such identifications of holiness. Moreover any person can receive these holy things, and he gets them directly through spiritual meditation, not from other mortals. If you are motivated by the spirit, then speak and preach and pray—otherwise, be silent.

I have had occasion to watch the Quaker's rituals. For their Meetings, Quakers enter a plain wooden house. They walk in quietly. The men sit on the right; the women sit on the left. Two or three seats are set on a platform at the end of the hall facing the other seats. Here the respected Elders sit—you may know two of the Elders from this region, Edmund Corrigan and Hale Fields.

Some white tribes are boisterous, loud, and wild. That is not the way of the Quakers. Quaker Meetings have no singing or dancing or music. The people sit quietly, perfectly still. Sometimes men wear hats, and sometimes they do not. If any visitors have come to town, they are expected to speak, to preach, or to pray aloud. Otherwise everyone waits. If no one feels the urge to speak, then in about an hour the Elders stand, they turn to one another, and they shake hands. The rest of the group then rises and leaves—"the Meeting breaks," as they say.

Sometimes a person stands and speaks—women as well as men can talk in the Meeting. The speech starts slowly. Then the person talks more and more rapidly as he warms to the subject. Sometimes a person chants. When there is silence, someone else may stand. If the speaker happens to recite a prayer, he may kneel—this is a signal for the others to stand. Everyone waits politely until the prayer is finished and then everyone sits again.

Weekday Meetings are also used for community business, after the silence and the speaking and the prayers. For the business session, the women meet with each other on one side of the house and the men meet together on the other. Once a month there is a more formal Meeting. This is when marriages happen. For the marriage ceremony, the man and his attendants sit in the Elder's gallery but on the woman's side of the house. At the close of the group Meeting, one of the Elders announces: "William and Jeanette are to be married today." The man and the woman stand in their places. Each declares that the other is to be a partner for life. Each pledges love and faithfulness till death. The Elder writes a marriage certificate, the paper is signed by the couple and their attendants, and the marriage is recorded formally in a register book. Then everyone files out in silence.

All of Quaker life is built around Meetings. Farm work is planned in order to leave Meeting times free. Quaker stores are closed during Meeting times. Extra food is stockpiled in advance, being set aside for entertaining the Friends who come from a distance for any of the major Meetings. Every three months, there is a special Quarterly Meeting, and the main Quaker event is the Yearly Meeting. I remember once talking with my young Quaker friend, the printer Jimson Smythe, in Mount Pleasant. He was looking for work as a journeyman, having just finished his apprenticeship. I said he should go to New Orleans because I had heard that many printers found work there and that they were paid good wages. "And," I remarked, "people say that it is an exciting city." Jimson shook his head. "No, it's certain to be dull and quiet now," he said. "Yearly Meeting time is over—there won't be much doing down there until next year."

The Quaker tribe has a level social structure. Any Quaker can attend most Meetings (although there are a few special sessions entitled Meeting of Ministers and Elders). At Meetings, all decisions are assumed to be unanimous if there is silence in response to: "Is the measure approved?" If someone does voice an objection, the matter is postponed for further reflection.

I cannot say much about the detailed religious doctrines of the Friends. The Quaker books that I have seen seem vague. They describe pious experiences or protests against other tribe's ceremonials and against the general extravagances of living and dress; however, they do not prescribe particular religious rules. Quaker writings focus on the freedoms of an individual and they describe the moral responsibility of one's behavior.

In Ohio country, Quakerism follows the strict teaching of an American named Elisha Bates. The Batesians are quite firm about everything—speech, dress, manners, daily commerce, and so on. Fasts and feasts, gaming, dancing, light pursuits, and theater are all forbidden. Jimson Smythe said that he knew Bates pretty well: Smythe had worked for Bates as a printer for a year. Mr. Bates disagreed with another Quaker Elder, Elias Hicks—but Jimson was more impressed with Hicks. Elias Hicks traveled about from his home base in New York. He was sincere but mild mannered and he smiled often. Hicks encouraged Quakers to follow the original example of George Fox, who was less formal than the present-day Friends. The Hicksite Quakers are informal, and they remind me of another white man's religious tribe called the Unitarians.

The Quaker Society of Friends uses the same religious tract, the Christian Bible, used by other white man's tribes. The Friends also add the personal inspirations that come from an individual's meditation and waiting in quietness. Quakers are more optimistic than other white man's tribes. Quakers are against bad behavior, but they help sinners rather than punish them. They imagine that a person can win the war with sin—people *can* be pure and good and right.

Old white-haired John Whitefeather was silent for a moment; he blinked and he nodded to himself. I have been talking on and on, he said—now I will end.

Among the white tribes that I have met, the Quakers are distinct. They rely on inner guidance. They avoid written creeds. They shy away from a formal priesthood. The Society of Friends tries not to interfere with the individual faith of its members. Often Quakers are blunt—but personally I like their openness.

Quakers are one large family. They respect each other; they help each other, especially the sick and the poor and the weak. Quakers consider each person to be important. If all white men were Quakers, I could imagine living closely with them.

Perhaps, concluded John Whitefeather, this is why I have watched them and have listened carefully whenever I have heard them speak.

·27·

The Natural Religion
of Johnny Chapman

SINCE THE MIDDLE of the last century, apples have been a staple of the Ohio diet. Settlers ate them fresh or dried. They ate them during the winter, after the apples had been stored for months in the root cellar. They ate them cooked, mashed, or fried, and they drank apple cider and apple whiskey. Ohio's Shakers made a special applesauce, mixed with spices and concentrated cider, and German settlers made apple kuchen and apple fritters, while Hungarians made apple strudel and linzer cake.

Apples are everywhere in Ohio—but I have to say a special word about apples from Defiance. Go up to the west, the northwestern corner of the state, and you find Defiance County, named for Fort Defiance. Once, much of the county was the Black Swamp, but now it's been cleared of the impassable damp forests and swamp water and no finer more fertile soil can be found this side of the River Nile itself. Barley, buckwheat, oats, potatoes, rye, and wheat are grown there. The Defiance farmers raise cattle, horses, pigs, and sheep. And also there are apple trees—but I'll come to that in a moment.

The county seat of Defiance is also called Defiance; it's laid out where the Maumee and the Auglaize Rivers meet. This was a good place for a fort, so General Anthony Wayne built one there in 1794. The fort was right next to a cluster of Indian tepees, bark huts, and council houses, and this Indian city was old even then. Water travel took you easily into the region from just about anywhere, so tribal chiefs from Canada, the far West, and the South

had met at that spot for generations. The great Chief Pontiac was born there about 1720.

The apple tale of Defiance County is known throughout America. The story begins in the East. It begins before the Revolutionary War, when there came to America from England a man named Nathaniel Chapman. Some say that Nathaniel was a Welshman, but his family tradition says that Nathaniel came (with his three brothers) from Scotland. In any case, the Chapmans first landed in New Jersey. During the war, Nathaniel was a captain and he sold his farm in order to support himself and his family while he served in the army; by the end of the military struggle, Nathaniel Chapman was a poor man.

Mr. Chapman married twice. His first wife had two children, John and Elizabeth; I don't know this wife's name or the exact dates when all the bornings took place. The second wife was Lucy Cooley. She had ten children, five boys and five girls. The boys were Nathaniel, Andrew, Parley, Timothy, and Davis: the birthdates are a bit vague, but I do know that Timothy was still living in 1875 in Washington County, Ohio, near the city of Lowell, when he was about seventy-eight years old. The girls' names we know were Lucy, Martha, Percis, and Sally. These ten are half brothers and sisters to John Chapman, who was said to have been born in Massachusetts near Bunker Hill in the year 1764. . . .

What's that? Why am I telling you all this? It's to record as much as is known about the relatives of John Chapman, probably the most famous Chapman in America.

Even from the beginning, John Chapman was smart and quick and he did well in school—Johnny could read and write with the best of them. When he was twenty-one, he got a kick from a horse that fractured his skull and the pressure on his brain had to be relieved by a surgeon. Johnny changed a bit from that time. He got serious and idealistic and single-minded. Seven years later, he persuaded his brother Timothy to set off on a western trek with him, and the two young men made their way on foot through the wilderness to Fort Duquesne, now Pittsburgh, Pennsylvania.

From Pittsburgh town, the Chapman brothers went up the Allegheny to the city of Olean in New York. Johnny and Tim stayed there a full year, but no one is still around in New York who remembers them. The country was woodsy and rough and completely unsettled. The two brothers never had any bread or grain. They hunted rabbits, squirrels, birds, and coon. Also, they tried fishing, but neither was very good at it.

The weather turned cold. Johnny was a roamer and wanted to see things, but Tim liked to stay put. They'd stocked up on firewood and dried meat, and Johnny left his younger brother to look out for himself. Some way or another—it's not remembered how—Johnny got hold of a muley steer that he walked all the way to Pittsburgh and back again. The whole trip took about four weeks, and when he came back he found that poor Timothy was thin as a rail since he hadn't been able to catch much game on his own.

Another time during that winter, Johnny wanted to go downriver a bit. The water was rushing and the ice was running. Johnny took their small canoe. The water was too much for it. After just a few minutes, Johnny got afraid that he'd capsize, so he managed to drag the canoe onto the center of a thick cake of ice. He was exhausted. He lay down in the canoe and fell asleep and, when he awoke, he was almost a hundred miles downstream. A few days later, he hitched a wagon ride back home.

The two young men stayed on the Allegheny River about one year; then they were getting a bit lonely, so they got word to their parents. Things weren't going too well back East and a few letters back and forth arranged that the family would meet in Pittsburgh—I guess the whole family had the pioneering spirit. At Pittsburgh, they dug out a large canoe from a poplar tree and floated down the Ohio River. The Chapmans landed at Marietta on Saturday, April seventh, 1798. They went up Duck Creek to a tract of land now known as the John Crop farm, and they built a cabin, where they settled in as farmers.

This whole area was a mighty good apple-growing region. The land had scratchy open fields, just the sort for apple trees. The local trees put out little apples only half the size of your fist. Those apple trees were round and short and bushy and spiny; the leaves were small ovals and had wavy teeth on the edges. In the spring the flowers were white, and each fall the branches were full of apples top to bottom. Johnny Chapman couldn't believe all the apples; they just grew there with absolutely no work from farmers. You could eat the apples straight from the trees. You could boil them and mash them and fry them. You could bake them into pies and breads. You could squeeze the cider juice out of them. Why, just one apple tree could make five children happy and keep a family full.

Johnny was overwhelmed. He was even more surprised when he found out that the cider mills around Marietta ended up with buckets of seed after pressing juice from the fruit. Johnny bought bushels of seed for next to nothing. He carted this seed to open fields and just started planting apple nurseries. Apple orchards growing everywhere in the wilderness—that was his dream. He planted seeds all over his Duck Creek farm, and, down in Washington County near Marietta on the Ohio River, there are still some of these trees standing, healthy and in good condition, just as planted by Johnny Appleseed himself.

After a number of years, Johnny's father died. Johnny became a walker, a roamer, an apple idler. From Duck Creek, Johnny went to Delaware, Ohio, where he made a small improvement on some school land and then planted an apple tree nursery. He carried his appleseed on his back in a large sack. When he ran out of seed he came back to the Muskingum River region. Johnny went 'round to the cider mills until he had all the seed he could pack. He sealed up his sack and off he wandered again. He found a good empty spot, he planted the seed, and when this supply gave out, he returned for more.

Johnny kept moving. Why? I don't exactly know, but I do know that he walked and walked and couldn't seem to rest long in one place. From Delaware, Ohio, he went to Sandusky. There he planted a large nursery and this took him about three or four weeks. Johnny planted completely by hand—he never worked a horse or other animal, except to transport his luggage from one place to another.

His next stop was Mansfield in Richland County. He settled for a few months in Perrysville on the Mohican River. Of course he planted patches of apple trees all around the area. At Perrysville, there were two vast, spreading Catalpa trees next to each other with intertwined branches. Johnny fastened his hammock in the trees, a practice he'd learned from some Indians. Then he slept in the trees. He even ate there, and he read and he sang to himself. Johnny took to wearing his pot on his head as a hat against the rain. He was quite a sight in his tree hammock, long-haired, bearded, pot-hatted, and happy as a king. Trees and especially apple groves were his kingdom.

In 1822, Johnny Appleseed turned up at Fort Wayne in Indiana. Somehow he bought a piece of land in his own name—there're records for John Chapman in the County Land Office. He planted a large apple nursery on the land. Then he made a whole passel of visits back to Ohio to pick up more apple seed. When he traveled, he wandered natural-like, following the flow of the land, building rafts and floating downstream whenever he came to a river. Johnny went here and he went there, and he planted apple trees all over.

Old Johnny's last visit to Ohio was in February of 1842. His brother Timothy was now a neighbor to my grandfather's father and they were good friends. Timothy was a general handyman. He'd moved to near the Ohio-Indiana state line about 1840. Johnny helped in the move. Tim's wife and one daughter, Rebecka, rode on a canal boat while John and Tim took turns riding the horse along the towpath. Timothy settled at a point called Ox Bow, a bend in the Maumee River, and he got a job with the government, taking care of Sailor's Lock in the Erie Canal near his home. Later Tim was a section foreman on the Wabash Railroad, which was also near his home—about a half mile south of the old Erie Canal and a half mile west of the state line.

For a time, Timothy's home was headquarters for Johnny Appleseed. Tim helped Johnny plant a nursery of apple trees up beside the Maumee River. Tim Chapman was the only relative present when John Chapman was later buried by the spring near Richard Worth's home in the old burying ground on the Cassel land. Timothy himself died on Sunday, May thirtieth, 1886, and was buried in the cemetery in Antwerp, Ohio, alongside the Maumee River in Paulding County.

Johnny Chapman's last years were spent up near the northwest corner of the state where the Maumee River gets formed from the St. Joseph River and the St. Marys River. In that area, not far from my great-grandfather's house, there lived a Mr. John Whitney. One summer, lightning struck a large black oak tree on Whitney's land. Branches cracked off and burned. The tree was completely split, as if it'd had been chopped by a giant, and some of the pieces were perfect wood pickets, so Whitney built a fence out of them.

Johnny heard about this and he said he had to see it for himself. So he and Tim came to my great-grandfather's house. Great-grandpa agreed to introduce them to John Whitney. As they started to leave, great-grandpa grabbed up his gun in case they should run into a bit of dinner trimmings, squirrel or rabbit or the like. But Johnny objected. He read great-grandpa a severe lecture on the subject of taking the life from any living creature. God, declared Johnny, is the author of all life, so everything belongs to Him—He'll decide when to demand it back. My great-grandpa shrugged and put up the gun, and the men moved on out the door.

Soon they came to a creek, cold and black and swift running with moss on the stones blowing in the icy current. Tim and great-grandpa crossed by stepping from one rough stone to another. Johnny had been persuaded to accept a pair of old shoes while he was with his friends but now he took them off and waded through the water. Snow was on the ground; it was freezing cold. Johnny's feet turned blank white. After getting through the creek, Johnny still kept the shoes under his arm, and he plodded on barefoot through the woods and briars till the three men arrived at the farm.

John Whitney took them to the fence. Johnny Chapman got down on his knees. Carefully he examined the wood. He felt the pickets. He stood. He counted them. He shook his head. Then he began to extol the virtues of the Lord, Who had seen fit to save Whitney untold labor. Said Johnny: "God's given you a large family of boys, they've cleared you a farm in the woods—and they worked hard to do it. Makin' rails is mighty hard and heavy work; so God pitied the boys and He sent the lightning to make your rails. Furthermore, He selected that old burly tree close by to where you most needed them—it's all clear as day, John Whitney."

Whitney shook his head. "No, I just can't believe that God did this specially for me; I think it was an accident," he said. "'Course, I'm always thankful when God has the chance to spread His kind care over me and my kin. But I never heard of God makin' fence for anybody."

"You must've earned His favor," said Johnny. Whitney just shrugged.

Johnny said that God always provides. Whitney said that God was a busy feller and couldn't be bothering with every little thing in the world. That's why bad things happen, he said. How could you imagine, he continued, that God was providing for you that time you got lost in the woods in the dead of winter and you had to dig a hole in the snow bank and crawl in, shiverin' and hopin' to save your life?

"Well," said Johnny, "I was a fool for puttin' myself in such a situation in the first place. But, inasmuch as I'd already done it, wasn't it a great mercy of God to send enough snow so's I could dig a hole and secure myself from freezing?"

Whitney shook his head. He mentioned other trials, tribulations, and hardships he'd heard that Johnny'd suffered. But Johnny Chapman maintained that, through it all, God had never forsaken him. When he was about to do wrong, he always had some warning, there was always a signal of the danger beforehand, and there was always some saving miracle—and Johnny gave a passel of examples.

"Even when it's not easy to see God actin', He's actin'," said Johnny. For instance, one winter he was in the wilderness in a terrible blowing snowstorm. It was colder than stone—bitter cold. At night, he found a large tree that had fallen, and lo and behold the tree was hollow. It was the perfect shelter. It was God's great providence. Johnny was about to climb in and sleep, when he saw that an old bear had already taken up living there. Whitney started to say something but Johnny interrupted.

"Now, listen here," says Johnny, "that bear had his rights and I never disputed them for one moment. The bear got there first, so I left him to enjoy his comfort. I just turned and set out to find other quarters. And, through the good graces and the wondrous providence of the benevolent Lord, I lived though it all, and I'm here today to tell you about it, amen."

God works in mysterious ways, and Johnny did admit that one thing that happened to him at Mansfield always seemed strange. Perhaps, he suggested, he'd misunderstood the language of God. You see, somehow Johnny'd accumulated ten ponies. One day, the

Indians came down from along Lake Erie and, without much ceremony, just carried him and the ponies off. The next day, the
Indians released Johnny but they kept all his ponies. He could
understand his freedom all right—it was due to God's great
beneficence. But how about the ponies? Johnny could only figure
that the Indians needed horses more than he did, so God had
decided to redistribute the wealth.

Johnny shook his head when he saw the extravagance of people in the world around him. For example, he couldn't understand
standard clothing. Sometimes his pants had legs made of two different types of cloth of two different colors. Johnny had his eccentrici-
ties; he liked buckskin, but he hated leather shoes. One time, he
got hold of a tough old coffee sack. He cut a hole in the bottom
and a hole in each side, then he turned it upside down and wore it
like a nightshirt. He was mighty sad when that sack finally wore
out after a year or two.

Yep, old Johnny Appleseed was an eccentric in everything he
did. He liked to eat alone and to eat out-of-doors. Usually each
meal was only one thing, like corn mash, apples, or cattail roots.
He preferred fruit and nuts and grain to meat or fish or milk or
cheese. Once he had hired a young man, Heywood Harding, to
help him in his apple-planting work. At meal time, Johnny took
Heywood back to his camp and set out a huge pile of black walnuts
for dinner; young Heywood raised his eyebrows and offered that he
really wasn't very hungry.

Johnny liked nature, but he was a reader too, and if you asked
him, he'd say his religion was Swedenborgeanism. Swedenborgeanism was called the New Jerusalem Church; it followed the teachings
of Emmanuel Swedenborg who actually saw the Last Judgment
anew and the Second Coming of Christ. Swedenborg was a Swedish
scientist, philosopher, and mystic. He studied paleontology, crys-
tallography, music, and astronomy. He invented an ear trumpet for
the deaf and a mercury-filled air pump, he improved the standard
house stove, and he proposed building a flying machine made of a

light frame covered with canvas. He also preached that good actions are required of all men, who, in this way, become direct agents for the Lord. Johnny Chapman followed this creed.

Johnny was good-hearted, and he tried to do good actions. If he met someone who was poor, he gave whatever money he happened to have in his sack, five, ten, fifteen, and even twenty-five dollars. And generally Johnny had money. He was no beggar—but he sure as shootin' looked like a beggar. He walked barefoot. He wore his old coffee sack coat. He didn't care how he looked, he just dressed, as he said, "practical." As I mentioned, Johnny wore a tin pot on his head like a hat. People talked quite a bit about this pot. It was actually a kind of kettle. And he ate everything out of that kettle. My great-grandfather saw him take it off his head, swish a bit of stream water 'round in it, and boil up some corn mush with a little maple candy added for sweetening.

Johnny was a strange one—he trusted other people more than himself. One time he'd accumulated fifty dollars from a couple weeks of work cutting trees for a farmer. He worried that he'd lose his money. He looked around for a safe hidey hole. Finally he settled on a rock under the roots of an old chestnut tree where the ground had caved away. Then Johnny set off back to eastern Ohio to collect more apple seeds from the cider mills. Somehow, with the planting and the wandering and various other things, it wasn't till three years later that Johnny returned to his chestnut tree. But sure enough, his money was still there, and Johnny said that he wasn't surprised.

Old Johnny tried his best not to hurt any living thing, but this led to some difficult calls. One time a rattler got hold of his pants. Johnny looked the other way and dropped his axe. Later, when he came back to get his axe, he found that the snake "just happened to have gotten crushed underneath." Johnny went out of his way to try not to hurt animals. When he made a fire, he looked at all the sticks. If he found any worms or ants he'd knock them off before burning the wood. "I don't exactly know how these bugs feel," he said, "but it sure makes *me* feel better."

Johnny Chapman never married, and he never set settled long in any one place until he died, when he settled forever in the good cool earth. In Johnny's last years, he usually stayed in a cabin belonging to Richard Worth. The cabin was alongside a stream near the city of Fort Wayne, Indiana, on a farm that then belonged to the Cassels and that now belongs to the Roebuck family. Johnny Appleseed was eighty-two when he died—he was skinny, wispy haired, and happy. That was on Saturday, March fifteenth, 1845. Johnny was buried on the east side of the St. Joseph River; Tim Chapman, Richard Worth, and one other man did the honors. At that time, there was an old graveyard about a quarter mile southwest of the spring and about five hundred feet west of what is now the reservoir on the Roebuck's farm. The three men didn't give old Johnny any fancy tombstone, just a granite rock. In the 1940s, a young spruce was set to mark the grave—but there's no question that it should have been an apple tree instead.

Joe Copperwing,
the Last Shawnee in Ohio

NATHANAEL GREENE WAS born to be a general. It was on the seventh of August in the year 1742 in the township of Warwick, Rhode Island, that Nathanael first opened his serious brown eyes to the world; his father was a Rhode Island Quaker, a farmer, and a blacksmith. Even when young, Nathanael was quiet and self-assured. He was a natural leader—other boys always wanted to follow him. Soon he was a soldier. Military strategy came naturally to him: innately he knew how to plan surprises, he knew how to use whatever he had at hand, and he never took ill winds or unexpected obstacles as personal attacks.

During the Revolutionary War, Greene was George Washington's right-hand man. He never came to Ohio country; nonetheless, Greene County, in the southwest of the state of Ohio, was named for him. In the eastern half, Greene County is flat and good for grazing, and, in the western half, it's rolling and good for farming. Greene County streams run strong and deep, just like their namesake.

The city of Xenia is Greene's county seat. North of Xenia—about three-and-a-half miles up the road—is a little village called Oldtown. Oldtown is on the Little Miami River. It was a famous Indian settlement, and you can find it on early maps, where it was called by the Shawnee name Chillicotha. In 1778, Daniel Boone visited Chillicotha. The next summer, General Clark came in with troops, and the Shawnee burned the village rather than let the European settlers take it.

For centuries, this region had been the center of Shawnee government and in early American days a number of Shawnee clans still lived there. In 1812, the Ohio Shawnee divided into two factions. One of them, Chief Black Hoof's band, was moved by the white settlers onto western reservations. The other Shawnee clan was made of many little groups (such as the Piquas) and some stayed quietly in Greene County, living as scattered families. Officially, however, all the Indians but Joe Copperwing were evicted from Ohio by the white settlers.

The European settlers were a self-centered tribe. They pushed and they pulled; they elbowed their way in, and they built houses, stables, towns, fences, farms, and roads. Eventually, the white men forced the Indians out of Ohio country. The Shawnee ended up in Indian Territory in Oklahoma, after temporarily being moved to the Auglaize River area in northwestern Ohio. Black Hoof's Shawnees left Old Chillicotha for the Auglaize. It was a sad day. They'd been born, raised, and bred there in the beautiful southern Ohio valley, and all their ancestors were buried nearby.

I don't know how they could go. They must have been broken people. But, go they did. Scattered Shawnee families stayed hidden in the hillsides, but only one Indian, Joe Copperwing, publicly refused to leave. Copperwing was a cripple: his left leg had never healed properly after a fall from a cliff when he was a child. He was given a home by Hannah and Thomas Aaron Paxson, who lived in a big round-log cabin less than two miles from Old Chillicotha. Years later their grandson, William Aaron Paxson, told my uncle what he remembered about Joe Copperwing, and I'd best write it down or it will be forgotten.

Old Joe had been a tanner of skins, especially groundhog skins. Joe finished skins both with the fur on them and without. He made soft leather pads and cloths and clothes, and he made sturdy rough-hides. Joe called his toughest product whang leather because he made whangs—thongs—from it.

Bill Paxson said that old Joe's method produced the absolutely perfect finish for any wild animal hide. Joe worked his hides in the streams, on rocks and logs, and in wooden troughs. Each spring he cut two new troughs out of the trunk of an oak. Joe's troughs were almost as special as his leathers: they were long and light and they were smooth and watertight. Joe hewed out one of these troughs, which could hold more than a barrel, for Bill's grandmother. Grandma used it for soaping, that is, for making soft soap. Pioneer women made soft soap once a year. The spring soaping started with household wood ashes saved through the winter. By April, the soap trough would be filled with ash; then came the "tug of war"—that's what the children called it—the young'uns had to carry water every day from the springhouse in order to keep the ashes wet. Eventually the soaked ashes made a gray, smoky lye solution that Grandma filtered and stirred into a kettle of melted cow fat. Finally, Grandma cooked the whole mess to make soft soap.

Joe also made watering troughs for Bill's grandfather. These were smoothly finished and considerably longer than the soap troughs. The men put the largest trough in the stream just at the edge of the springhouse. Water came in at one end and flowed out the other end and into a highway of smaller troughs that channeled fresh water to the fenced-in cattle and pigs and sheep and horses. No stock ever had finer running springwater every day of the year, even during the winter.

The Paxson springhouse was damp, mossy, cool, and cavelike with big black spiders in the corners. It was also used as a general wash house. Just to the right of the springhouse was a bosky dell with briars and reeds and cattails. Indian Joe used it as a "soaker." Joe would collect willow branches from just over the hill along Ludlow Creek and drag them into the bog where he set them to soaking. After a week, Joe pulled out the black sticks, carried them back to his sitting bench, and stripped the bark. It was the bark he wanted because he wove it into baskets.

Patiently Joe twined the large willow bark strips into feed baskets. From the small strips, he wove ladies' work baskets. Joe's baskets were neat, even, and long lasting and you could find them in Xenia homes for years afterwards. Faith Faerwether collected as many of these baskets as she could find, and twelve of them are still in her niece's house in Yellow Springs.

Joe Copperwing was an all-round craftsman, woodsman, and artisan, but leather was his finest craft. How did an Indian work his leather? Well, I'll tell you. First Joe took a hide and cut it to an even shape with no bad spots. Sometimes he cut off the hair, but if it had especially fine fur then he left it as it came. Second came the soaking—Joe soaked the skin for twenty-four hours, weighted down by rocks in Ludlow Creek.

The next day was scraping. Joe took the hide from the stream. He had a log about eight inches in diameter and eight feet long and he had it tilted at an angle—one end on the ground and the other hiked up in a forked stick high enough to reach Joe's hips. Old Joe Copperwing stood with the skin draped over the high end of the log. He took his flat wooden tool and he scraped the surface. Joe scraped evenly and smoothly, with the same calm motion that he used for everything from eating to walking to talking. Old Joe fit in smoothly with the world; he moved along the edges of the wind just like a light spring leaf.

Joe used groundhog skin for thongs and whang leather and even a kind of woven rope (groundhogs are about as tough as animals come). Other hides were made into soft leathers. Joe started the softening with another soaking. He mashed oak bark juice in an old iron kettle over a low heat. He added oak leaves every couple of hours; then he pounded the whole mess with an oaken club. This made a mighty smelly brew. The oak mash got poured into a soaking trough, which Grandpa Paxson made Joe keep far from the cabin. The hides soaked there for days. Joe took them out after about a week. He washed them in the stream. He rubbed them, he pounded them, and he stretched them, and he got into a rhythm and could work on his leathers for hours at a time.

Then Joe let the hides sit and rest—they would relax for a day or two, and so would Joe. Joe said that he was a bit hard on the skins in the first steps and that they needed time to recover. Then, when the sky was high and the clouds were white and the air was cool, Joe would carry the hides over to his sitting bench where he sat and rubbed the hides in tallow from cows or hogs. That could take all morning for a single skin. The next day, Indian Joe used the animal spirits. You see, whenever someone brought him a skin to tan, Joe always had them bring the head of the animal too. Old Joe Copperwing rubbed the animal brain into the hide. Joe said that brains had a special kind of spirit fat in them; this made the finished leather soft and smooth and comfortable—it carried the soft thoughts of the animals forever and ever, so they were unaffected by harsh wind or weather.

All told, old Joe's tanning was mighty slow. But he made fine, smooth, durable leather. He made leather that lasted and that wore well and that was better than your own skin. Joe's leathers were like a blanket or a cloud. All the womenfolk thereabouts wanted Joe Copperwing's clothes and belts and harnesses and hats and vests—they wanted his bits of trim and wall hangings, they wanted his shirts and purses and moccasins. In those days, southern Ohio people all came to Indian Joe for their leather finery.

As a tad of a boy, Bill Paxson sat and watched Indian Joe working back behind the big cabin of Grandpa Paxson's farm. Bill was wide eyed. To him, Joe was wonderful, magical, mysterious. Joe was as old as a tree or a hill or a rock. Joe was part of the outdoors and the day and the night. His voice was the wind. His arms were tree branches. His hair was like the long leaves of the willow trees. Bill would jump up if Joe needed anything; he would fetch water or a bucket or a tool or a stone. Joe Copperwing never smiled, but he talked quietly and he told Bill stories of the old days of the Shawnee.

Joe told Bill Indian stories from way back in time. He talked about the Sun, the Moon, and the Stars. These were all shining animals. They lived in Star Land, the realm of Star Chief, on peaks of the blue Cloud Mountains. Joe said that the Great Spirit was the first being who ever lived. Great Spirit was the uncle of Star Chief, and Great Spirit lived in a log house high up in the sky. The shining animals who were the Sun, the Moon, and the Stars were his family—in fact, the Moon was his wife. The Moon watched over the star children day and night. Great Spirit had given all the land on the earth to the Indians long, long ago. Indians were the caretakers. Now the white men were going against the natural way as it had been established once upon a time and as, after a time, it would be reinstituted and would go on forever and ever and ever.

Down in the Xenia region of Ohio, there were tiny night lights that looked like flames in the air over the marshes. White men called them will-o'-the wisps and friar's lanthorns. Local folk said that these were spirits, tiny wisps of stillborn children who flit between heaven and earth never resting and looking for their parents. Old Joe called them jack-o'-lanterns. Joe Copperwing told Bill that the tiny jack-o'-lantern lights that flashed and glowed over the Ludlow Creek bottoms were small stars. They'd come down too low and had gotten their wings damp with the fog. For a while they couldn't fly back up to the other stars where they belonged—it wasn't till they'd dried off that they could get back onto the cosmic tides and fly and float up to heaven. Joe said that the lightning bugs that came by the thousands every summer were the children of these jack-o'-lantern stars. These were shining little boys and girls who visited their parents and told them all the news from Star Land where the poor jack-o'-lanterns could not go until they were completely dried off, which could take weeks or months or even years.

Joe told young Bill Paxson that the sun came out of a groundhog hole up at Hickory Point. (Hickory Point was a small hickory grove on the east side of Bill's grandfather's farm—you can still find it, above a steep cliff with a stream that has cold black rocks and tadpoles and salamanders and crawfish.) Joe Copperwing even took Bill to Hickory Point and showed him the groundhog hole. The rim of the hole was hard, brown clay worn smooth; Joe said that this was due to the sun pushing out of the hole each morning. And where did the sun set? It went down into the earth behind the big stone on Steel's Hill.

I guess I'd also better say a word about Old Baldy. On the

Paxson farm there was a tree that Joe called Old Baldy. It grew on a hillside in the middle of other oaks. Old Baldy was eighty feet tall and it was the largest chinkapin in those parts. It had light gray bark and there was a black swirling slash of a scar twenty feet above the ground. In the fall, its leaves suddenly turned reddish brown all at once; you couldn't miss it. Old Baldy's hill was just across the road from Grandpa Paxson's gate—this was near the property line and, to prevent the tree from being cut, Grandpa Paxson had set his fence over a considerable distance.

Is Old Baldy still there? It's possible, but I don't know for certain. Indian Joe said that it had been a sacred tree to the Shawnee for as long as he could remember. Joe Copperwing would not leave on his annual spring pilgrimage until the tree had leafed out. This was Joe's first sure sign of spring, usually early in April. During the spring after Joe died, Old Baldy didn't put out its leaves till well into May—Bill Paxson said that this was the first time Old Baldy had ever been so late. All the years before this, when Joe returned from his pilgrimage, he would stop first and greet the tree. Joe would say something quiet and low; he would chant with a rumbling hum. And Old Baldy was a cold weather tree too; it never lost its leaves in the fall till well after the first frost.

Bill thought of Joe as an ancient tree like Old Baldy, but Joe's skin wasn't like a tree trunk at all—no, Joe was lightly wrinkled and as soft as his softest leather. Over the years, Joe Copperwing got worn and more and more wrinkled and he grew to be an old man with a gimping limp. Still, he sat in the yard with his skins. Sometimes he would sit for hours, silent, thinking or listening. Sometimes he would chant to himself. Every once in a while, Joe got talkative. There weren't many other people around, so Joe talked to Bill. He told Bill about the Indians, how they lived and hunted. He said that when a Shawnee died, he went to a cool woodland hunting ground where he was never disturbed by white men. After that, Joe looked at Bill a moment. Some white men were good, said Bill—Bill's grandfather Thomas Aaron was one of the good ones.

The Shawnee were always suspicious of the European settlers—and I'm afraid it was rightly so. Joe Copperwing was quiet
around white men. He was the last native Indian of the Shawnee
tribe that anyone knew living at Oldtown. Joe lived there after
Graybag Willie and Bitter Deer. He lived there after Kawati and
Greenriver Gar-man. He even lived there after Seth Darkblades.
These and all the other Shawnee, now passed on to the glorious
woodland hunting ground, were children of the Algonquins in the
East and were Ohio's great native Indians.

Grandpa Paxson was respected by the Shawnee. He'd learned
some of the Indian language and he stopped to talk whenever he
ran across a native. Thomas Aaron traded with the Shawnee hon-
estly, so when the other Shawnee left it was natural that Joe Copperwing came to Grandpa Paxson. This was in the fall, and Joe
asked to stay the winter on the Paxson land. Well, Thomas Aaron
Paxson would never turn away a good man, so Joe stayed that
winter and then he stayed many a winter afterward. I don't know
how many years Joe Copperwing actually lived there—but I do
remember a bit of the story about when he died.

Did I tell you that Joe would always go away in the spring after
the weather was settled? He never said where he was going. Perhaps
it was out west to Oklahoma where there were other Shawnee.
Maybe it was north to Canada. I really have no idea. In any case,
he took his blanket and his buffalo-leather robe. Those were for
sleeping. Joe never slept in a bed. Wherever he was, at home, out
visiting, or camping, he wrapped up in his robe and his blanket.
Inside a house, his favorite place was to lie down on the floor in
front of the kitchen fire. But he rarely slept indoors. On his long
camping trips each year he was always out-of-doors. Besides his
blanket and robe, he always took exactly the same things on these
trips: bacon, bread, and fishing tackle.

Old Joe set out each spring, and some years he did not come
back until the beginning of the fall. One year there was a very early
spring. Old Baldy put out its shiny oval leaves "as big as a squirrel's
ear" in the first week in March. Not long after, when the tiny

yellow chinkapin flowers were hanging like golden hair from the branches, Indian Joe left Oldtown.

Joe Copperwing was gone all through the summer. The fall stayed late and there was a surprising hot spell. The folks living in Xenia were sweating in the evenings and fanning themselves in the shade all day. Then, in just two days time, the weather turned. Suddenly it was cold with snow. There was a bitter wind and frost. Old Joe came back coughing. He had catarrhal fever of the lungs. He set himself down to rest but he had pneumonia quick as a flash. The disease came on all at once—at sunset Old Joe began to shake and shake. Then he stopped shaking and he began to cough. He coughed a rusty cough. He breathed fast. He grunted and he groaned. He had pains in his chest. He had the sweats. Bill's grandmother said that Joe talked a bit in Indian and then in English, saying something about "home."

Well Grandma Paxson did her best. She doctored Joe Copperwing but he grew worse and worse; he was feverish and weak and coughing all the time, and finally he died. This happened on the last Sunday in November. There was snow on the ground. Joe had said that he didn't want to be placed in a coffin; instead, he wanted to be wrapped in his robe and blanket and buried in the ground. He also wanted his fishing line and hooks and some bacon and bread buried with him.

A couple of neighbors came over: they were Uncle Abie Beal, Andrew Walls, Billy MacIntosh, and Dave Keifer. With Bill's grandfather, the men wrapped Joe Copperwing all nice and neat in his robe and his blanket. They put the things he asked for with him in a buckskin sack. Then they hauled his body on a sled across the field and up the hill to the burying ground on the Paxson farm. The men buried Indian Joe, with a gray-brown boulder over his grave. The rock is still there, down in Nathanael Greene's County; it sits tired and small and as smooth as the wind in the old Ohio country of sometime long ago.